SILENT WATER

A JAGIELLON MYSTERY 1

P.K. Adams

IRON KNIGHT PRESS

CONTENTS

Cast of Characters

The Royals

Zygmunt I

King of Poland and Grand Duke of Lithuania

Bona Sforza

Queen Consort of Poland and Grand Duchess Consort of Lithuania. Daughter of Duke Galeazzo Sforza of Milan and Isabela of Aragon

Poles

Aleksander Stempowski

Crown Chancellor. Leader of the pro-Habsburg faction that Queen Bona opposes

Sebastian Konarski

Junior secretary in the king's household reporting to Chancellor Stempowski

Jan Dantyszek

Courtier and diplomat. Member of the *bibones et comedones* semi-secret society

Adam Latalski

Courtier and poet

Kasper Zamborski	Courtier and member of the *bibones et comedones* society. Engaged to be married to Chancellor Stempowski's daughter
Piotr Gamrat	Queen Bona's advisor
Archbishop Jan Łaski	Primate of Poland. Queen Bona's political ally
Mikołaj Firlej	Commander of the Polish forces during the Teutonic War
Helena Lipińska	Queen Bona's maid of honor
Magdalena Górka	Queen Bona's maid of honor
Konstanty Konarski	Knight in the Polish army and Sebastian Konarski's cousin
Princess Anna	King Zygmunt's daughter from his previous marriage
Princess Jadwiga	King Zygmunt's daughter from his previous marriage
Princess Izabela	King Zygmunt and Queen Bona's first-born daughter
Beata Kościelecka	King Zygmunt's illegitimate daughter
Stańczyk	Court jester
Michałowa	Chief cook at Wawel Castle
Maciek Koza	Servant

Italians

Caterina Sanseverino	Lady of the Queen's Chamber
Ludovico Mantovano	Queen Bona's private secretary
Giuseppe Baldazzi	Queen Bona's physician
Antonio Carmignano	Queen Bona's advisor
Giovanna d'Aragona	Queen Bona's cousin and lady-in-waiting
Lucrezia Alifio	Queen Bona's maid of honor
Portia Arcamone	Queen Bona's maid of honor
Beatrice Roselli	Queen Bona's maid of honor
Father Marco de la Torre	Queen Bona's confessor

Rules of Pronunciation Relevant to This Story

Letter ł (capital Ł) is pronounced like w in *water*

Letter w is pronounced like v in *vat* (thus the river Wisła is pronounced "Viswa," and Wawel Castle is pronounced "Vavel")

Letter c is pronounced like ts (thus *noc* (night) is pronounced "nots")

Letter j is pronounced like y in *young* (thus the name Mikołaj Firlej is pronounced "Meek-o-why Fear-ley")

Letter ǵ is pronounced like ǵh in *ghost* (thus Jagiellon is pronounced "Ya-ǵhye-lohn")

Letter e is pronounced like eh in *egg* (thus the name of the village of Niepołomice is pronounced "Nye-poh-woh-mitseh")

Common diphthongs
Sz is pronounced like sh in *shop* (thus the name Dantyszek is pronounced "Dan-tysh-ekh")

Cz is pronounced like ch in *check*

Ch is pronounced like h in *hang*

Rz is pronounced zhe"

-cki" – a common ending of Polish last names is pronounced "tsky"; unlike in English the c is not silent.

Glossary of Terms

Szlachta (pronounced shlah-ta)—lower nobility, equivalent of England's landed gentry.

Sejm (pronounced seym)—the lower house of the bicameral parliament, whose members were lower nobility (szlachta). The upper house, the Senate, consisted of wealthy aristocracy (magnates) and high-ranking church officials, and served as the royal council.

Wojewoda (pronounced voy-e-voda)—chief administrative officer of a province, a territorial governor.

Pan—Sir. *Note:* like all Polish nouns, it is subject to several conjugations, hence the form "Panie" that appears occasionally in the text. That happens when someone is addressed directly (vocative case) as opposed to being referred to in the third person (nominative case).

Pani—Lady, if the woman is married or widowed.

Panna—Lady, if the woman is unmarried.

PROLOGUE

The nightmares did not start until my old age, when sleep becomes elusive for some, while for others it is burdened with images from their past they would rather not remember. The stone cellar, dank and malodorous; the glint of a blade; the killer's cold eyes; the victim's pleading ones over the dirty rag stuffed in his mouth ... I reach for that gag, but my hand can never get close enough—it is like trying to move through water, the effort of it frustrating and futile.

I wake up covered in sweat, cold fear gripping my throat like a fist.

For years I slept soundly. It is strange, given the terrible events I witnessed at the royal court in Kraków that fateful Christmas and New Year's season forty years ago. I was still new to that northern kingdom, having arrived in the spring of the year 1518 as part of the entourage of Bona, the daughter of the late Duke Galeazzo Sforza of Milan, who was newly married to King Zygmunt of the great Jagiellon dynasty, which rules Poland and Lithuania.

I did not mind going so far from home. I had been recently widowed, still in my early twenties, and although my marriage had not been a particularly happy one—I was married at seventeen to a much older man of my parents' choosing—I did not relish the idea of returning to my family. By then my father had died, the family fortune was declining, and I knew that my enterprising mother would soon be searching for another wealthy—and probably old—husband for me.

As a member of the Sanseverino family, the Princes of Bisignano, by marriage, I first became a lady-in-waiting to Bona's mother, Isabela d'Aragona, the Duchess of Bari and former Duchess consort of Milan. She was a lady who valued education in nobly born women and was impressed by the fact that I had spent four years as a young girl at the Convent of Santa Teresa outside Naples, where I learned Latin and history, studied the church fathers, and even read a bit of Cicero and Virgil. So after I was widowed and Bona became betrothed to the King of Poland, Duchess Isabela offered me a place in her daughter's new household. To me, that seemed like a chance to escape another marriage and to see the world beyond Bari and Naples.

The union started off smoothly despite a difference in age and temperament between the royal couple. King Zygmunt was past his fiftieth year, already grizzled and filling out at the waist. Despite his stern appearance, he was a man of exceedingly mild manner who always sought to avoid confrontation with friends and enemies alike. He was also given to bouts of melancholy, during which he would not be seen for days, or he would remain pensive and silent, withdrawn into his inner world.

His new wife, by contrast, was four-and-twenty. Short in stature compared to Zygmunt, she had a slightly beaked nose, a determined mouth, and sharp blue eyes. Bona Sforza, true to her name, was sturdily built, strong of body, and forceful of will. She had received an excellent education, far more wide-ranging than mine, at the ducal court in Bari and was keenly interested in affairs of state, of which she demanded to be appraised daily and in detail by her secretary.

Yet the two seemed to complement rather than contradict each other. Already in those early years, many envoys, senators, and nobles of the Sejm—the lower house of the kingdom's parliament—sought the queen's counsel whenever the king was overcome by his darker moods. Gradually, Bona carved out a place for herself as an informal co-ruler, a role that would only strengthen over time as her royal husband aged.

Most importantly of all, nine months to the day of their first meeting in Kraków, the queen gave birth to a daughter, Izabela, the first of the six offspring they would have together.

So things proceeded apace, as expected. The future of the monarchy looked assured, and everyone seemed satisfied.

Until that festive winter's night that haunts my dreams again.

1

Kraków, Kingdom of Poland
April 1518

The day we arrived in Kraków was the coldest I had ever known. It was April 16th. In Bari, it would have been full spring, almost summer; but in our new home, a cold wind blew from the east, and patches of snow covered the mud of the streets or perched precariously on the city's slanted roofs. Like all the other ladies, I was wrapped tightly in my new marten-fur cloak and shivered despite riding in an enclosed carriage. In my companions' faces I saw the same silent question that had accompanied us through the miles and miles of thick pine and oak forests of Bohemia and Poland, so different from the sun-drenched wide-open hills at home: what if summer did not exist at all in this northern land, and we would never be warm again?

"I'd heard winter is harsh in these parts, but I didn't realize they would still be in the middle of it when we arrived." Lucrezia Alifio, the seventeen-year-old maid of honor who sat across from me, grimaced as she brought her face closer to the window. The thick greenish-tinted pane steamed slightly from her breath.

"It *must* be coming to an end," I said hopefully. I had never seen snow before and therefore was not sure if the amount I was looking at was a lot or not. But it did seem to be melting—surely that was a good sign?

Lucrezia sighed in a way that suggested she did not share my optimism, but she did not contradict me. I was six years older than she, a countess, and a lady-in-waiting. In Bona's household respect for hierarchy was strong, and everybody knew their place. It was just as well, for I had been promised—on the strength of Duchess Isabela's recommendation—the appointment as the Lady of the Queen's Chamber, which would also put me in charge of the maids of honor. Watching over a gaggle of adolescent girls would be a formidable task, and I would need all the help I could get.

"Kraków is bigger than I thought," I said, partly to lift Lucrezia's spirits, but also because I was pleasantly surprised. At first glance the city seemed so different, yet on closer inspection, it was not unlike the merchant towns of Italy. The remnants of ancient structures and stone-paved streets left to us from the time of the Romans were absent here, and most of Kraków's buildings were of brick and wood in the style of a hundred years before. Its churches had narrow pointed windows and tall slender towers. But now and then an ornate stone edifice of a nobleman's dwelling came into view that looked much like any wealthy *palazzo* in our parts.

"It is." The girl's face brightened. "I was afraid it would be small and boring—a fortress with a few old houses surrounded by a wall, and forest for miles in every direction, like most of the towns we have passed along the way." There was genuine relief in her voice.

"Remember Lady Bona told us that there are quite a few Italians living in Kraków," I said as another *palazzo*-like mansion came into view. A few days earlier we had stopped at the castle in Vienna, and during a late-night chat, Bona informed us that there was a vibrant community of Italian artists and artisans living in Poland's capital. They had been commissioned by King Zygmunt to beautify the city in the vein of the new construction that was popular in the south and that drew its inspiration from the Roman and Greek structures of the past. Now I could see that the scale of it was not comparable to Rome or even Naples, but the influence was unmistakable, and it warmed me with its familiarity as much as the brightness of the limestone.

"Yes, but they are probably all old men who prefer sculpting women out of stone to dancing with real ones." Lucrezia sighed.

"Probably," I said pointedly. Lucrezia—small, plump, and perpetually smiling, her present mood notwithstanding—had few thoughts in her head, save those that concerned entertainment and flirting. I should not have mentioned the Italians—I was not at all sure if her assessment of their age and interests was correct, and she should not get any ideas.

I turned to the window again and watched the streets lined with cheering crowds. Despite the festive occasion, I could see the signs of a busy, bustling town, located as it was at the crossroads of major trading routes. From the eastern lands to the Low Countries, and from the ports of the Mediterranean to the Baltic coast, Kraków was a transit point of many merchant trains. The cold air carried with it not just the smells of meat pies and roasts sold to the gathered crowds, but also more pungent scents of spices, herbs, and oils emanating from stores and apothecaries' workshops. I thought I even caught—from one of the many taverns along the way—that peculiar heavy but sweet odor of tobacco, an increasingly popular smoking substance brought by the Spaniards from the newly discovered world.

That, even more than the *palazzos*, caused a swell of nostalgia to rise in my chest. But though I missed Bari, I reminded myself that I was embarking on a new life here. If things went well and the queen was satisfied with my service, perhaps I might avoid marrying again in order to secure my future. It was not that I did not want marriage at all—rather, after my first experience with it, I had come to a firm belief that money or titles were not the right motivations for it. Of course, most women I knew had done it for exactly those reasons, including the heiress to the Duchies of Bari and Milan, who rode a few carriages ahead of us.

But Bona had been born to one of the most prominent aristocratic families of Europe, and she had a role to play. Her destiny was never going to be in her own hands, a fact which—as far as I knew—she had never questioned. On the contrary, she had seemed satisfied with the match when it was first announced, and excited during her marriage-by-proxy ceremony at Castel Capuano in Naples the previous December. But she would become queen and help perpetuate a dynasty, and perhaps that was worth the price. I had no such pretensions, and although I knew what my mother's expectations were and how women of my station viewed these matters, I somehow believed that I should marry for nothing other than love.

"Donna Caterina," Lucrezia's voice broke through my musings. "Do you think Lady Bona is eager to meet her new husband?"

I stared at her, amazed at how her words reflected my own thoughts. "Of course," I said, careful not to sound hesitant. "She talks about him all the time and has been writing him letters every day from the road."

"But is she really *eager* ..." There were emphases, albeit slightly different ones, on both "really" and "eager." She stopped herself just in time, though the corners of her lips trembled with suppressed laughter.

I sent her a stern look to convey how I felt about her speculation. But before I had a chance to say anything, the carriage abruptly stopped. Behind us, the same thing was happening like a ripple all through our cortege of several hundred. It included officials from Poland, the Italian states, Hungary, and Bohemia, as well as imperial envoys, mounted men-at-arms, pages, and courtiers. We also brought with us a hundred fine coursers from the Duchess of Bari's famous stables, each caparisoned in red damask with golden tassels, their bridles sparkling with gold. Mule-drawn wagons filled with thirty-six carved chests bearing the coats of arms of the Sforza and Aragon families contained the first installment of Bona's dowry of fifty thousand ducats, in addition to furniture, gowns, linens, books, and paintings. The weight of this treasure allowed us to make only a slow progress toward Wawel Hill, where the centuries-old royal castle stood overlooking the city.

Now all of it screeched to a halt.

That was because Bona was about to leave her carriage, pulled by eight white horses, for the last stretch of the journey so her new subjects could see her in all her splendor. Though she was out of our sight, I knew she was going to mount a gold-cloth caparisoned steed to ride onward, erect and proud, her head of plaited blonde hair covered with a loose velvet cap sewn with pearls and aquamarines. She would look magnificent in her blue satin gown decorated with miniature beehives forged of gold plate: undaunted, impervious to the cold, calm, and regal.

In the streets, the noise momentarily abated as the townsfolk lining the route and leaning out of the windows craned their necks. I knew she had left her carriage when they erupted in cheers again, waving, throwing their hats in the air, and shouting, "*Niech żyje! Nasza Królowa!*" Long live! Our Queen!

We stopped three more times en route to receive welcome from city officials in robes and chains of office, and from representatives of guilds, also clad in robes and the various insignia of their trade—goldsmiths, stonemasons, wheelwrights, drapers, brewers, and many others. In the arcaded red-brick courtyard of the University of Kraków, we were met by Stanisław Biel, the provost, and all the teachers. I would later learn that the school, which had been founded a hundred and fifty years earlier, had received a major boost from one of Bona's predecessors, Queen Jadwiga, who had donated all of her jewels to the university shortly before she died in the year 1399. It allowed two hundred students to be enrolled in courses of astronomy, law, and theology.

After the introductions had been made on both sides, a booming salute from the cannons placed along the city walls rumbled through the air. We moved on only after Provost Biel had delivered a long and tedious speech, praising Bona's beauty and the virtues of her mind and character, one of several in that vein that we had to listen to that day.

As we finally began the ascent toward the castle amid the pealing of the bells of all of the city's churches—their metallic clangs both solemn and joyous—the clouds parted, and a brilliant sun came out. The royal hill was wide and flat, its southern part occupied by a large flagstone-paved ceremonial forecourt. The castle, a self-contained structure of limestone built around an inner courtyard, stood to the north. A gate led from the forecourt to the castle through one of its wings, and it was wide enough to allow six mounted men to ride in side-by-side.

We came to a halt in the forecourt. Along its far side, overlooking the river that flowed placidly from the west only to turn north past Kraków on its course toward the Baltic Sea, were the armory and the royal stables. Brightly dressed grooms rushed toward us to take charge of the horses. On the opposite side, near the gate to the castle, the grand Wawel Cathedral overlooked the forecourt. Built more than two hundred years earlier, it was an amalgam of diverse styles and materials—gray stone, limestone, and brick—surrounded by chapels and topped with tall copper-domed towers, each with a bell of its own.

Outside the cathedral's open doors, King Zygmunt, cloaked in scarlet edged with ermine, waited to greet his new wife for the first time in person. He was flanked by the kingdom's highest nobility and its most important church officials. A little to the side, surrounded by a group of ladies, were two small girls, golden-haired and plump-cheeked, neither older than five. They were clad in little cloaks of white fur bordered with gold, with matching hats on their heads. They were the king's daughters, Jadwiga and Anna, from his previous marriage to the Hungarian noblewoman Barbara Zapolya, who had died three years earlier. Bona was thus arriving to join a small family already, a stepmother before she had ever become a mother.

Bona dismounted and offered her husband a deep curtsy, and we all followed her example. The king planted a kiss on both her cheeks. He took her by her left hand, on which sparkled a large diamond ring she had received from his envoys on her wedding day, and he led her into the church for a mass of thanksgiving for her safe arrival. Two days later, Bona Sforza would be crowned Queen of Poland there.

I joined the rest of the court in following the royal couple inside to the sound of the hymn *Te Deum laudamus* sung by a boys' choir. Earlier, while alighting from the carriage near a stone statue of a saint, I had swept my hand over the pedestal to gather a bit of snow and shivered at the cold wetness of the lumpy mass. I dropped it and dried my fingers on my fur, then looked up at the sky to find it almost—although not quite—as blue as that over our southern Italian land. I felt another pang of longing for home, and again it was followed by a thrill of anticipation for the new life that awaited me here.

But even in my wildest dreams, I could not have foreseen what it would bring me.

The festivities following the coronation on April 18th lasted for a full week, with many speeches delivered and poems declaimed for the occasion, and daily feasts, music, dances, and tournaments. The royal couple even went for a hunt to nearby Niepołomice together, where the queen—whose mother's stables in Bari were renowned throughout Europe for breeding excellent steeds—impressed many with her equestrian skills.

When the celebrations were finally over, we began settling into our new quarters set up on the second floor of the castle, in the wing above the gate that connected the forecourt and the courtyard. They consisted of the queen's private apartments; the chambers of her maids of honor; and the offices of the queen's advisors, her treasurer, and her private secretary, Don Lorenzo Mantovano. They were all ranged along a gallery whose windows gave onto the colonnaded inner courtyard, surrounded on three and a half sides by the castle. The remaining half side, to the south of the gate, was occupied by service buildings, including an entirely separate royal kitchen. It had been moved there a few years earlier from the main residence due to the risk of fire, which had been breaking out with some regularity in the centuries since Wawel Castle had been built.

I assumed the role of the Lady of the Queen's Chamber with some trepidation, mindful that while I had obtained it with Duchess Isabela's help, I now needed to prove myself. My old patron was thousands of miles away, and my position depended wholly on the young queen's continuing favor.

I had it—so far. Bona tended to be loyal to those who served her well, but she could be tempestuous and capricious, especially when things did not go her way. Thus I could take nothing for granted. Unlike the other ladies-in-waiting—who did not need to do more than accompany the queen during official receptions and entertain her with conversation in her chambers—I would have to work hard to maintain my privilege. Although I was Countess Sanseverino, I was also a widow, and thus in a more precarious position than any of them.

The maids of honor I was put in charge of were a mix of young Polish and Italian noblewomen. In short order I had to learn how to be strict and maintain discipline over sixteen- and seventeen-year old girls whose relatives had entrusted them to us in hopes of securing good marriages that would strengthen their families' power. I had to be on alert day and night because any hint of impropriety could be detrimental to a girl's reputation, and to my own standing. There are women who relish having that kind of control over other women's lives, as I know only too well from my time as a pupil at the convent in Naples. But I was never one of them; no amount of Suor Modesta's droning about the need to uproot evil wherever we saw it had turned me into that. Yet, without a husband, father, or brother, I had to do what it took to secure my own future.

My role proved difficult from the beginning. As soon as the girls settled into their new surroundings, their minds turned toward the pleasures of the court. The abundance of choice foods and sweets; dances, hunts, and other amusements; and easy access to gossip and the latest fashions were all at their fingertips. But it was the proximity of young men and the opportunities for flirtation it presented that soon became their chief preoccupation.

When a handsome courtier—or, at times, even just a courtier—entered the queen's antechamber, they would cease their chatter and lower their heads over their embroidery, but never so low as to prevent them from sending the man long glances accompanied by much batting of eyelashes and puckering of lips. Of course, not all of them were like that. For every Lucrezia Alifio or Magdalena Górka—whose sole preoccupation when not serving the queen was gowns and jewels with which they could turn heads in the great hall—there was the pious Portia Arcamone, whose only adornment consisted of a necklace with a gold crucifix that she kissed many times a day, or Beatrice Roselli, who always volunteered to read from the Bible when the queen was in need of spiritual elevation.

And then there was Helena Lipińska.

Helena was diligent in her duties, but quiet and aloof, and she kept mostly to herself. She arrived from her father's estate near the town of Baranów, northeast of Kraków, to join Her Majesty's household a month after the coronation. But she showed no signs of wanting to become close to any of the other girls, and as the year 1519 arrived, I could not say that I knew her any better than I had in the spring of 1518. All I could say was that she was not particularly devout—I caught her yawning into her sleeve several times during mass—and did not seem to have any interest in the men of the court. In fact, more than once I had seen her shoot disdainful looks toward her companions as they simpered in the presence of a young knight or widowed baron. On that account, at least, she was unlikely to give me trouble.

Still, I had my hands full. Just a few nights before that fateful Christmas of 1519, I had gone into their bedchamber late at night to make sure they were all there. As I opened the door, there was a frantic scrambling around Lucrezia's bed, which was the only one where a candle still burned on a nightstand. Her bed neighbored that of Magdalena Górka, a slender yet full-bosomed beauty from one of the most prominent families in Wielkopolska. Magdalena's bare feet flashed as she hastily slipped between the covers. Walking between two rows of canopied beds, I caught sight of Lucrezia hiding something under her pillow.

Lucrezia had rich black hair and the smooth, olive-hued complexion common in our parts, which made her—to her unending delight—the object of a great deal of attention from Polish courtiers. To them, she must have appeared quite exotic compared to the golden-haired, ruddy female looks, much like those of Magdalena, to which they were accustomed in this kingdom. Now she lay straight and immobile, pretending to be asleep, even though traces of mirth and mischief still flickered around her mouth. I came to a stop by her bedside. After some moments, she opened her eyes and guiltily reached under the pillow to pull out a small volume, which she put in my extended hand.

"I am sorry, Donna Caterina, we couldn't sleep and we were just reading a bit—" She broke off as I opened the book to the title page. It was a Latin version of the fictional love letters written by Theophylaktos Simokates, a Byzantine writer. *Epistolae morales, rurales et amatoriae* had been translated by Nikolaus Kopernikus, who was a frequent guest in Kraków in those days. Some years later, he would gain notoriety for propagating theories about the universe that would scandalize the world.

I straightened my spine and gave Lucrezia my best Suor Modesta look. This was not her first infraction. Early on, I had gone through their chests—as my role required—to make sure they had not brought anything inappropriate for the court with them. Among Lucrezia's belongings, I found a dog-eared copy of Boccaccio's *Decamerone*, which I then confiscated.

"Well, you won't be reading anymore tonight," I said in a firm but low voice so as not to awaken the others. I tucked the book under my arm. "Blow out your candle, and do not ever let me catch you with these sorts of writings again." I directed the last words to both of them, sending Magdalena what I hoped was an equally stern look. She pulled the covers up to her chin.

"*Sì, signora.*" Lucrezia made a better show of humility.

"In the future, if you wish to have a book to hand for a sleepless night, I am sure Her Majesty will be glad to lend you one of her volumes of Petrarca."

"Oh, I wouldn't dream of that," she assured me with a fear in her eyes. A fear of boredom most likely. "What if she fancies a read herself and it's not there, and then she has to send for it and wait?"

"I wouldn't worry about that. She knows it by heart."

I went back to my chamber, and, after a short deliberation, opened the book and began reading. I had to admit that the translation of the love poems was quite artful, and my pulse quickened more than once at the images they invoked in my mind. The candle was burning low when I finally went to bed. My dreams that night included scenes from my married life that made me blush at their recollection the next morning. I put the book in the chest by my bedside, next to the *Decamerone*, where it would remain until the day I left Kraków.

What I did not know was that that day would come less than a year later.

2

Wawel Castle, Kraków
December 25th, 1519

The Christmas banquet started at three o'clock in the afternoon, after a two-hour mass in the cathedral. The celebration brought together the entire court and scores of guests from all corners of the Jagiellonian realm—the Grand Duchy of Lithuania, Mazovia, Hungary, Bohemia, Moldavia, and Ducal Prussia. The tables in the banqueting hall, the walls of which were paneled in gilded walnut and lined with mounted bronze sconces, creaked under the weight of choice dishes. Their appetizing fragrance mixed with the balsamic scent of the spruce and juniper wreaths hanging on the walls and twined around the great chandelier that could hold two hundred candles.

We were served smoked hams, roasted boar, succulent venison in a variety of herbal and spicy sauces, pheasants on beds of greens surrounded by slices of fresh Italian oranges, an array of cheeses, and a dizzying assortment of sweets, for which the queen had a particular weakness. Everywhere trays were heaped with candied walnuts, sugared plums, apples and pears baked in honey, and delicate flaky pastries filled with jellied strawberries and almond paste. All of that was accompanied by excellent Lombard wines.

Queen Bona and King Zygmunt, along with a few select guests, were seated on a raised dais by the windows that gave on to the balcony that ran the perimeter of the castle enclosing the inner courtyard. It had snowed a few days earlier, and the wide ledges of the balcony's ornate railings were covered with a white coating, now sparkling with a reddish glow in the last rays of the setting sun. The queen looked resplendent in a golden brocade gown with puffy sleeves slashed with white satin. Her large headdress was like a halo trimmed with pearls and rubies. It was covered with a short veil of white silk so light and translucent it seemed like gossamer floating about her head.

She had brought new fashions with her from Italy, especially in her preference for comfortable wide sleeves and low-cut square necklines that revealed the lace of the chemise underneath. Gradually noblewomen in major cities like Kraków, Gdańsk, or Vilnius—who until then had worn tightly buttoned gowns and old-style fitted sleeves that constrained the movements of their arms—had begun to imitate their new queen. Lately the more daring ones at the court had taken to competing with one another for who would show more bosom, an aspiration that delighted some courtiers but scandalized many others. It was a controversy, if such it may be called, in which the king, true to his nature, preferred to take no sides.

The guests at the main table reflected the kingdom's political priorities. On the queen's right sat the *wojewoda* of Vilnius, the capital of the Grand Duchy of Lithuania, along with the ambassador of the Kingdom of Hungary, which was ruled by the king's nephew Ludwik. On the king's left side were the *wojewoda* of Gdańsk, the main city on the Baltic coast, and Prince Bogusław of Western Pomerania, a distant Jagiellon kin. He had offered his lands as a fief to Poland, and some—though by no means all—advisors hoped that the king would accept it. It would, the argument went, protect the kingdom's access to the Baltic Sea, which was forever threatened by Poland's long-standing feud with the Teutonic Order. That

Christmas the hopes of the Pomeranian faction must have been very high indeed.

In the corner farthest from the royal dais, the children's table had been set up, presided over by Princesses Jadwiga and Anna. Long before the sun went down, shrieks and chases were under way, and the nurses were poised to intercept any food pellets that might start flying. At one point Princess Izabela, almost a year old, was brought in from the nursery. Dressed in a miniature gown of red and white silk, with a starched white cap adorned with ribbons on her head, she looked like a cherub. After she had received kisses from her parents, her nurse brought her to the table at which I sat with the maids of honor. We passed her around, cooing and smacking our lips at her. She smiled back, exposing her toothless gums and making gurgling sounds in her throat, until suddenly she went still, grew red in the face, and started grunting. She was promptly removed back to the nursery.

We laughed and waved after the little princess. We were in a cheerful mood, despite the looks sent our way by some of the Polish noblemen, unhappy with the way we Italian women talked and laughed rather than being quiet and demure. I knew that they deplored the fact that the Polish maids of honor imitated us in this, but it was Christmas, the short winter day was coming to an end in a fiery glory, and I did not care much. The traditional Advent fasting period was over, and, dressed in all our finery, we enjoyed ourselves and were happy to sample the delights of the table.

All of us except Helena, it seemed.

I had noticed that she appeared subdued and preoccupied. She spoke little and ate even less, every now and then casting anxious glances toward the hall entrance, as if expecting—or fearing—someone's arrival. She sat at the other end of the table from me, and several times I meant to ask her if everything was well, but I kept getting distracted by conversation. At one point I noted that her place was empty, and from Magdalena, who was seated next to her, I learned that she had gone to visit the privy.

The system of lavatories at Wawel was better than in the castles of Bari and Naples. Better even—if courtiers who traveled around Europe were to be believed—than in France and England. Each of the residential wings had a bath chamber into which water was pumped from the castle well to be heated in large vats on a hearth. Doors on each floor lead to recesses in the walls, where openings covered with wooden seats could be found. Helena would not have had far to go, yet she remained absent for so long, I was beginning to worry she had become ill.

When she finally returned, she was much changed—her face was flushed and her eyes shone with a strange light, although that may have been the effect of the candles that had been lit in the sconces around the hall as the winter sun dipped behind the woods across the river. Perhaps she had indeed felt sick and purged, which often brought relief in mild cases of indigestion. Yet that would have been unlikely to bring color and light back to her face; it would have done rather the opposite.

As I watched her talking with a newfound animation to Magdalena, I was forced to acknowledge that it could only be one thing: she had a lover. I had seen that look often enough. A part of me felt sympathy and even curiosity—I had never had a chance to experience a youthful flirtation; I had been married to a man who was introduced to me on the eve of our wedding day. Nonetheless, I was disappointed in Helena. She was one of the few girls who had not given me any trouble, but now I would have to have a talk with her. And I would have to keep an eye on her in the future. Soon that would be all I would do from dawn to dusk.

I was about to look away when Helena gazed at her still-untouched plate of food and absentmindedly brought her right hand to her stomach and rubbed it gently, as if to calm a roiling inside. I felt sweat breaking out at the base of my neck—if she was sneaking around to secret assignations with some courtier *and* was suffering from nausea, that could mean only one thing. And if that proved to be true, it would be both our downfalls. The queen would blame me for having failed in my oversight duties, and she would send me back to Bari, where, I had no doubt, my mother already had a list of eager—and aged—candidates to claim my hand.

My eyes went instinctively to the dais, and in that same moment, the queen turned to me. She beckoned me with two beringed fingers, and my heart sank. Did she already know? I walked up to her on such weak knees I feared I would not be able to rise from my curtsy.

"I do not see the Master of Ceremonies anywhere," Bona said impatiently as I leaned toward her. "Go and check if Kappelmeister Gąsiorek has set up in the throne chamber yet. The company is getting sluggish; it is time for them to revive to some music."

Unlike many in the hall, the queen had eaten lightly, not only because she was still not used to the cuisine full of meats and heavy sauces, but also because there were signs that she was with child again herself. But she liked her Italian wines, which she could drink in prodigious amounts without appearing any worse for it. In fact, when it came to revels, Queen Bona could outlast the hardiest of the Polish nobility, she was that robust. In the two years I had served her, she had never had so much as a sniffle.

Bowing in relief, I did as I was bid, and I returned shortly to inform the queen that the musicians were ready. She gave a signal, and everyone rose with a scrape of chairs and benches. Those who were not so drunk that they had to be taken home by their attendants began to drift to the throne chamber, where formal receptions were held. It was smaller than the banqueting hall, but with its gilded coffer ceiling, floor covered in shiny mosaic tiles, and colorful tapestries lining the walls, it exuded a stately magnificence like no other chamber of the castle.

The musicians had set up in a corner close to where the two thrones stood under a fringed canopy of red damask sewn with stars and moons in gold and silver thread. As soon as the king and queen were seated, they struck the first notes of *Ave Maria, Virgo Serena,* and a four-man choir began to sing. As the vocal lines weaved around one another, we all stood transfixed, listening to the sound, pure and sublime, expanding and filling the chamber.

When it was over, we applauded enthusiastically. Talk and laughter gradually resumed when the musicians intoned Dufay's *Ave Maris Stella*, which is less spectacular and more melancholy. More wine was brought in and poured from ornate silver flagons, and piles of sweetmeats were carried around on gilded trays.

I floated around, greeting friends and exchanging words with acquaintances, including Bartolomeo Berecci, a Florentine architect who had been commissioned to build a new chapel in the cathedral. I was surrounded by conversations in Italian, Latin, German, Lithuanian, and most of all Polish, a language I had been studying diligently since my arrival in Kraków. I enjoyed its melodic rustling sound, even as its bewildering number of declensions still largely eluded me.

In a corner of the chamber, under the painting of Ghirlandaio's *Adoration of the Christ Child*, which the queen had brought with her as part of her dowry, I spotted none other than Nikolaus Kopernikus. He was wearing canonical garb and was deep in conversation with two elderly men who, with their white beards and frowns creasing their foreheads under plain black caps, exuded a scholarly air, most likely teachers at the university. Kopernikus was very tall, long-haired, and long-faced; in fact, everything about him seemed elongated and oversized.

With a sudden blush spreading over my cheeks, I remembered the poems he had translated.

Turning on my heel, I took a few steps in the opposite direction only to find myself almost in front of Jan Dantyszek. He was a young and ambitious diplomat who had been part of the group of Polish envoys who negotiated the queen's marriage to King Zygmunt. Dantyszek was handsome, with a neatly trimmed dark blond beard and intelligent if slightly mocking blue eyes. His slender figure was clad in tight hose gartered with ribbons of white silk, elegant black breeches, and a matching doublet slashed with blue. The snow-white lace of his shirt was visible at his wrists and collar. He wore not one, not two, but three feathers in his cap and stood in a pose of disengaged ease, confident and suave.

He was a known seducer, and although not the type of man I personally found attractive, I could see why others would. Dantyszek also fancied himself a poet. Two years earlier, he had published a collection of rhymes titled *Elegia amatoria*. It circulated around the court and was said to be far more scandalous than the volume of Kopernikus's translation. I had already noticed Lucrezia's interest in him, which seemed to be reciprocated. I watched her closely whenever Dantyszek was around, for I suspected he would not be eager to make an honest woman out of a conquest if she found herself in the family way.

But it was not his person nor his intentions regarding the maids of honor that stopped me in my tracks; rather, it was the subject of his conversation. I grabbed a goblet of wine from a passing servant and stood near enough to hear, pretending to be enjoying the ruby sweetness of the drink while admiring a tapestry depicting a bucolic hunting scene.

"What Reverend Luther postulates is worth serious consideration. I don't necessarily agree with all of it, but he makes several good points," Dantyszek said in German, a language

I understood well, though I spoke it poorly. His interlocutor was a narrow-shouldered slip of a man with wispy brown hair whom I recognized as Georg Fugger, a banker. "For example, the theses that condemn clerical greed—"

"You shouldn't speak of such things, and during the Christmas season!" Fugger interrupted him nervously, and I understood why. He came from a wealthy family from Augsburg and had only recently settled in Kraków, some said because of his devout Catholicism. The last thing he would want was to be accused of reformist sympathies.

"What better time to discuss matters of religion than Christmas, eh?" Dantyszek laughed and slapped Fugger's spare shoulders, visibly enjoying his discomfort.

"You are jesting, Herr Dantyszek." He sniffled. "But imperial jails are full to bursting with men who have come under the spell of that preacher."

Dantyszek made a subtle gesture with his head toward the throne. "Our gracious king is a man of learning and curiosity, and he encourages debates even when views contrary to his own are argued," he added with the smooth assurance of a seasoned courtier.

The banker leaned toward him and dropped his voice so that I had to take a step closer to hear. "That may be true, but seeing as this push for religious reform shows no signs of abating, I have it on good authority that His Majesty is considering a proclamation that would ban this kind of talk at court."

"Well, he hasn't issued it yet." Dantyszek chuckled, unfazed.

I admired his self-confidence, but Fugger was likely correct. The king's devotion to Rome was well known. Indeed, his coronation vows had included a pledge to uphold the tenets of the Catholic faith and defend the Holy Church. And what once had seemed like a relatively harmless manifestation of disobedience on the part of an obscure German cleric was now—if the reports from foreign courts were to be believed—a cresting wave, ever more difficult to tame. Crackdowns were happening all over Europe, as Fugger had said. Dantyszek should indeed have minded his tongue, for we lived in dangerous times.

As those reflections went through my mind, I had no idea that for one among us at the castle that night, the danger was far more immediate than I could have imagined.

I glided back to the dais and seated myself to the right of the queen, next to her senior ladies. It was fully dark outside, and I was beginning to feel tired from the wine and the heat of the chamber. All I wanted was to rest while listening to the music, but it was not to be as the queen's cousin Giovanna d'Aragona, Princess of Montefusco, turned to me. She was a beanpole of a woman with thick graying hair that she could barely fit under her headdress. Once she started talking, it was difficult to stop her. She immediately launched into the story of her arduous journey to Poland, which she had undertaken in the autumn only to now suffer the bitterest winter cold in her life. I listened with half an ear, as I had already heard the story twice. The complaints about the cold and snow were so common among the Italians at the court that nobody paid them heed anymore.

The princess paused midsentence as the large figure of Grand Chancellor and *wojewoda* of Kraków Aleksander Stempowski emerged from the crowd. Stempowski bent his knee before the throne with the slowness of an arthritis sufferer, pressing his hand to the thick gold chain of office that rested on his chest. The king motioned for him to approach, and the chancellor leaned in to whisper in the royal ear. I did not catch a glimpse of the king's face, obscured as it was from my view by the princess's headdress as she leaned forward to see if she could hear anything. She was not one to miss a piece of gossip if she could help it. This lasted only a moment, then we were all scrambling to our feet as the king rose, kissed the queen's hand, and excused himself to her.

The music stopped, and the chamber fell silent as he descended from the dais, wearing his habitual expression of pensive sadness. The crowd parted with a low bow until the door closed behind him. There was a momentary murmur as the courtiers exchanged puzzled looks, but conversations soon resumed, as did the music, for it was known that, contrary to his wife, the king disliked prolonged festivities. Most likely he had retired. I was quietly envious, for I wanted nothing better at that hour, but I had to stay until the queen was ready. Yet there was no sign of that, despite her condition.

At least the princess turned her attention elsewhere. I was free once again to observe, which was my favorite way to deal with large court gatherings. By now the musicians had moved on to playing *frottolas* in a nod to the queen, who enjoyed music from her native land. With a surge of homesickness, I listened to the melancholy tones of the lute, harp, cornett, and viol, and the clear voices of the singers that told of airy woods, sighing winds, and the vain hopes of separated lovers.

I could not help marveling at the beauty of the performance under the direction of Stanisław Gąsiorek, who had been born a peasant. Earlier in the evening, I had seen Bishop Erazm Ciołek holding a lively debate with Archbishop Jan Łaski, a political rival and opponent of Chancellor Stempowski. Ciołek was a son of a wine merchant, and I wondered at this singular kingdom of many nationalities and languages that allowed men to rise from such humble origins to positions of great power and prestige.

I was still ruminating over that when another courtier approached the dais. I recognized him as Sebastian Konarski, a junior secretary in the king's household and a nephew of Jan Konarski, the Bishop of Kraków, who had officiated at the queen's marriage at Castel Capuano two years before. I had first met the young Konarski six months earlier, during *noc świętojańska*, the Midsummer Eve celebration when we all went down to the river to light bonfires. But we had not spoken since then; he always seemed busy with the king's business and did not appear to be one for small talk at court gatherings. Now I considered him again from up close. He was shorter than the chancellor but well-built, with a slim waist and broad shoulders encased in a tight-fitting black velvet doublet with leather trimmings. He had wavy dark hair, brown eyes rimmed with thick eyelashes, almost feminine in their length, and a clean-shaven face. It was a rare choice not to wear a beard, but it suited him, for it showed the fine line of his jaw and chin, neither too large nor too weak, but of perfect proportion to the rest of his face and body.

"Your Majesty, I bear disturbing news." I was jolted from the contemplation of that jaw by Konarski's words, pronounced as he bowed before the throne. The ladies' chattering ceased, although the crowd behind him still hummed like a beehive.

"Tell me," the queen commanded with a flick of a hand.

"One of His Majesty's men has been found dead inside the castle," he said. "By tomorrow morning the entire court will know. His Majesty wanted Your Majesty to learn about it directly, rather than from gossip."

"I thank you, Signor Konarski." Bona's face remained impassive, but I could see curiosity shining in her eyes. "Who is the man?"

"Kasper Zamborski, Majesty," he replied.

My head, which had been swimming in fumes of wine, suddenly cleared. I knew him, or rather I knew *of* him—everybody did. He was a courtier and a prominent member of a semi-secret group known as *bibones et comedones*, tipplers and devourers. They were a society of men and—rumor had it—a few women as well who enjoyed a lifestyle centered around drink, good food, and amorous pursuits. The king tolerated it as long as they were discreet about it—and they were, for nobody knew the true extent of its membership beyond the few who did not care to hide it, like Jan Dantyszek, who also happened to be their leader. Perhaps the royal indulgence was due to the fact that some of the highest-born youths of the realm were said to belong to the group, and King Zygmunt liked to avoid confrontation wherever he could.

The queen's women exchanged looks of consternation, covering their mouths or pressing their hands to their bosoms. "Zamborski? Was he not engaged to be married to Chancellor Stempowski's daughter in the spring?" someone asked.

With her usual self-importance, the Princess of Montefusco started nodding—she was already up to date on all of the court matches and upcoming nuptials—when a woman's cry rose up to the ceiling.

We all turned as the crowd parted to reveal young Celina Stempowska crumpled on the floor in a heap of carnation silk and white lace, sobbing uncontrollably. Those closest to her held out their hands to raise her and lead her to a chair by one of the tapestried walls, and someone brought a goblet of wine for her. Konarski was wrong—the court would not know about it by tomorrow morning; it would know before midnight.

I thought about how strange it was that the chancellor, when he came to speak to the king earlier, had looked serious but not particularly distressed. Then again, as a longtime courtier and a skilled politician, he must have been adept at hiding his feelings.

All at once, I remembered that the king had been ushered through the door on the left, which led to the State Chambers where he conducted official business, rather than through the right-side door that opened onto the corridor leading to his private apartments.

And then I knew that this was no ordinary death.

3

December 26th, 1519

The court, as expected, was abuzz with all manner of talk by the following day. The queen forbade us to report on gossip, but she was not going to be kept in the dark. In the late morning, she started sending her secretary, Don Ludovico Mantovano, to find out more from the king's men. Eventually, Mantovano returned, accompanied by Secretary Konarski.

Dressed more plainly during the day in a dark blue doublet, open at the neck to reveal the frilly collar of his shirt, Konarski still cut a dashing figure. He wore a black velvet cap adorned with a single sapphire brooch on the side, and I was struck once again by how he eschewed predominant fashions. It was a rare courtier who did not wear feathers in his cap or rings on his fingers, and it made him look somehow fresh, more intriguing. I glanced at the maids of honor sitting on both sides of the queen and on the cushions at her feet, and I saw avid curiosity on their faces. I doubted that poor Zamborski's fate was the only reason for it.

"Majesty." The secretary bowed. "The hunt for the killer has been launched, but I cannot report any progress yet. It's still early." His face was polite but reserved, a perfect courtier. "We are pursuing many leads," he added in a tone of assurance.

"We?"

"Chancellor Stempowski was charged by His Majesty with finding the man responsible. Doctor Baldazzi will be helping him."

The queen's eyebrows went up in surprise. "Why is Baldazzi involved in this?"

"Pan Zamborski's body was discovered by Adam Latalski, who raised alarm and sent for a doctor—"

"And Baldazzi was the first one they found?" Bona interrupted with a snort. "What help could he have been to a dead man if he has never helped a living one?"

Konarski cleared his throat. Baldazzi was the queen's personal physician.

"He will never find out who did it," she went on, waving a hand dismissively. "He can barely find a vein to bleed me when I have a headache." I imagined her plump white arm, now encased in a sleeve of embroidered red velvet tied with lace ribbons at the wrist, and I felt a twinge of sympathy for the doctor. Bona despised physicians in the way that people who never needed them did. She would not keep Baldazzi about her, either, if he had not been sent by her mother from Bari. "How did Zamborski die?" she demanded.

"He was stabbed, Your Majesty."

There was an audible gasp from the women, although the queen did not even blink. "Where?"

"In the service wing, in a passageway near the delivery doors—"

"*No, no, no.*" The queen shook her head impatiently. "Where on his body?" She made a circular gesture that roughly outlined Konarski's midsection.

The secretary looked uncomfortable. His gaze swept the ladies and rested on me for just a moment too long, and I felt warmth rising to my cheeks. I hoped fervently that the others were still staring at him.

"I hardly think it is a—" he started.

"It doesn't matter what you think, signore. I want you to tell me which part of his body was attacked."

He made a small apologetic bow. "He was stabbed in the back, Your Majesty."

"And . . ?"

"That is all I know," he said with enough firmness to be polite, but also to make it clear that he had no more information.

The queen tossed her head. By the frown creasing her forehead, I knew that she was thinking intensely. One way or another, she would have the answers she wanted. There was a long silence, then she asked, "Where is the body now?"

"In the mortuary chapel under the cathedral."

"I want to see it."

"Your Majesty?"

"You heard what I said. You will take me there and show me the body."

Konarski looked pained. "It is not a sight for Your Majesty's eyes or for anyone else of the delicate sex." His eyes wandered toward me again.

"Nonsense." Bona flicked her wrist impatiently. She looked around, and the girls dropped their heads to their embroidery in unison. "Caterina, you will come with me." She gestured toward me. "And you—" She turned to a young page, scarcely more than a child, who sat on a cushion in a recess of one of the windows, picking at a thread of his brightly colored doublet. The boy grabbed his cap from the windowsill and jumped to his feet. "Go find Signor Latalski and tell him to meet us in the crypt in half an hour," the queen ordered, and it was settled.

Our cloaks and gloves were fetched, and tightly wrapped against the cold, we crossed the inner courtyard surrounded by a newly built colonnaded arcade, splendid even in the fading light of a winter day.

A guard carrying a halberd walked ahead of us and Secretaries Mantovano and Konarski behind. As we approached the gate to the forecourt—where Master Berrecci had recently added the Sforza coat of arms, two azure serpents and two imperial eagles, next to the double yellow cross of the House of Jagiellon—we passed the new brick structure that housed the royal kitchens. I had heard that it was built on the site of an old church. Now its windows blazed with an orange light from the ovens inside, and the appetizing smell of meat stewing in herbs wafted toward us on the frosty air. Given a choice, I would rather have gone inside for a cup of mulled wine. Instead, we were headed for the cathedral that loomed majestically over the forecourt, and where only a cold, stabbed corpse awaited us.

When we stepped inside, Konarski beckoned to a passing deacon and bid him lead us down into the mortuary crypt. When the cleric recognized the queen among us, he executed a series of bows before opening an iron-bound door in one side of the nave. We walked carefully in single file down a winding flight of stairs, barely wide enough to accommodate my and the queen's voluminous skirts. Then one of the cathedral bells struck four o'clock above our heads. The sound was muffled by the thick walls, but it was somehow more sinister for that.

It was cold outside, but below the floor of the cathedral, an even greater chill assailed us, seeping through our fur-lined cloaks even before we were halfway through the maze of passages dimly lit by flickering oil lamps. The crypt was a low-vaulted chamber supported by thick columns, and it must have been very old because some of the stone of their capitals was chipped, and the flags under our feet were worn smooth. It was lit by similar lamps as the passages, except for one area toward the back where there was more light from a torch set in a bracket.

There, in a recess of the wall, a body covered by a white funeral shroud lay on a stone slab. As we came closer, I noticed that another man was there, hidden by one of the columns. It was Doctor Baldazzi. He was a short, pudgy man of nervous disposition who always seemed to be in motion, even when he was not moving. Something about him always waved or jerked or shook, whether an arm, a leg, or his head, covered with a cap from under which his perpetually unkempt hair escaped in all directions. When he realized that the queen was with us, Baldazzi gave a low swaying bow.

Bona ignored him, gesturing to the guard to lift the shroud. He hesitated a moment, then did as she bade him. I held my breath. The body was naked to the waist; I had never seen anyone so pale, so white in my life. I vaguely remembered the fair-haired Zamborski as having had a ruddy complexion, but here he looked like a marble statue from one of the sarcophagi up in the cathedral. His lips, which had a slightly bluish tint to them, were barely darker than his skin.

The queen gazed at Zamborski for a long while as I tried to keep my gaze fixed on the flagstones of the floor. Next to me, Secretary Mantovano stood motionless, a thin, dark-clad figure whose lips had twisted in disgust when the body was first uncovered. Perhaps that was his way of masking his fear.

When I raised my gaze, I met that of Konarski. I saw a tinge of concern and an unspoken question in his eyes. *Are you all right?* I gave a slight nod, wondering, incongruously, if the king's secretary was also a member of the *bibones et comedones* as Zamborski had been.

"Show me the stab wound," the queen ordered Baldazzi.

The doctor seemed disconcerted for a brief moment, then he gathered his wits and motioned to the guard to help him. Together, the two of them turned Zamborski on his side. And there it was, in the middle part of his back, below the shoulder blades—a single entry mark about half an inch in length.

"Is that what killed him?" the queen asked.

"*Sì, Maestà.* It punctured his lung. He would have bled inside and suffocated quickly. There are no other wounds or bruises anywhere else that would indicate a beating or strangulation."

"What weapon caused it?"

"A dagger."

"Hmm." It was clear that the queen had more questions but did not want to ask them of Baldazzi. Still, next to Konarski, he was the only one among us who was up-to-date on the investigation. "Who do you think would have done such a thing, *dottore?*" she asked finally.

Baldazzi smiled unctuously, flattered to be asked his opinion. "Perhaps a jealous fiancé or a cuckolded husband?" He spread his hands in a jerky motion. "Signor Zamborski was known for seducing maids and matrons alike. A great many of them, they say."

"*Basta.*" The queen waved her hand, and Baldazzi took a step back, bowing as Mantovano sent him a withering look. The queen's secretary was a stiff and officious type, with the long, habitually sour face of a man who had devoted everything, including his own family, to his career. He was always dressed in black, with a single ruby ring and a plain silver chain of office as his only adornments. At least there could be no doubt about *his* aversion to the tipplers' and devourers' antics.

A sound of footsteps rang out in the passage behind us, and we turned to find a wiry young man with a scholar's cap set on his head of fine colorless hair. He wore a heavy cloak that made him look even thinner.

"Ah, Signor Latalski," the queen exclaimed, a warm note entering her voice. "We have been waiting for you."

Queen Bona was fond of Adam Latalski. A poet and a writer, he was one of the best-educated courtiers. Having studied law at the university in Padua, he could converse with Bona in our native tongue, which greatly endeared Latalski to her.

That, and his friendship with Castiglione, whose *Il Cortegiano* he reputedly wanted to translate into Polish.

He bowed with a flourish, but it was obvious that he was uncomfortable in the crypt. "Your Majesty."

"We have come to have a look at poor Zamborski. A dreadful business." She gestured toward the corpse, but the poet's blue eyes remained on the queen.

"Indeed, madam. Very unfortunate." The torchlight cast dancing shadows on his features, but I could have sworn that he went a little pale. But he was pale by nature, like most scholars unaccustomed to the sun and the outdoors.

"They say you were the one who found him?"

"Yes. In a ground-floor corridor not far from the delivery doors."

"And what were you doing there?" She raised an eyebrow. It was a good question.

"I needed some air as I'd had a little too much wine at the Christmas banquet, but I went through the wrong door and ended up in the back passage instead of the courtyard," the poet replied apologetically. Then he added, anticipating the next question, "I didn't see anybody except for Kasper crumpled on the floor." The familiar way in which he referred to Zamborski made me wonder if he, too, was a member of the society. He did not look the part, with his unimpressive physique and rather morose disposition, but appearances could be deceiving.

Latalski then explained that Zamborski was already dead when he found him, blood dried and crusted on his lips, beard, and shirt collar. I could not help but gaze back at that white face, imagining the scarlet flow that had marred it only yesterday.

"And the dagger?" The queen wanted to know. "Who removed it from his back?"

"It was not there when I arrived," he said. "The killer must have taken it with him." He puffed out his meager chest at being able to offer a little theory of his own.

"Is the chancellor aware of that?" the queen asked Konarski sharply.

Again, the king's secretary looked uncomfortable, and I realized that he was probably under orders to keep the details of the inquiry secret. But denying any knowledge of an important fact like that would have been an obvious lie, and he could not lie to the queen so openly, with all of us as witnesses.

"Yes. The chancellor believes that it was Zamborski's own dagger."

A stunned silence fell on us. "And what makes him think that?"

"Because it was missing from his belt." He added that the chancellor had already interviewed Jan Dantyszek, Zamborski's close friend, who described the weapon. It had a finely wrought silver hilt studded with rubies—an expensive piece. "His purse was gone too."

Before anyone could react, Don Mantovano's voice rang out, strangely high in the echoing chamber of the crypt. "Your Majesty, if I may—"

The queen motioned for him to speak.

"It is clear that the dagger was the motive," he said authoritatively. "A servant or page must have coveted one, and not being able to afford so fine a weapon, killed Signor Zamborski, who most likely had also wandered into the passageway drunkenly"—he sent a contemptuous look toward Latalski, who scowled at him—"and was killed with it and for it. He would not be the first man to have met his end due to too much drink," he concluded sanctimoniously.

"Is that your opinion also, Signor Konarski? That it was a robbery?" There was a subtle note of flattery in the queen's voice, enticing the junior secretary to prove his importance in the king's household.

But he did not take the bait. "The investigation hasn't been concluded yet," he replied diplomatically, impressing me with his apparent lack of vanity, a rare trait at court. "We are keeping all options open."

On our way back, I wondered why the queen was so interested in a case that involved a relatively minor figure. The court in Kraków—like, I imagine, all courts since the beginning of time—reveled in drama, liked a good scandal, and appreciated a juicy piece of gossip. But Bona's cultivation, the upbringing and education she had received in anticipation of her elevation to the ranks of royalty, rendered her above all of that. And yet, perhaps it was that fact—that she had been bred to reign but had to satisfy herself with the role of a mother and hostess—that made her bored, restless, and searching for something to occupy her mind. Even if it was a murder case.

As if she had read my thoughts, the queen enlightened me on her motivations when I was undressing her for bed that night.

"Zamborski's death is very convenient for Chancellor Stempowski," she said as I unhooked the bodice of her gown. She had dismissed the parlor maid Dorota, who normally helped me with the queen's toilette, so we were alone.

"In what way, Your Majesty?" I asked, genuinely surprised.

"His daughter fell madly in love with Zamborski, but he was a rascal and a drinker, and not very bright to boot, from what I heard. It is said that Stempowski didn't want him for a son-in-law." She exhaled with relief as I removed the bodice and brocade skirt so she stood in only a flowing chemise of embroidered Cambrai linen. "It would not surprise me if he had hastened the boy's departure into the afterlife," she added.

It was a serious allegation, one only a queen could get away with. I needed to speak cautiously. "Are there no easier ways to ensure a daughter does not marry an undesirable man?" I asked, taking the rings off her fingers and putting them into an ebony case. "Like withholding the father's consent?"

The queen snorted. "She is his youngest child, and he would satisfy her every whim. Most likely he could not say no to that angel face," she added sarcastically. "But after the thing had been decided, he realized that he could not have it. So he sent an assassin to dispatch Zamborski quickly while making it look like a robbery."

I reached for a bottle of the oil of olives mixed with almond essence to rub into her hands, wondering why the queen was so convinced that the crime had been ordered by Stempowski, why so eager for it to be true? It was no secret that she was not fond of the chancellor. The fact that he combined the highest crown office in the land with the position of the *wojewoda* of Kraków, despite a law to the contrary that had been passed in the year 1504, was a source of constant irritation to her. No doubt he was able to get away with it on the strength of the enormous trust the king had in him, and no doubt Bona was jealous of their friendship. All the same, it was hardly a good enough reason to accuse him of such a grievous sin. There had to be something else.

"That kind of conspiracy would require a truly devious mind," I reflected.

"And he has one! He is a Habsburg partisan; you cannot trust him as far as you can spit."

Was that it? The chancellor's advice to the king did indeed tend to favor Emperor Charles V. Although related to the Habsburg ruler, Bona was a proponent of a closer alliance with France, like all the Sforzas. But was that reason enough to be so suspicious of Stempowski? And, if her suspicions turned out to be correct, was it sufficient to cause his fall from grace? Zamborski was a minor courtier, after all, largely unknown outside the Wawel circles.

✐

She never asked me *my* opinion that night, but if she had, I would have told her that I found the jealousy and random robbery explanations to be unsatisfactory. My late husband—a kindly man, even if he was old and rather boring—had served for some years as a judge in Bari. His work was the only thing about him that I, a girl of not yet twenty, found interesting. He knew that, and he often regaled me with details of the cases brought before him, which to me were more absorbing than gossip and dances. Many of those cases involved crimes of passion or opportunity, common enough on the streets of our city, where passersby could often see the corpses of the unfortunates lingering for hours, or even days, before being removed. I had seen them myself from the carriages in which I accompanied the old duchess. Even without my husband's stories, I had seen enough bruises, bloodied faces, and knife wounds, often multiple, inflicted in haste. Such things were messy.

That was not the case with Zamborski, from what I had seen in the crypt and from what Latalski had described. This murder seemed to have been committed with precision, as if the perpetrator had given it some thought beforehand. As if it had been *planned*. Perhaps the queen was right, after all.

But there was something else that bothered me about it. Try as I might, I could not put my finger on what.

4

December 27ᵗʰ, 1519

I summoned Helena to my chamber the next morning. Her flush was gone and the pallor had returned to her skin, enhanced by the dark green color of her gown. There was a sluggishness in her step I had not seen before, for despite her slim figure, Helena was strong and athletic. She had accompanied the queen on hunts in Niepołomice a few times, showing herself to be an excellent horsewoman capable of controlling even the liveliest of the mares in the royal stable. She was also a very good archer, as I had seen during a contest held among the courtiers before the bonfires were lit on Midsummer Eve. She had been the only lady to enter it, and she came second— right before Zamborski, in fact. She was her father's only child, which likely explained why she had been trained in such manly skills.

We stood in silence for some moments, and she gazed at me steadily with eyes as gray-green as our Italian sea on a sunny day. Helena was not a beauty, but her eyes, complemented by dark auburn hair surrounding a delicate oval face, gave her a striking appearance.

I walked to the sideboard and lifted a majolica decanter I had brought with me from Bari. I poured a cup of wine for myself and held the decanter above the second goblet, lifting an eyebrow in Helena's direction.

She shook her head, and her hand went to her stomach. "Thank you, signora. I have not yet fully recovered from my earlier indisposition."

I took a deep breath, my gaze lingering on her hand. "What do you think is the cause of it?"

"I don't know," she replied, averting her gaze for the first time. "I must have eaten something unwholesome."

I walked to the window, which faced north toward the city of Kraków at the foot of Wawel Hill. As a capital as well as a merchant town, its streets were busy year-round with foreign visitors to the court, and with traders and carts laden with spices, silks, cloth, fur, and exotic fruit. In that, if not in the weather, it reminded me of where I came from. Now its roofs were covered in snow, melting after a thaw had started that morning, droplets of moisture glistening like jewels in the sun. It looked like the beginning of spring, although we were still months away from it. Normally I would have enjoyed that view, but now I was steeling myself for a conversation I never wanted to have with any of the women under my supervision.

I did not like confronting them about their little amorous intrigues because deep inside, I could not bring myself to consider them to be wrong. In fact, I felt a certain sympathy for them, far from home and lonely as they must have been. There was another reason as well: I had once—when I was about the same age as Helena—wanted to have a child, even though I did not love my husband. Perhaps it was *because* I did not love him that I wanted it, to have someone on whom to bestow tenderness and affection. But I had not been blessed that way. I did not know whose fault it was, but it was true that my husband had not fathered any children in his two previous marriages either.

As a result, the idea that a pregnancy could be either a joy or a curse seemed deeply incongruous to me. Depending on the circumstances, it could solidify a woman's position in a family, or it could render her an outcast, despoiled of dignity and reputation, and condemn her to a terrible fate. And it all depended on how others—and not the woman herself—judged her situation. What if Helena was indeed in love—or even just thought she was—and wanted this child despite her mistake? I did not want to condemn her for it. There were plenty of others in the world who were ready and eager to do so. Perhaps they should have had my role—they would certainly have performed the duty better. But I needed this position; it afforded me a degree of security that being an ordinary lady-in-waiting did not. And so I had no choice—I had to do it.

I turned back to Helena. "I think I know what it is." Her face tensed, and a hint of wariness crept into her eyes. But she said nothing, and I went on, "I think you have been sneaking out to meet with someone." I sensed her go still, like a statue. "I don't know who he is, but I do know the purpose of such assignations, and I am disappointed in you. I thought you had more sense than the rest of them." I pointed with my chin toward the adjacent chamber where the girls slept.

The tension in Helena's face eased slightly, but the wariness remained. There was an interval of silence during which I imagined her struggling to decide whether to admit it or not. "It is true, signora," she said finally. "I have made an error of judgment. I promise I won't see him again," she added, holding my gaze.

Half-relieved that there would be no tearful scene of pleading and justification—most young girls believe that their first *innamoramento* is true love destined to last a lifetime—I was nonetheless dismayed. For if my suspicions regarding her condition were correct, she clearly did not even care about the man. She would bring us both down, and for what? A momentary weakness, nothing more.

"You can promise all you want," I said harshly, and the sound grated in my own ears. I pointed an accusatory finger at her stomach. "The evidence of your liaison will soon be in plain view to all, and then what will you do?"

What will we both do?

Her eyes followed the line of my finger. She looked momentarily puzzled, then she lifted her head. "If you are suggesting that I have fallen with child, signora, I assure you I have not." There was a mix of relief, fleeting amusement, and something else in her voice, a slight thickness that betrayed an emotion bubbling just under the surface.

I studied her, my confusion growing. The fact that she did not blush or lower her eyes at my line of questioning suggested a more daring and defiant nature than I had suspected. She'd had a secret, and she was not ashamed when it came out. Yet her denial sounded genuine.

"Well . . ." I said, then I took a draught from my cup to hide my perplexity. "I will wait a few days to see if your appetite and your color return. If you are not better by the year's end, I will have Doctor Baldazzi examine you." Helena grimaced—an understandable reaction—before composing her face again. "Then I will have more than your word to rely on."

Helena dipped her head, her eyes never leaving my face. "As you wish, signora." Again, she sounded confident. There was not a trace of apprehension in her voice.

"I am going to keep an eye on you," I warned her. "If I see any indication that the affair continues, I will inform the queen and you will be sent home immediately." I paused to let it sink in. "You may go."

She turned to leave.

"And Helena."

She stopped with a hand on the doorknob.

"If you find yourself in a delicate condition," I said, more softly this time, "know that he—whoever he is—will deny it, and you will be left to fend for yourself with your reputation damaged beyond reprieve. You will carry your dishonor for the rest of your life, while he will go on enjoying his."

The darkness that came over Helena's face lasted only a heartbeat, but it terrified me nonetheless. I turned to the sideboard as she closed the door behind her.

I put the goblet down on the tray with a loud metallic clang and ran a hand over my forehead. Between this business with Zamborski's murder and Helena's little love game that could spell disaster for both of us, this was not a joyous season for me.

Yet it was about to get much worse.

5

December 27th, 1519

We may have been in the middle of Christmas celebrations, but the business of the realm must continue, especially when that realm is surrounded by enemies. Two days after Zamborski's murder, the king received a delegation from the Sejm, which had declared war on the Teutonic Order on December 11th. Along with the deputies came Crown Marshal Mikołaj Firlej, who was to lead the army on that campaign. After Muscovy, the Teutonic Order—a fief north of the kingdom's borders on the Baltic coast and closely allied with the Habsburg emperor—was Poland's greatest foe. This was despite the fact that its Grand Master Albrecht von Hohenzollern was King Zygmunt's own nephew.

The queen was a known opponent of the Habsburgs; alongside Jan Łaski, Archbishop of Gniezno and Primate of Poland, she campaigned for expanding Polish influence on the coast. She had therefore persuaded the king to include her in the war council. But I suspected she had another motive as well. Since the previous autumn, she had been spending a great deal of time with her secretary Mantovano and her trusted advisors Antonio Carmignano and Piotr Gamrat. They were planning a series of agricultural reforms in the eastern principalities of Pińsk and Kobryń that the queen had received as a royal grant upon her arrival in Poland. Those improvements would raise

yields and boost her revenues, so any talk of war was of interest to her. Moreover, although she had not admitted it openly,
everyone knew—and not everyone was happy—that the queen
wanted to acquire more lands.

At the appointed hour she made her way to the council
chamber. I was the only one of her attendants to accompany
her and had to swear on the Bible that I would not divulge
anything I heard there. The deputies, the marshal, and Archbishop Łaski were already waiting when we arrived, and the
king joined us shortly afterward.

"Marshal, Your Grace. It is a pleasure," he greeted his guests
as he entered the chamber together with Chancellor Stempowski. "Madam." He kissed the queen's hand.

I noticed that Stempowski—normally haughty and self-
assured, due not just to his high position in the kingdom, but
also his close friendship with the king that went back to their
childhood—looked rather sullen. It was no wonder, I thought,
for as the leader of the pro-Habsburg faction at the court, he
must have opposed the war and had failed to persuade the
parliament against its declaration.

The gentlemen and the queen moved to the center of the
chamber occupied by a large walnut table on which a map of
the kingdom and her neighbors was spread out. Little blue-and-
yellow flags, the color of the Jagiellons, were tacked into several
points on the map. From the corner where I sat, I could see the
king tracing a line with his finger from a location I assumed
was Kraków, pausing at the first of the flags to the north.

"Are you all set for the assembly at Koło?" he asked Firlej.

"Yes, Your Majesty." The marshal said. "We have nearly
four thousand men. The *wojewoda* of Kalisz is yet to make a
pledge, but I expect it within days. We will also have a banner
from Bohemia and two sent by the Duke of Mazovia."

Mikołaj Firlej was a sinewy man of medium height and
looked to be in his fifties. He was dressed modestly yet with

care in a soft black leather doublet, black hose, and dark brown boots fashionably loose about his bony calves. I recalled that even though he had successfully fought against Muscovy in the previous five years, he had started his career as a courtier to the king's father and later became a respected diplomat. The bottom half of his face was obscured by a thick gray moustache and beard, so the voice that came out was gruff and somewhat muffled, but it was firm and confident.

"That is good." The king seemed pleased, but then his habitually beneficent face hardened. "Our vassals are doing their duty, for we must curb the ambitions of the Order once and for all." He paced to the window and back without looking at his chancellor, who stood with an inscrutable look on his face although he could not have liked what he was hearing. Across the table, I could see a small smile playing on the queen's lips as she shifted her gaze from the chancellor to the archbishop, her ally.

The king returned to the table. "And from Koło we will be marching toward Pomesania?" he asked, pointing further north on the map.

"Weather permitting," Firlej cautioned.

"Your Majesty," the chancellor finally spoke, "would it not be better to wait until the spring, when we can be sure that the snow is behind us?"

The king frowned. It was obvious that he was eager for the war, but either because of his friendship with Stempowski or his innate caution, he stopped to consider this.

Seeing her husband's hesitation, the queen intervened. "Your Majesty, the Order is conniving with Muscovy *and* the empire. If we put off stopping them, the knights will take Royal Prussia and Warmia from us before we know it. There is a thaw abroad," she added, "but even if it snows again, it is hardly reason enough to delay a campaign that will protect the kingdom from grave danger from the north *and* the west." The emphasis was clearly for the chancellor's benefit in both cases.

Stempowski scowled but held his tongue.

The king nodded. "We have been fighting them for more than a hundred years, since the very founder of this dynasty was still on the throne." He tapped the middle of the map with his forefinger, looking determined. "It is time to deal them a final blow."

The tension on the queen's face eased. The archbishop, too, looked pleased.

"We have been praying to God for fair weather every day," the king declared. "So far, it seems, our prayers have been answered." With a hand adorned by a single gold ring engraved with the Jagiellon double cross, he gestured toward the windows. There, the water from the melting snow was dripping from the eaves and arches of the courtyard so fast it seemed like a light rain was falling.

"Indeed." The marshal inclined his head. Then he cleared his throat. "But I have a request to make of Your Majesty." He paused. The king, still studying the map, motioned for him to continue. "It appears that no reinforcements for the knights have yet arrived from Moscow, and therefore the Grand Master is not ready for war—which favors us. However, the Order's cities are well fortified."

"Yes, yes, we know that." The king waved his hand.

"Some more heavily than others," Firlej went on. "We should be able to take Sztum, but for bigger towns like Marienwerder, we will need cannon."

A new frown creased the king's forehead, this time skeptical. "Are you sure, marshal?"

"Yes." The firmness of the answer left no doubt about it. "It is also a persuasive weapon. The very threat of its use is often enough for a fortress to surrender. That is what happened,

Your Majesty will recall, when the French marched on Naples in the year 1495."

Marshal Firlej may have been a diplomat once, but today he was a general, determined to advocate for this army and mindful of nothing else. But the deputies shifted uncomfortably, casting glances in the direction of the queen. The French campaign that the marshal had alluded to had been conducted with the help of the queen's great-uncle Ludovico Sforza of Milan. Thus, many on the peninsula, and especially the then-pope Alexander VI, considered it a treachery. Some still did. But those words had no effect on Bona, who remained royally impassive. She was proud of her ancestry. She was, and always would be, a great supporter of alliances with France.

The king was too preoccupied with Firlej's request to notice any of that. "How many cannon are we talking about?"

"As many as can be spared."

The king tugged at his beard. "That would require significant additional manpower, horses, and wagons to transport and operate, would it not?"

"Indeed."

"It would put a significant strain on the treasury," the chancellor chimed in eagerly.

Everyone knew that the kingdom struggled financially, and a silence fell on the chamber. Even the queen could not directly contradict that statement, but when her eyes went again to the archbishop, I knew something was coming. She gave Łaski a barely perceptible nod.

"Not if we impose a new tax," the archbishop said.

The chancellor snorted, and the queen stifled another smile. Her face was alive with anticipation for the king's response. All at once I understood what she wanted and how she planned to make her case for it. It was brilliant.

"It would be worth it"—Firlej picked up on the suggestion—"if it could buy us peace and security in the north, not to mention an unfettered access to the sea. Then we could focus on the eastern borderlands and the threat from the Tatars."

"I have levied a poll tax twice in the last ten years for the war against Vasili of Muscovy. I cannot do it again." The king shook his head. "My merchants and burghers will not abide it. And the Jews! I had to break the agreement their forefathers had struck with my grandsire when he permitted them to settle here. Their payments to the Crown were fixed at that time, but I forced them to accept new terms." The king looked unhappy, and I sympathized with him, knowing his non-confrontational nature. "If we tax the Jews again, they might pick up and leave. We benefit from their presence as much as they do from our protection."

"The last land tax was the highest in memory," Stempowski stated preemptively. His concern was understandable: he was one of the largest landowners in the kingdom. "Any more, and there will be no profits left."

"The yields are not enough to support a new levy on the land, either." The king spread his hands as he turned to the marshal.

"The yields are low because the land is worked inefficiently," the queen put in.

This time it was not just the chancellor but also the deputies from the Sejm who looked uncomfortable. Many, if not all of them, were landowners themselves, although as members of the parliament's lower house, they were not the same wealthy old aristocracy to which Stempowski belonged. They were only *szlachta*, the lesser nobility, but that did not mean that they would be any more eager to pay another tax.

"And what can be done about that, madam?" the king asked. The question was put in earnest, for he was aware of the queen's reform plans for her estates.

Before she answered, Bona swept the gathering with her gaze to heighten the sense of anticipation and to make sure that she had everyone's attention—which she most definitely did.

"I ordered a detailed report from each of the dower lands Your Majesty saw fit to grant me," she began, and the king nodded in acknowledgment. "They have given me and my advisors valuable insight as well as ideas for improvements that can be made." Another pause. "We will begin by installing competent and trusted administrators where such are lacking, then we will measure the size of all the estates in a uniform fashion and merge those that will benefit from it."

She paused again for effect, ignoring the skepticism on the faces of everyone except the king and the archbishop. I had to admire her confidence. "In Kobryń and Pińsk we will introduce a system whereby an estate will be divided into three parts, one to be sown with winter crops such as wheat and rye, one with beans, lentils, and peas, and one will be left fallow for a year. These assignments will rotate every season, allowing each field to rest and replenish. My advisor Carmignano studied this way of farming across Italy, and we believe that if we adopt it here, it will increase yields very quickly."

The landowners did not look pleased. "That will require more plowing than the current method," the chancellor protested, and the deputies nodded in agreement. They knew that what the queen was saying applied not just to her, but potentially to all of them. They had little appetite for such an upheaval, not to mention the costs associated with it. "We can barely get what we need out of our peasants as it is."

"It *will* require more plowing," the queen responded, "and I will ensure that I have enough men, oxen, and plows to do so. In fact, there is a new type of plow that can help make the process faster. I am having one sent to me for inspection. It should be here next month."

"It will take years to see benefits from the scheme Your Majesty proposes," the chancellor said with due deference, but he was unable to hide his satisfaction at pointing that out. "None of it will help raise the funds for the artillery Marshal Firlej believes is needed now." It was his turn to look triumphant as he turned to the king. He, too, was confident.

"That is true," the queen retorted, "but the treasury, depleted though it is, can surely withstand the cost of sending a few cannon north. In the meantime, you can start by making changes that, come harvest time, will already bring enough extra revenue to reimburse the Crown." This time there was no doubt as to whom she had in mind. "For example, you can collect more dues in coin rather than in kind. That is what I did last year."

And just like that, she made everyone in that chamber unable to contradict her. The king could not deny that the funds could be advanced, while the chancellor and the deputies could no longer claim that there was no way of raising additional money. It would be the equivalent of saying that they did not want to make improvements on their estates that were likely to result in higher profits—and more income for the Crown—in the long run. But most of all—and that was the master stroke—she had joined forces with Łaski. The archbishop was a rabid anti-Habsburg who also happened to be one of the only top clerics to support a greater taxation of ecclesiastical estates. If Stempowski so much as mentioned the light burden of taxation on the Church, I had no doubt the archbishop would offer to share the burden.

The chancellor's face darkened, and the deputies looked disconsolate. The prospect of having to reorganize the way their families had farmed for centuries was becoming real, as was the fact that any rewards for that inconvenience would be eaten up by a new levy.

But I could see that the king liked the proposal, though he was careful not to be overtly enthusiastic about it. "It is an idea worth considering," he stated diplomatically, then he turned to

Firlej. "Prepare a cost estimate for the use of the cannon you need, marshal. And before we authorize the funds, we will wait for your report from the field. We will only send the artillery if the campaign stalls. Go with God, and may He bless your effort."

It was a typical way the king made decisions—satisfying few but offending few also. Instead, I saw some dark glances, not least that of Chancellor Stempowski, trailing after the queen as we left the chamber. I knew that, whatever the outcome, she would be seen as the power behind the throne—or the power itself.

When we returned to the queen's apartments, Bona wanted to play a game of chess. She sent for the Princess of Montefusco, who played well enough to be entertaining but not so well that the queen would not win most of the time.

Portia set up the chessboard by the hearth, where a log fire was blazing briskly, spreading the refreshing scent of pine throughout the sitting chamber. Only half of the candles were lit in the sconces in each corner, giving it a warm but subdued light, and the queen ordered music to be played. Helena was the most accomplished musician of us all; she picked up a lute, seated herself by one of the two mullioned windows, tilted her head to one side, and began to pluck the strings, filling the air with the high sentimental notes of *La Villanella.*

In the meantime, Magdalena was pouring wine into Venetian glass goblets, talking in a low but excited voice to Lucrezia, who was arranging honey cakes on a tray. It was the usual idle chatter, but I pricked up my ears when I heard the name Sebastian Konarski. Magdalena was telling Lucrezia that he was the youngest of three brothers and had two sisters besides, though none of them served at the court, as far as she knew. He, on the other hand, had been with His Majesty for four years and was thirty years old.

"The perfect age for a man"—she gave a sigh—"when he has reached full maturity, but his stomach has not yet begun to strain the buttons of his doublet."

They covered their mouths with their hands to stifle a burst of laughter, and I asked myself how Magdalena had managed to learn so much about the king's junior secretary in just two days.

As the queen and princess seated themselves at the chessboard, the latter inquired about the war council. The queen limited herself to mentioning the cost concerns and the king's unwillingness to raise a poll tax, especially on Jewish merchants. They played in silence for a while as the rest of us listened to the music and night fell outside. By the time Helena moved on to a livelier piece by Francesco Canova da Milano, the queen's favorite composer, the princess was losing. I could see that she was distracted. As I wondered what new piece of gossip was on her mind—for it could not have been the nuances of funding the Teutonic War—she lost her second rook, and her queen was in peril.

Contemplating her next move, the princess said, "His Majesty's concerns remind me of something I've heard ..." She leaned forward, her eyes shining conspiratorially in her over-rouged face. She even lowered her voice to enhance the dramatic effect of what was to follow, although not so low that all of us could not hear her loud and clear. "They say Zamborski was killed by a Jew."

Helena's fingers slipped on the strings, the sudden disharmony ringing in our ears as she murmured an apology. Portia made a quick sign of the cross and kissed her golden crucifix.

The queen lifted a skeptical eyebrow. "Who says that?" she asked as Helena resumed playing, more softly than before.

"My maid told me last night when she brought me my bed warmer. She said the servant quarters talk about nothing else, and most of them agree it was a disgruntled Jew." She nodded vigorously, leaving us with no doubt as to where she stood on that. "They bring their goods to the delivery area, and they know that passageway well. And—as His Majesty said—they are still angry at the higher taxes. It makes sense."

I tried—and failed—to see the point of killing a courtier, especially one unconnected to the king's tax-collecting authorities, to protest the kingdom's fiscal policies. I looked at the queen. She, too, was thinking, the game forgotten, a skeptical frown marring her forehead.

"But what would a Jew be doing about the castle on a day when we were celebrating the birth of Our Savior?" she asked, and I shifted my gaze to the princess.

"Why, murdering a king's man, of course!"

I groaned inwardly and saw a shadow of irritation pass over the queen's face. She had little patience for her cousin.

"Your Highness," I said, my tone duly deferential. "I think what Her Majesty is saying is that the merchants would have delivered their goods days before the feast, rather than when we were all already at the table." The queen nodded, and I went on, "There would have been no way for any of them to be here on Christmas Day without arousing suspicion. If a Jew had wanted to kill Zamborski, he would have chosen a different day."

The princess shrugged, her face assuming a look of offended indifference. All she had wanted was to share a piece of gossip, and she was clearly disappointed that it had not had the desired effect.

She would have been more satisfied later than night, for when I went into the girls' bedchamber, I found them gathered in a knot around Helena's bed, debating vigorously in their nightgowns. They fell silent as I walked in and took stock of their flushed faces and shining eyes.

"It seemed fanciful what the Princess of Montefusco said today, and your point was well taken, signora," Helena said to me. "But we have been wondering—what if it *is* true?" A look of anxiety stole over her face.

"I do not believe it," I said. "You should not excite your-selves with such speculation, especially at this hour. Go to bed."

"*I* believe it!" It was Magdalena. Color rose to her face as it contorted with fear and hatred. "It is well known that Jews drink the blood of Christian children at Christmas."

I felt their eyes turn to me, but I kept mine on Magdalena. I remained deliberately silent to give her time to think about what she had said. But she only raised her chin defiantly and, realizing that I was not going to back her, looked fiercely about to find support elsewhere. None of them spoke, although some heads nodded timidly.

"Pan Zamborski's body showed no sign of being drained of blood," I said, trying to keep the memory of the corpse in the crypt at bay. "And besides," I added pointedly, "he was not a child."

Lucrezia burst out laughing, but she went quiet when I sent her what I hoped was a withering look. Magdalena blushed again but did not back down. "I still think it was a Jew."

I sighed. "Go to bed. I want the candles put out by the time the cathedral bell strikes midnight." Which, I hoped, would not be long.

There was no point in arguing this any further. In truth, none of us had any idea who the murderer was. It could have been anyone who had ever set foot inside the castle, Jew or not.

6

December 28th, 1519

"Donna Caterina."

It was still dark outside, but I was already dressed and on my way to the queen's chamber. Bona liked to rise before dawn, when most of the castle was still quiet.

The voice startled me amid the silence, but its familiar sound was reassuring. I turned to find Secretary Konarski walking toward me, past the guard who waved him through.

"Good morning." I made a small curtsy and was mortified to feel the heat of a blush rise to my face. Silently, I thanked God the gallery was still dim, with only a few small torches set in the brackets. Just in case, I did not move from the shadowed alcove where I had stopped.

Konarski returned my curtsy with a bow. I wondered what had brought him to the queen's apartments so early, as he did not seem to be in a hurry and was not carrying his customary sheaf of papers.

Perhaps he read that question on my face, for he hesitated, and I thought I saw slight color come out in his cheeks. But that may have been a trick of the light and shadow playing on his features. "I—I have come to inform you that an arrest has been made in connection with Pan Zamborski's murder. I know Her Majesty has an interest in the case."

"Oh." I tried to gather my thoughts. "So fast." In the back of my mind, I wondered why he would need to bring this news to us at such an early hour. Unless the suspect was someone connected to our household. The thought made my heart flutter with sudden anxiety. "Who is he?"

"A servant. A burly young fellow who helps with unloading deliveries. He was found skulking about the passageway last night, long after his work was done," he added when I did not respond.

"Oh," I said again, trying to make sense of this information. Zamborski was killed near the delivery entrance, so it would not be surprising if someone working there was responsible. A servant was always in need of coin, and a fine dagger would fetch a handsome price, not to mention the money stolen from the purse. A quick and neat solution to the case.

Except he had been arrested for being there two nights *after* the murder.

"Do you believe him to be the culprit?" I asked, conscious of the skeptical note in my voice.

Konarski hesitated again. "I don't know." I almost smiled at how diplomatic he was. "He will be interrogated, and we must trust that the truth will come out."

"Where is he now?"

"In Baszta Sandomierska," he said.

The *baszta*, or tower, stood at the foot of Wawel Hill on the southern side of the castle. It was a royal jail, and a place with a history as grim as its appearance. It was a tall and narrow brick structure with slit windows that admitted little light into the cells inside. During the previous century, it had infamously housed several city councilors in the wake of the murder by a group of Kraków burghers of a magnate who had assaulted a local craftsman for the poor quality of a piece of work he had ordered. The councilors were beheaded after a swift trial, but they were said to be innocent of any involvement in the crime.

It was rumored that their souls still haunted the tower, pulling on chains in empty cells, jangling keys on their hooks, and causing candles to light up or extinguish of their own accord.

The prospect of setting foot in that place made me queasy. But I was overcome by a feeling, similar to the one I had experienced after the visit to the crypt, that what I heard did not make sense. For one thing, catching somebody at the scene of the crime two days after it had been committed was hardly proof of his involvement. And then there were the queen's suspicions regarding the chancellor. If she was correct, this arrest might serve as a distraction from the true perpetrator of the murder. I knew the queen would be very interested in this development, and if I managed to find a way to get into the jail and speak with the arrested man, I might bring her some valuable information.

It was a daring idea, of course; it was not my place to question anyone intended to be brought before the king's justice. Yet I had to give it a try. The way things were going with Helena, my future in the queen's household seemed more precarious than ever. Helping Bona and having her gratitude, I reasoned quickly, might go some way toward strengthening my position and shielding me from the consequences of my ineptitude in supervising the maids of honor.

"Panie Konarski," I addressed the secretary with the polite Polish appellation. "I must see this man."

He looked at me as if I had spoken in some unknown tongue. In his expression, I read the same reasons I should not do this as had just crossed my own mind.

"It is not a place for a lady—"

I seized his arm. "Please," I entreated him.

"The chancellor will never grant you permission to see him," he said reasonably, taking hold of my hand but not removing it.

"I know he won't. Which is why I am not going to seek it." My mind was working fast, even as I was acutely conscious of his touch. "But you can take me there; you have the authority as a royal secretary." I squeezed his arm until my own fingers hurt, the leather of his doublet soft and yielding but the muscles underneath it taut. "You can tell them I am his sister."

Konarski laughed, a small and indulgent sound. It was an outlandish idea, and we both knew it. I withdrew my hand. "Please," I repeated, and the warmth rose to my face again. But I did not avert my eyes. "Help me have a few words with him. It won't take long."

We stood like that for a few moments, our faces only inches apart, and I recalled all the feminine wiles my girls employed to perfection to wrap this courtier or that around their fingers. I possessed no such talent, so I just held his gaze, my breath coming fast between my lips. What would Magdalena or Lucrezia do?

Konarski stepped back, and I could see his Adam's apple working under the skin of his throat as he swallowed. "I'll see what I can do," he said in a low voice, then a small smile crossed his lips. "But you will have to dress more plainly than that." He gestured toward my bodice of blue satin trimmed with lace, over which hung several strings of creamy pearls. Then he turned on his heel and walked away before I could throw my arms around him in gratitude.

As I watched him disappear around the corner, I was glad I had not done it, but also vaguely disappointed.

I relayed Konarski's message about the arrest to the queen. She dismissed it as an attempt by the chancellor to blame his crime on someone else, as I had expected she would. When I offered to visit the tower to find out more, she gave me leave but warned me to be discreet about it.

Konarski, having concerns of his own, arranged it exactly that way. The next morning, he sent me a note instructing me to meet him by the gate to the queen's private garden an hour before vespers. Mindful of his suggestion, I put on the only linen gown I had, removed my pearls, earrings, and headdress so that my hair was covered only by a white coif. But my two winter cloaks were lined with marten fur and had silver clasps at the neck; one of them, a gift from the queen, was studded with small turquoises. In the end, I borrowed a woolen cloak that fastened with strings from one of the chambermaids, but I made sure to attach a purse with silver talons in it to my belt in case we had to bribe the guards to get inside. At the appointed time, I took a servants' staircase down and left by a side door.

The secretary was waiting for me at the end of a narrow passage that connected the courtyard with the garden, the expression on his face eloquent in his skepticism of my undertaking. I pushed down my hood and spread the folds of my cloak to reveal my modest attire, and he gave me a curt nod of approval that nonetheless sent a vein in my throat pulsing. I pulled the hood back on as he cleared his throat and turned to open the gate with a key he fished out of a pocket inside his cloak.

The garden was in the Italian style, with flower beds laid out like the squares of a chessboard, a marble fountain in the center, carved stone benches along the gravel paths, and a trellised loggia which, in the summer, was shaded by the leaves and flowers of the rose bushes that entwined it. It was the queen's favorite retreat when she was not away hunting in Niepołomice, for it reminded her of the gardens surrounding the palace in Bari, where she grew up. But the plants were bare now, and the ground was covered with patches of grayish snow that we tried to step around as we cut to the far side. Konarski unlocked a small iron-studded door in the outer wall, and I admired how efficient and quick he was about it for a scribe who spent most of his time copying court documents. Within moments we were outside the castle.

"We must hurry." I looked up at the sky. Out in the open it was still light enough, but the shadows of the night would be rising soon.

"Darkness favors us, signora," Konarski said, and I realized that he was right. If someone spotted us, we would have much explaining to do. He lifted a small unlit lantern I had not previously noticed. "For the way back." He grinned, and I found myself smiling, too.

We went down a narrow unpaved path made more perilous by the softness of the sodden ground. Our boots made squelching sounds and were caked with mud within moments. When I slipped and nearly fell, my companion slackened the pace. He took my arm to help me remain steady until we arrived at the cobbled road that started at another, much larger door in the southern wall of the castle. It was the delivery entrance. We took that road all the way down to the foot of the hill, arriving at the tower door. Once there, Konarski advised me to take off my calfskin gloves and hide them inside my cloak.

When he knocked on the heavy oak door, my anxiety returned. Everything was quiet for a long moment, and just as he raised his hand to knock again, a pair of red, bleary eyes appeared through the iron grille. They took some time to focus, then considered us for a while before vanishing. Soon, we heard the sound of bolts being pulled back and the clang of keys being turned in the locks. The door opened with a groan of its rusty hinges to reveal a fat guard whose mouth moved around in a chewing motion. Everything about him was greasy, from his hair to his hands, down to his boots.

"Wha's your business 'ere, sir?" he asked without pausing the chewing. Pellets of saliva-moistened bread flew in our direction, accompanied by a whiff of sour wine. I took a step back.

"I am a secretary to Chancellor Stempowski," Konarski said, and the guard's bloodshot eyes became instantly more alert. "This good woman's brother, Maciek Koza, is being held at the king's pleasure, and I have leave to take her to his cell so she may have a word with him." He produced a piece of paper that he waved in the guard's face as he pushed past him. I followed swiftly, trying to hide my surprise.

The guard hesitated, but Konarski's posture exuded so much confidence that he shrugged. "You will 'ave to leave your weapon wi' me." He reached out a calloused palm, and his fingernails were rimmed with black. "It's the rules."

Konarski removed his dagger from his belt. It had a shapely wrought-silver hilt and a well-polished blade without any traces of tarnish, but no gemstone decorations. Its plain elegance was something I had already begun to associate with the king's secretary. "Mind that it is here when we return," he warned the guard, "or you will take up residence here yourself soon enough."

"I will also 'ave to check the lady for a weapon." The guard took a step toward me, a slimy smile beginning to spread over his lips. My hand instinctively went up to where my cloak was tied at my neck, and I shuddered at the thought of those greasy fingers touching me.

But Konarski lifted a hand before he took another step, his open palm landing on the guard's chest with a soft thump. "You will do no such thing." He pushed him back and waved the paper again with his other hand. "Must I remind you on whose authority we are here?"

Again, I was surprised, for the chancellor could not possibly have given us this permit, but as the guard stared blankly at the paper, I realized that he could not read. I glanced at Konarski with renewed appreciation for his clever ruse.

The matter of the search thus settled, the guard placed the dagger in a chipped wooden tray, mumbling under his breath, or possibly just resuming his interrupted chewing process. Then he motioned to his companion, a pimply youth with equally greasy hair and a massive set of keys at his belt, to take us to the cell. Before we were through the inner door, I heard the older guard drop back into his chair with a groan followed by a loud belch.

The guards' room had been warmed—although barely—by a small brazier, but when we stepped into the inner stairwell of the jail, it was as if we had found ourselves in the crypt under the cathedral again. I pulled the chambermaid's cloak closer about me, wishing I could put my gloves back on. But I tried to find solace in the fact that at least the foul smell hanging in the air was made less aggressive by the icy cold.

The stairwell was dark, with only infrequent torches guttering on the walls, and Konarski lit his lamp from one of them as we climbed to the third floor. I kept my eyes on the back of the young guard's worn jerkin, the stories of the tower's ghosts rushing unbidden to my head as the shadows danced around us. From somewhere below us came a faint cry and a moan, and my heart quickened nervously as I wondered if it was one of the damned spirits of my imagination or some poor wretch, still alive, being stretched on a rack to extract a confession.

Finally, our guide stopped in front of a door and opened it after some fumbling with the keys. As we entered, Konarski bid him to remain outside and closed the door in his face with another reminder of the chancellor.

The cell was small, no more than four paces across, with not even a pallet to sleep on. Its floor was strewn with dirty straw that rustled and squeaked suspiciously, leaving me with no doubt as to the kinds of companions with whom the inmate shared that dismal space. But at least it had a tiny window to let in a little bit of fresh air. Not that it made a big difference.

Maciek Koza, large and fleshy despite his sixteen years, was slumped in a corner. When he heard us, he raised his head. It was covered with thick, bristly hair, and the movement—slow and wary—made him look oddly like a bear. The small, closely set dark eyes that squinted at us in the lamplight showed a mix of dullness and fear, like a beast brought to slaughter. My chest tightened—the boy was obviously slow-witted.

He saw that I was not one of the jailers and laughed briefly, and it was in that moment that I recognized him. My mind traveled back more than a year, to the autumn of 1518, about six months after we had arrived in Kraków. One evening, well past eleven o'clock, I heard a patter of feet past my door and looked out just in time to see Lucrezia reach the end of the queen's gallery. But instead of taking the right turn onto the main corridor of our floor of the castle—assuming she had any business being out of her chamber at that hour—she pushed open a small door on the left that led to the servants' staircase. I hastily wrapped my dressing gown around me and followed her.

When I entered the staircase, I could hear her steps fading on the top floor, where the servants slept, but it was empty when I arrived there. As I stood wondering if I would have to knock on every door and rouse everyone to find her, a door opened in the middle of the corridor and a boy came out, closing it carefully behind him. He was large but moved slowly, murmuring some words under his breath that were punctured by small bursts of laughter, idiot-like and inno-cent. It was the same boy who now sat in front of me in the corner of the cell.

I remembered pushing past him into the chamber and finding Lucrezia in the embrace of his roommate, a dark and handsome fellow who often served at the lower-ranking tables in the banqueting hall. Only a few weeks earlier, I had seen Lucrezia chatting with him during the reception for the Muscovite envoys and admonished her against it. Clearly, she had not taken it to heart. When she saw me, she screamed and pulled away from the man, gathering the folds of her dressing gown that had come loose around her neck. Even before I had a chance to say a word, she ran around me and out into the corridor, where I caught up with her.

"What were you thinking coming here in the middle of the night for a tryst with a servant?" My voice shook with indignation at the deception. Out of the corner of my eye, I saw the boy cowering against the wall, whimpering, although he must have been stronger than both of us combined.

Lucrezia put her hands to her face and started crying. "I'm sorry, signora," she sobbed. "I really am!"

"You will be even sorrier when I tell the queen." I grabbed her by the arm as doors along the corridor began opening. The last thing I needed was for us to be seen and start the gossip mill. I steered her toward the staircase. "When she learns about what you have been up to, you will be sent home with the next group leaving for Bari," I added as we began our descent.

By then she was wailing loudly and clutching at my gown, and I had to stop on the landing lest we both tumble down the stairs. She kept promising that she would not do it again and imploring me not to tell the queen, and she calmed down only after I said that I would think about it.

I never did tell the queen. Lucrezia's lover was soon dismissed from service anyway, but that event was the reason I had taken to checking on the girls every night at midnight to make sure they were all in their own beds. Not that that was a sure way of keeping them there—to be certain, I would have to stop sleeping altogether.

I ran a hand over my eyes and crouched beside the boy. Both of his wrists were shackled in iron bracelets chained to the wall. He recoiled slightly as our eyes met at his level. "Maciek?" I said gently. I wanted to put a hand on his arm, but he shifted and the chains clanged, and I felt a momentary panic as I moved back. Behind me I could hear Konarski take a step toward us, but I raised my hand to signify that I was fine.

"My name is Caterina," I enunciated the Polish words more carefully than I did with Konarski. "I am a lady-in-waiting to Her Majesty the Queen," I added in what I hoped was a reassuring voice. I made sure to keep it low because I would have bet every coin in my purse that the pimply guard was listening at the keyhole.

"The queen." Maciek nodded, smiling like a child. "A beautiful lady."

"Yes." I smiled back. "Do you know why you are here?"

His face darkened. "There was a murder, and they say I done it." He rocked back and forth, then shook his head as if to convince himself. "But I done nothing!"

I considered him for some moments. He was big, which was why he worked as a carrier, but there was a gentleness and vulnerability to him that made it hard to imagine that he would be capable of killing someone. He was a bear, but one without claws. Besides, he did not have the wits to plan a murder, and Zamborski's killing was nothing if not deliberate.

"What were you doing by the delivery door so late when they arrested you?" I asked.

"I been there to see that the doors was properly locked up for the night. It was not me who done it!" From his seated position, he bowed so low that his forehead almost struck the ground. When he looked up again, I saw tears pooling in his eyes, but they were tears of bewilderment more than fear. "I swear!" He pulled on the chains, and Konarski stepped up to my side.

"It's all right. I believe you," I said soothingly, and this time I touched his hand. It was icy cold. He was wearing only a linen shirt and a sleeveless jerkin, an outfit he must have had on when they brought him here from the castle. "I believe you," I repeated and felt him calming down.

After a moment, I asked, "Do you remember what you were doing during the Christmas feast?"

He raised his head, his eyes wandering along the wall behind me as he tried to recall. "I stayed in our chamber with the other carriers. There was no deliveries to take."

"And did you stay there all evening?"

He nodded. "We ate and drank, then we sang carols." He gave a wan smile, his eyes roving to a metal plate sticking out of the straw near his feet, licked clean by him or the rats.

I rose to my feet. "Thank you, Maciek. I hope that the truth will out and you will be released soon," I said, even as I began to fear that would not happen. Whatever Stempowski's motivations, the boy was a perfect scapegoat.

"I only left once," Maciek spoke again just as I was about to turn away.

Konarski and I exchanged a look. "Left to go where?"

"To piss." Maciek's forehead creased with a deep frown. "And I seen somebody."

"Who? Who did you see?" My heart quickened.

"A man in a cloak."

"A man in a cloak?" I echoed. "By your chamber door?" I squatted down again, and it was all I could do to not shake him by his shoulders. "What did he look like?"

"Didn't see his face, only the cloak."

I took an exasperated breath. "You only saw a cloak? No person?"

Maciek nodded. He was thinking hard, the effort obvious in the tension of his face. "He was turning a corner down the corridor when I came out. I just seen a bit of cloak, fluttering-like, and then he was gone." He shuddered. "Like a phantom." He huddled his broad shoulders into himself.

I felt sorry for forcing him to remember what clearly had been a disturbing experience, but this was too important. "What color was the cloak?"

"Black," he said in a muffled voice, his chin still pressed to his chest.

A thought occurred to me: was it the hem of a man's cloak or a woman's gown he had seen? Perhaps it was Lucrezia up to her old tricks again. But she had stayed at the table all evening.

Then my heart stopped. Was it *Helena*? She had been absent for some time, and by her own admission, she had gone to meet someone. But no, it could not have been her. She would not carry on with a servant, of that I was certain. She *had to* be more discriminating than Lucrezia. No, most likely Maciek had seen the back of the killer, but that was all I would get from him. It was almost as if he had seen a ghost—no face, no body, just a sweep of cloth disappearing into the shadows.

Back downstairs, I clenched my jaw so as not to shout at the fat guard and his underling. Instead, I held out a hand with two silver talons. "Fetch a wool blanket and some food for M—my brother."

The guard looked surprised that I would dispose of such a sum, but he took the coins readily enough, trying them between his teeth before pocketing them. "There will be more if you treat him well," I added as Konarski ushered me out the door with more than a slight pressure on my back.

"What are you doing throwing silver around like that?" he hissed. "You are supposed to be a peasant. Do you want to get us in trouble?" He fastened the dagger the younger guard had restored to him back at his belt.

"I'm sorry," I said. I would never forgive myself if Konarski's position was put in jeopardy because of me. "But you saw that place. I would not let a dog sleep in that cell."

He grunted, and we set out on our way back as the cathedral clock struck six, the clangs echoing heavy and somehow louder in the dark. We passed a whipping block and a pair of stocks on a low hill on the other side of the delivery road, where the punishments of the tower's inmates were carried out. In warmer months, the stocks were occupied daily. Only a few days earlier, two men had been flogged for getting into a knife fight in one of the city's taverns.

Whenever capital crimes were dealt with, the block was replaced with a scaffold or an execution block, depending on the condemned man's status. The owners of the nearby town-houses made a handsome profit renting out windows facing the hill, which offered a prime viewing location. Townsfolk who could not afford it but were still eager to participate in the entertainment crowded the streets below, attracting hawkers of all manner of goods as well as pickpockets, both in search of profit. It saddened me to think that Maciek might soon make for that sort of spectacle.

It was colder now than when we had come down, the thaw seemingly over. The ground was not as soft anymore—the mud had begun to congeal as the temperature dropped—but it was not any less slippery. From the woods across the river, a wolf's lonesome howl reached us, and I shivered.

"Do you think he did it?" I asked as we began to pick our way back up the hill, first over the cobbles and then over the unpaved path, Konarski holding me by the arm and lighting the way with the lantern in his other hand.

He thought for a while before answering. "I want to say no, but"—he searched for the right words—"appearances can be deceiving."

"What do you mean?"

"When I was a boy," he said, "my father's groom had a son who was much like Maciek. He was large and strong, but he had the mind of a child." There was a note of sadness in his voice as he cast his mind back. "One day, a milkmaid was found smothered in the barn, a girl of barely eleven. There were no signs of any other violence on her, and after an inquiry, it was found that the groom's son had done it. He said he only wanted to play with her ..."

I patted the hand that held my arm. "Even if Maciek had some interaction with Zamborski that night—and there is no proof that he did—that murder was no accident."

We continued for some time in silence.

"He says he was with the other carriers the whole evening; surely that proves he could not have done it?" I said. "They can testify in his defense."

"The chancellor interviewed them on the night of Maciek's arrest. I was there. They confirmed that he had stepped out claiming he needed to relieve himself, but what time it was or how long he was gone, they could not say as they were all drunk by then."

I snorted. "But if he had killed and robbed Zamborski, would he not have pawned the dagger the next day, then take off with the money, never to be seen again?" I was breathing faster from both the effort of the climb and the frustration building up inside me.

"He will be put before a jury, and we must trust that they will make the right decision—"

"I will ask for a meeting with Chancellor Stempowski."

Konarski halted abruptly, and I almost slipped. "What?"

"I will ask to meet with the chancellor so I can speak for Maciek. I will say his family petitioned me to do that."

"Caterina." He tried to sound stern, but the familiar address softened the effect. "You should forget this matter." I started to answer, but he raised his hand. "Listen to me." He took a breath. "The queen has detractors in the king's household, advisors who are unhappy with her involvement in state affairs and with her push for farming reforms, which they see as unwarranted meddling." I wanted to protest, but he was right. It had all been on display during the war council meeting. "If you seek to speak with the chancellor, it will be seen as another interference, not just by you, but by the queen," he warned me.

"Then we will let the boy die for someone else's crime?" I asked indignantly.

He took me by the elbow again, and we resumed our ascent. "I will talk to the chancellor," he said at length. Then he added, lowering his voice to a near whisper, "I shouldn't be telling you this, but ... let's just say the chancellor wasn't happy with his daughter's engagement. He had been hoping for someone better connected and higher placed. But he is a devoted father, and Celina had set her heart on Zamborski, despite his reputation as a scoundrel."

That, too, I already knew. Having it thus confirmed by Konarski made me wonder again if the queen might not be right about Stempowski after all. Perhaps there was more to her suspicions than a desire for a political opponent's downfall?

"So you see," he went on, "whoever killed him did the chancellor a favor. I hope to God I am wrong, but he might just pin this on Maciek out of convenience." There was a hardness in his voice, and a touch of bitterness. I had the sense that, competent and diplomatic though he was, Konarski did not like the scheming and the intrigues that were so much a part of life at the court. I was curious why he had come to serve in the first place. But it was a good career for a man from a noble family, who, as the youngest of three brothers, likely could not count on much in the way of land inheritance.

Still, I was dismayed. If he was right, Maciek's fate was sealed. There was nothing either of us could do. But that did not mean that I should stop searching for the truth, especially now that nobody else seemed to be interested in finding it.

We reached the door to the queen's garden, the bare branches of ivy coiling around it like gray snakes. Before Konarski opened it, we stood facing each other, our breaths steaming between us. The lantern cast a small circle of light, but beyond it a black and moonless night pressed in on us, unrelieved by the sound of birds or insects in the middle of the winter season. Even the wolf had stopped howling.

"None of it makes sense," I said. "That cloaked figure—if, in fact, that was the killer—wandering around the servants' quarters far from the scene of his crime . . . Why?"

"To make himself harder to recognize if he encountered anyone?"

"In that case, he is a nobleman."

"Yes."

"But if he had just killed a man, why not leave the castle, flee as far away as he could before the body was discovered? Why stay?"

Konarski lifted the lantern higher and the flame flickered, causing his face to swim in light and shadow. "Perhaps because he lives here." He pointed with his chin toward the castle, and a shiver ran through my body again. But this time it was more than just the cold.

7

December 30th, 1519

It was a court tradition to hold *sanna*—a sleigh ride along the river to the royal hunting lodge in Niepołomice—on the day before New Year's Eve. It was the unofficial beginning of that celebration, but in the year 1519, it almost did not happen. For days it had looked like there would not be enough snow on the ground, but the thaw had come to an end that same evening we visited Maciek in the jail, and it snowed that night—a cold, hard type of snow, not abundant but compact enough to allow the sleighs to run smoothly.

King Zygmunt decided to hold another war council as the attack on the strongholds of the Teutonic Order was to start in a matter of weeks, and he called off his attendance. The queen joined him, and for a while it seemed like the ride would be canceled after all. But the king proclaimed that tradition must be honored, the court deserved the entertainment, and the *sanna* would go on, albeit without the royal couple. Only the most essential staff and those attending the council were ordered to remain in the castle, and everyone else who wanted to go to Niepołomice was free to do so.

I never liked New Year's Eve, with its sense of something passing, irrevocably ending, of time slipping from our grasp and taking away a part of ourselves as it floats into the dark gaping maw of the past. And, of course, that New Year's season was marred by the still-unsolved murder of one of the courtiers. Few believed that a slow-witted servant was responsible for it, yet the investigation seemed to have stalled. The queen persisted in her belief that Chancellor Stempowski was involved and that he wanted to shut the case down, but she could offer no proof. Nor could I, for that matter.

With all that hanging over us, I was especially happy that the day was bright and sunny, the winter sky pale blue and cloudless after the snow. I took my seat in a four-person sleigh with Lucrezia, Helena, and Jan Dantyszek, who had jumped in at the last minute, having run down from the castle among the stragglers. I was disappointed, for I had hoped that Sebastian Konarski would show up, and I had kept the seat empty for as long as I could with vague excuses. I guessed that he had been held up on the king's business, or the chancellor had called him to attend the council.

The sleigh was a large and sturdy vessel carved out of mature oak and painted elegant shining black, with gilded finishes around the edges and gilded knobs on the little doors on both sides. Four people could fit inside, facing each other in pairs, propped on soft cushions and with wool blankets piled on their knees. The ladies and I were wrapped in cloaks lined with marten fur, with fur hats on our heads and gloved hands in fur muffs. Dantyszek sat cavalierly with only a small feathered velvet cap on his head, the better to show off his wavy hair that shone golden where the sunlight touched it. But like us, he was wrapped in a thick cloak, which he informed us was bear fur from a beast he had slain himself.

It took a while for the sleighs to be tied together and prepared for departure, and as we waited, I took a flask filled with hot water mixed with raspberry syrup out of a leather pouch that servants had placed in each sleigh. I filled everyone's cups, and between our wrappings, the sun, and the warming beverage, the cold was not so biting anymore; in fact, it was rather invigorating.

Finally, we moved, leaving behind the slanted roofs of the city with their gleaming red tiles. The stone walls of the castle seemed brighter in the sunlight, almost as white as the surrounding snow. The village of Niepołomice lies four leagues east of Kraków, and the journey took us along the winding riverbank. It was here, according to ancient lore, that *smok wawelski*, the mighty Dragon of Wawel Hill, had come to drink from the Wisła to quell a fire burning in his stomach. He had dwelled in a cave on the slope of the hill and terrorized citizens and peasants from the surrounding countryside until a clever cobbler came up with a plan to slay the beast.

To that end, he stitched together a calfskin which he had stuffed with meat and a mix of smoldering sulfur, tinder, tar, and pitch, and he laid it outside the cave like an offering. When the hungry dragon next came out, he swallowed the calfskin whole, and soon an inferno was raging in his belly. Unable to quench his thirst no matter how much water he drank from the river, the dragon died breathing fire from his mouth, and the city was saved.

Some think it a legend, but others believe that a creature like that had indeed lived many centuries earlier when Kraków had just been founded. Whatever the case, the riverbank looked quiet and pristine now, its snow sparkling in the sun as if it had been dusted with crushed diamonds.

How different it was from its midsummer aspect, when townsfolk and courtiers came out to sing and dance on its lush grass speckled with violets, dandelions, and clover. The maids of honor made garlands of daisies and persuaded me to wear one. "You look so young, Donna Caterina!" they exclaimed when I took off my headdress and cap and pulled out the pins that held up my hair. The garland sat like a cool fragrant cloud around my head, and I did feel like a girl again, in fact, the lightness of it lifting the burden of my present life off my shoulders, if only for one afternoon. "Someone who didn't know you would think you one of us!" They laughed.

I laughed too, casting a discreet glance at a nearby archery target. There contestants were preparing for the competition, and Helena was among them. Zamborski stood in line as well, but my attention was attracted by a dark-haired man with an air of quiet confidence about him, without the cockiness or the aggressive loudness of the other men. That man was Konarski, as I would soon find out. He was not the biggest of them all, but his figure was lithe and his movements quick and precise. He made it look easy, whereas the others strained, the veins in their necks bulging. And he won the contest, besting Helena and Zamborski—in that order. A little later, as I congratulated Helena on her second place, he happened to walk by. I congratulated him on the win, and he bowed and introduced himself. That was the first time we spoke. I hoped to see him again after that, but as the dusk fell and the bonfires were lit, he disappeared. We went down to the river to sing and float the garlands at sunset, a beautiful ceremony punctured, for me, by a faint sense of disappointment.

After that day, I only saw him a few times in the banqueting hall on big court occasions. He always acknowledged me with a nod, but we never exchanged any other words. How strangely ironic that it was only this terrible event of Christmas night that had brought us closer together.

Now those lively images of the summertime faded before my eyes, replaced once more by the peaceful gleaming blanket of whiteness, and I began to be aware of Dantyszek flirting with Lucrezia. He was leaning toward her so that their shoulders brushed, and he was pointing out tracks in the snow, pronouncing which animals they belonged to.

Next to me Helena sat quietly, gazing into the distance. I thought she looked better than the other day, although that may have just been the cold giving her cheeks a faint pink color. Only once did her eyes turn to the couple opposite us. Lucrezia dropped her gaze in feigned modesty when Dantyszek, his voice low and throaty, stated that her eyes were shining like two black coals. A small smirk, almost of pity, lifted one corner of Helena's lips.

I was still stuck on trying to remember whether coal did in fact shine, when Helena's voice broke through some new nonsense Dantyszek had come up with. "Panie Jan," she said in a similarly low and breathy voice, a mix of subtle seduction and not-so-subtle mockery that made me lift my hand to my mouth to hide a smile. "I was sorry to hear about the death of Kasper Zamborski. I understand you were friends."

Dantyszek broke off in the middle of a sentence, blinking. "Yes, it was quite unfortunate and tragic," he mumbled. "He is sorely missed." Anyone could tell that Zamborski's murder was one of the farthest things from his mind at that moment.

He began to return his attention to Lucrezia, when Helena asked again, "Do you think it is true what they say: that he was killed by an irate husband who had found himself a cuckold?"

I stifled a gasp as Lucrezia rolled her eyes and gave a dramatic sigh. "Must we talk about such awful things on this beautiful morning of the *sanna*?" she complained, her tone whining. "We are here to have a good time, aren't we?" She looked eagerly to Dantyszek for confirmation.

A ghost of another smile touched Helena's lips, but she did not even glance at Lucrezia; she kept her eyes fastened on her companion, demanding an answer.

Dantyszek frowned. "That is not an altogether unreasonable assumption." He chuckled. "He did like the fairer sex," he added, sending Lucrezia a smoldering look that made her giggle.

I thought their behavior was rather tasteless, and I began to feel irritated. I would have to have a talk with Lucrezia tonight.

"If that is so, are you not worried that other members of your little society are in danger?" Helena pressed.

Dantyszek's smile faded. I know I should have scolded her for such a disrespectful question, the mockery and the very subject were unbecoming of a young lady, but a part of me was curious to hear his answer.

For some moments, his face was inscrutable. I was not sure if he was angry, offended, or confused, for his courtier's training did not allow him to show emotions he did not want to share. Then he laughed his usual charming laugh, in full control again. "Panna Helena has a very active imagination for one so young," he said, still smiling, his eyes swiveling in my direction as if to underscore what his tone had already made clear—namely that imagination was not a desirable or attractive quality in a lady.

"It's better to have an overactive imagination than none at all," she replied before I could think of how to put an end to this conversation.

Dantyszek's face became a blank mask again. Next to him, Lucrezia laughed her toothy, high-pitched laughter, which she often did when she was nervous. "It is a sentiment that is difficult to argue with," he said at length, but I could see that Helena's retort left him rattled. He must have a very high opinion of himself and did not suffer humiliation, especially from a woman. "But to answer your question," he added to dispel the negative impression, "no, I am not concerned. The harmless pastimes our members indulge in are not worth damning one's immortal soul."

Helena did not reply, her sea-green eyes turning back toward the river that was passing us on the right. The Wisła flowed slow and stately, belying the strong currents underneath its placid, gently shimmering surface. Each summer, those unseen and treacherous vortices claimed the lives of pages, servants, and young farmers who ventured into it in search of an outdoor pastime or respite from the heat. I recalled Helena once telling me that she was a swimmer too, an astonishing and unheard-of skill in a woman. She used to swim in the ponds on her father's estate in Baranów, and she had told me that she would love to go for a swim in the Wisła if I ever gave her permission to do so. I had no intention of doing that, of course. It was not an appropriate activity for a lady, requiring as it did the stripping to one's undergarments; but equally, I would be terrified if she set foot in those benign-looking waters that were, in fact, deadly.

In the sleigh, there was an uncomfortable silence for a while, then Dantyszek reached into the folds of his heavy cloak and pulled out a flask. He poured the spirit into each of our cups, and Lucrezia and I drank from ours eagerly as soon as he filled them. Helena never touched hers.

Lucrezia and Dantyszek tried to resume their earlier banter, but the mood was soured, and by the time we arrived at our destination, nobody was talking.

The lodge was in a river valley close to dense forests abounding in a variety of stag, as well as boar, rabbits, foxes, and numerous species of birds. The last king of the Piast dynasty had built it there due to the valley's proximity to the rich hunting grounds, but its three crenellated towers with arrow slits testified to a defensive purpose as well. The lodge was currently being renovated by King Zygmunt. A new courtyard surrounded by balconies crowned with round arches was nearly complete, and it bore an uncanny resemblance to Wawel, though on a far smaller scale. But its chambers could not be more different in their austerity; they were paneled in dark wood, with no gilding or tapestries, and had small windows. Ancient bows, crossbows, spears, and shields were displayed along the walls and above the hearths.

With those hunting implements glinting around us in the firelight, we ate a meal in the great hall—deliciously rustic fare of wine-colored borscht, wheat and onion dumplings, roasted boar, and more venison. To my relief and to Lucrezia's visible disappointment, Dantyszek sat with the other young men at the far end of the long table, where the mood soon became boisterous and where the servants refilling the cups were the busiest. Afterward the group decided to take advantage of the fine weather and stay behind to hunt for partridges, though with the amount of ale in them, I had little fear for the birds' safety.

Still, that required a few of the sleighs to be left behind to bring them back later. As a result, those who had ridden in them but were returning to Wawel had to find spots in other sleighs. That was how we ended up with Don Mantovano, the queen's secretary.

"I thought you had gone to the war council, signore," I said, for I had genuinely not noticed him before.

"Her Majesty only requested Signori Carmignano and Gamrat to accompany her today," he replied sourly. "She told me to go on the *sanna* and get some air."

I regarded his face, even paler than usual in the bright light. He squinted against it fiercely, and I could see why. I smiled, trying to make it as welcoming as I could—for I would have preferred to return with just the two girls in the sleigh— as he settled himself next to Lucrezia. From his glum expression, it was hard to deduce if he was glad to be going with us or not. Probably the latter.

As we set out on the return trip, I was overcome by that pleasant languor that comes from consuming rich food and drinking ale, even though I'd only had one small mug at the lodge. But we had barely cleared the forest and emerged onto the open road alongside the river when Lucrezia began to flirt with Mantovano. I observed it lazily, for I knew that this time it was less from any true attraction than from her irritation with Dantyszek's decision to stay behind, and possibly also a desire to amuse herself at the hapless secretary's expense.

Soon, her amusement was all too evident as Mantovano grew more and more uncomfortable. I saw him cast furtive glances at Helena, who thus far had completely ignored him. I do not think she looked at him once, and I wondered what he wanted with her.

Perhaps, given her indifference and aloofness, she was the type of woman next to whom he would have preferred to sit and be left alone. But we were already moving, so he was forced to listen to Lucrezia's chatter and endure her gloved hand on his arm, which he did with the expression of someone who had swallowed something bitter.

I am ashamed to admit it, but I found it amusing too. After a while I took pity on him. "Have you enjoyed your day so far, signore?" I asked to extract him from what he must have considered the oppression of Lucrezia's attention.

"*Abbastanza*," he said. *Enough.* Nonetheless, he sent me a grateful look. "What about you, ladies?" He glanced at Helena again to include her in the query.

"I don't think we could have asked for a more beautiful day for the *sanna*," I said, and I meant it. It was now the middle of the afternoon, the wind had died down, and the sun, unobstructed by a cloud, sent sufficient warmth to make me comfortable and cozy under the blankets that covered my lap.

"Pan Zamborski's death has not been far from our minds, unfortunately," Helena spoke for the first time since Don Mantovano had joined us. "We discussed it on our way over."

Lucrezia shook her head with a *not again* look and turned demonstratively to look out over the river, shading her eyes against the sun's glare. I, too, felt a surge of irritation at Helena's bringing up the murder again to mar the pleasure of the ride. It was as if she was trying to ruin the day.

To my surprise, Mantovano blushed, a pink tint rising from his starched collar, the only white part of his otherwise black attire. I had never seen him do that. With the previous glances cast at Helena, did he have a secret crush on her? It was such a ridiculous thought that I laughed.

Helena gave me a quizzical look, then turned her gaze back on the queen's secretary. "There seems to be an agreement that he had a mistress whose husband took exception to the affair, and Zamborski died as a result. Is that your view also, Master Secretary?"

Mantovano's blush deepened. It looked so incongruous under the dry sallow skin of his cheeks, on which the first lines of age were beginning to show. "Yes, well"—he stammered—"I suppose that is possible. Although—"

"Although what, signore?" Helena awaited his reply keenly. Why did she have such an interest in this murder? She had never shown signs of being interested in gossip before.

Mantovano lowered his gaze, clearly disconcerted. "It is hardly a transgression worth killing for—whoever Zamborski had an affair with, her husband probably also had a mistress—it happens all the time." He cleared his throat. "If courtiers killed their romantic rivals, half the court would be dead," he added, still staring at the floor of the sleigh.

Lucrezia turned back from looking out, and as our eyes met, I saw in her face the same sentiment I felt: Mantovano was right. Of all people, that dull colorless man who did not even partake in similar liaisons had made one of the truest statements I had heard on the matter. It laid to rest any lingering doubts I might have had about that explanation for the murder.

"Tomorrow night, of all nights, new affairs will form, so everybody better watch their back." I had intended this as a joke to lighten the mood, but it fell flat.

"Not me." Mantovano laughed, a mirthless, forced sound. "I will be working on Her Majesty's agricultural reform plans. We will be designating fields on her estates that will be sown with summer and winter crops later this year, and those that will be left fallow. I will likely not get much sleep," he added, his voice pitching higher with an oddly boastful note.

Lucrezia made a mock yawning face and shot me a *what-did-you-expect* look before turning back to the river.

The atmosphere turned heavy again and I felt tired, even though it was still early. I wondered once more what was going on with Helena. She had brought up Zamborski's death twice today. Had *he* been her lover and—possibly—the father of her child? If so, and if their relationship had soured over his infidelity, I would have understood her mockery of Dantyszek, Zamborski's comrade in the games of love. But Mantovano? What could he possibly have to do with it?

Suddenly, I wanted to be back and—if the queen was still in the council—spend some time alone in my chamber, listening to fire crackling in the grate and rereading old letters from Bari. Not for the first time, my official role weighed on me. Being constantly alert and aware of the girls' behavior, having to deal with such extremes of personality as exemplified by Lucrezia and Helena, was exhausting and unsatisfying. I began to suspect that I was not cut out for this. But what *was* I cut out for?

As we approached Kraków the weather changed, a broad veil of clouds moving in from the east and hiding the sun. We took a different route and rode by Baszta Sandomierska— where Maciek still lingered—its rust-colored bricks like dried blood. Above the tower, on top of the hill, the walls of the castle were no longer gleaming as they had in the morning but loomed dull and gray and somehow lifeless.

It was a strange impression to have, yet apt, as I was about to be reminded.

8

January 1ˢᵗ, 1520

I usually rose before dawn, but on the morning of the first day of the year 1520, I slept until the sun had risen well above the city's red-tiled roofs. The night before, I had not returned to my bedchamber until the clock struck three hours past midnight.

The New Year's Eve celebration had started with a feast, followed by dances in which the queen herself participated. Bona had been an accomplished dancer since her youth, known throughout Bari and Naples—and even the papal court in Rome, which she had visited as a young girl with her mother—for her skill and grace.

One such dance found the queen, Dantyszek and me on one side, and Konarski, flanked by Lucrezia and a very excited Magdalena, opposite us. I watched Magdalena and Konarski, telling myself that it was for the sake of her virtue, which was my responsibility. All the same, I was aware that it was his reaction to her proximity that I really tried to discern. He smiled and gave her a small bow when she arrived at his side, and she curtsied while fluttering her long eyelashes expertly. Did he smile again? I thought he did, but maybe I imagined it. I held my breath. Would he speak to her?

To my great relief, Gąsiorek's musicians struck up *La Gatta* just then. The ladies curtsied, the gentlemen bowed, and, holding hands, we moved forward with small steps to the rhythm of the melody. When we were two paces apart, we bowed and formed a circle, moving three steps to the left, then three steps to the right. After that we broke up into pairs, two ladies at a time dancing with the two gentlemen, turning in place for three steps, palms touching high. During that pass, the other two ladies awaited their turn.

My first partner was Dantyszek, who gave me a dazzling smile, beyond what was required of the dance convention. I could not help but return it, for the man was truly charming, even as I was surprised at how he enjoyed himself only days after one of his friends had been murdered. After our steps were completed, Dantyszek glided on to dance with Lucrezia to my right with an even bigger smile, and I had a moment of pause as I awaited Konarski's arrival. For the moment, he was paired up with the queen to my left.

I glanced around the hall. Joy was painted on every face, and food, drink, music, and conversation fueled the mood as we prepared to bid goodbye to the year 1519. It was as if nothing had happened at all to change the pace and purpose of life at the court. Most people still wanted to enjoy themselves while working to pursue the privileges that came with such a proximity to power. It was quite possible that the killer lurked among us in the banqueting hall, a betrayed lover or paid assassin, but that night it would have been impossible to form even the smallest suspicion by looking at the smiling faces, smacking lips, bright eyes, and flushed cheeks.

My open palm touched Konarski's, sending a small flutter through my chest. We had not seen each other since our visit to the jail two nights earlier. He inclined his head, and I could only hope that I was not blushing too much. I gathered my skirts in my left hand, and we took our three steps round, pausing briefly on the balls of our feet after each one. As we did so, I asked, partly to cover my fluster and partly because my mind was still on the murder and its possible culprits, "How fares Chancellor Stempowski? I haven't seen him all night."

"He is at his palace in the city," Konarski replied, his back straight and his right hand on his hip. "His daughter is in mourning, and he wanted to be with her until the New Year."

He glided on to Lucrezia, and as I waited for Dantyszek, who was dancing with the queen, I remembered the chancellor's opulent home on the outskirts of Kraków where he held frequent banquets. I had accompanied the queen there once when she joined her husband for a supper with the chancellor shortly after they were married. As Bona laughed and chatted with the noblemen at the table, the chancellor's wife, Zofia, barely raised her eyes from her plate, and when she spoke it was to women only, as was the custom. The royal couple enjoyed their lords' discomfiture, but that was the last time the queen had visited Stempowski's home, or that of any nobleman. From then on, she would receive them at the castle or other royal residences throughout the realm, where she made a point of displaying her Italian manners. Already, some of the nobility were imitating her, and nowhere was it more visible than at Wawel.

When Dantyszek arrived, I caught the queen's eye and saw the slightest nod of approval. She must have overheard my exchange with Konarski, although the image of Stempowski as a devoted father missing a festive occasion to console his grieving daughter was not exactly in line with her belief in his murderous nature.

When Konarski and I came together again, I asked, "Has the investigation been closed?"

He hesitated. "Not officially, but it will be soon."

"Because there are no other suspects?"

"Yes." *I thought we had discussed you staying out of it,* his face seemed to add.

"Then why close it?"

"I am sure the chancellor will be glad to reopen it should any new leads come his way," he replied. It was a bland answer; he, too, must have been aware that our conversation was not private. We said no more as the dance came to an end, and we all joined hands for the final circle and bow.

I danced several more times that night, including a *saltarello* with Konarski shortly before midnight. He proved remarkably competent at it for a non-Italian, our performance earning us a round of applause. But no sooner had the cathedral bell finished ringing twelve times and the shouts of well-wishes died down than the queen decided to leave, her condition finally making her tired. I went with her, followed by the maids of honor, but I was not ready to retire yet. After seeing the queen to bed and leaving Portia on chamber duty, I returned to the hall.

It had emptied somewhat, mainly of women. Dantyszek and his companions greeted me with beaming smiles, but I also attracted some surprised and not-so-friendly looks. In Poland ladies were not expected to participate in nighttime revels. But I'd had just enough wine not to care, and, in truth, I had come back for only one reason.

I stood uncertainly, trying to keep disappointment at bay as I looked around the tables. They were heaped with chicken bones, remains of lamb chops, orange peels, unfinished bowls of sweet cream, and overturned cups, the white cloths stained red and brown from wine and sauces. Revelers—though not the one I had hoped to find—still sat at some of the tables, drinking and talking, but with the candles burning low and the musicians gone, the hall had a weary, somewhat melancholy look. The feast was coming to an end.

Dantyszek waved to me to come over, and I hesitated. I had no wish to be associated with his group; on the other hand, why not have one last cup of wine, a small one ...

"I thought you had gone to bed." The voice behind me stopped me before I took a step.

"I wasn't tired yet," I said, turning around. "I was going to join Pan Dantyszek for a while," I added, and the frown on Konarski's forehead gave me an unexpected pleasure. Was he jealous? Afraid that I would become a member? Or—I thought, suddenly crestfallen—did he think I was one already?

"Then I will not detain you." He made a small gesture with his hand, a mockery of a courtier's flourish. But he looked amused.

I no longer wished to go. Still, I asked, "Will you join us?" I waited for his answer with bated breath. It would tell me a lot.

He shook his head. "I have nothing personally against Pan Dantyszek—he is a skillful diplomat. But his is not a society I like to keep outside of the State Chambers."

His choice of words was not accidental, I was sure. He was not a member of the *bibones et comedones!* The joy this gave me took me by surprise.

"Nor I," I said. Then I hastened to add, "Outside of the Queen's Chamber, that is—I mean—" I broke off, mortified to find myself suddenly tongue-tied.

Konarski laughed. He pointed to a table that was not too messy and signaled for one of the servants to bring more wine. Out of the corner of my eye, I saw Dantyszek and his troupe scrutinizing us. They would hardly be scandalized, but I imagined what the others in the hall were thinking.

As we awaited the wine, Konarski said, "I spoke with the chancellor regarding Maciek. I told him that his sister had petitioned me, and that I had gone to see him in the tower."

"And?"

"I have a sense that he doesn't believe in the boy's guilt either. It's not likely that Maciek will be hanged."

"Oh, thank God." Relief washed over me. "It would be a grave miscarriage of justice."

"But he might be kept in jail for a while until the matter dies down."

"In the meantime, the true murderer will remain free?" I could not hide my indignation.

Konarski spread his arms, and I knew that my anger was not fair. He had done all he could. For a moment, I contemplated telling him of the queen's suspicions regarding Stempowski, but perhaps wine is not always a tongue-loosening agent, for I wisely held my peace.

The servant arrived with a new flagon and cups, and we did not speak of the chancellor anymore, or of Maciek. Instead Konarski told me how his pompous uncle the bishop of Kraków had a weakness for communion wine, and how, for visits to the family's ancestral seat at Konary, he always brought a barrel of it with him, which he insisted the youngest and prettiest maids pour into his goblet at supper.

Later, when my tongue was a bit slurry, he tried to teach me the proper pronunciation of Polish words like *mistrz* and *deszcz*, with little effect but with much laughter. And later still, when there were only a few of us left and we were both quite drunk, he confessed that he preferred the old-fashioned fitted sleeves, rather than the increasingly popular puffy ones, for they did not conceal the shape of the female arm. It was a comment that makes my heart race even all these years later, not least because of the terrible events that followed.

I remember returning to my bedchamber when most of the castle was already asleep and hearing the cathedral bell ring three times as if from a great distance. Two guards were always posted at the entrance to the queen's wing, but that night both were snoring, one slumped on a bench, the other on a stool. On any other night and in a better state, I would have woken them up, but it was the New Year, and everyone was drunk.

I slept uneasily, someone shouting, running, and slamming doors in my dreams. I awoke to a pain splitting my head and rose with a groan. Silently, I vowed never to drink again. Once I saw to my morning duties, I would send for Doctor Baldazzi to make me one of his concoctions.

It would be an informal day, and everyone would feel much as I did, so I dressed more hastily than usual, forced my hair under a headdress with less care, drained the remaining water in the jug on the sideboard, and went outside.

The moment I stepped into the gallery, I became aware of a commotion at the far end of the wing, where the queen's advisors' offices were located. A group of men—courtiers, servants, and guards among them—came in and out of those chambers, talking in animated but hushed voices. It was a strange enough mix of people to be found together in one small area of the castle, and something in their demeanor conveyed a sense of gravity.

With a bad feeling, I went to see what the matter was, noting that the guards were not the same ones I had seen asleep at their post during the night. One particular chamber seemed to be the focus of the commotion, and it was the one where Secretary Mantovano worked. But as I walked in, I saw nothing amiss. Like the queen's apartments, it was filled with furniture brought from Italy, lighter and more ornate than the large and heavy desks, chairs, and settles found elsewhere at Wawel. I liked it, for it reminded me of home, so much that I often imagined these rooms sunnier than they really were because of the memories they evoked. But that New Year's morning, the feeling was absent because the mood was subdued, despite the unusual number of people crammed into the small space.

In addition to Piotr Gamrat, one of the queen's advisors, I found Chancellor Stempowski there, who I later learned had been summoned urgently from his palace. Having eschewed the previous night's revels, he looked bright-eyed and alert, unlike most of the others in the chamber. With him were two young men from the king's household whose names I did not know, but they looked like underlings.

I was thinking that Konarski was probably still sleeping off the festivities, when I noticed Lucrezia sitting in a chair by the far wall. She was hastily dressed, without a headdress, and her face was swollen and blotchy from crying. In her distress, she looked nothing like the carefree chatterbox who had nearly got herself onto Dantyszek's lap in the sleigh two days before. Next to her was a cedar table with a flagon and goblet of wine. The chancellor must have sent for it because Mantovano was not a drinker. But if the wine had been placed there for the girl's comfort, she had not yet availed herself of it, for her goblet was still full. Perhaps that was because her hands, when she raised them to wipe her eyes, were shaking.

It was as if someone had died.

"Oh no." My hand went to my mouth. I had a terrible notion of what had happened, even before anyone spoke, even as a small part of me still held out hope that whoever it was had died a natural death, peacefully in his bed ...

"Contessa Sanseverino." The chancellor made a small bow, but his face remained impassive. "A prosperous New Year to you."

"My Lord Chancellor." I curtsied. "And to you also." The fire had been made up in the grate and the chamber was warm, but icy sweat broke out at the back of my neck. "May I ask what is going on? Is Her Majesty safe?" I cast a glance at Lucrezia and tried to keep my voice even.

"She is, God be praised," Stempowski replied curtly. "She is in her bedchamber with Father de la Torre, Don Carmignano, and uh"—he hesitated, trying to remember the name, and failing—"her physician. I'm afraid there has been another murder."

Dull dread twisted my stomach, and a spot of perspiration came out on my upper lip. I gazed around the room—the somber faces of the chancellor and the advisor, the fearful ones of the young courtiers, and Lucrezia's terrified expression—and wished that Konarski was there with his calm, reassuring demeanor.

I did not have to ask who had been killed, although the body had clearly been removed already. Three men worked in those offices: Carmignano was with the queen, and Gamrat was there with us.

"Don Mantovano," I whispered.

The chancellor nodded grimly, and Lucrezia pressed a handkerchief to her mouth to stifle a sob.

Stempowski turned to her. He was a big man, taller than anyone else in the room, with thick eyebrows, a roundly trimmed graying beard, and a fine-boned, lined face that must have been handsome in his youth. He had a booming voice that enhanced his natural air of authority, and as a result he could be quite intimidating. His young courtiers cowered whenever he so much as glanced at them. "Signorina Alifio discovered him earlier this morning," he explained.

"*Dio mio.*" I walked over to Lucrezia and put a hand on her shoulder, and she clung to me. "*Povera ragazza, che tristezza,*" I murmured as I smoothed her dark curls, unpinned and disarrayed. I reached for the goblet and gave it to her, and she took a small sip. After a few moments I felt her calming a little.

"I was just going to interrogate her," Stempowski said. "If you feel up to it, signorina," he addressed Lucrezia with surprising gentleness. "Either now or when you have recovered from your shock, we will have to have a full account of how you came upon the body."

I looked down at her. Yes, how had *she*, of all people, found him?

She met my gaze, her red-rimmed eyes swimming with tears, then she turned to the chancellor. "I want to tell everything now and then forget it," she said, drawing a deep breath. Her voice trembled. "I don't want to have to remember it all over again."

That was wise, I thought, as Stempowski nodded to one of his courtiers. The man picked up a portable desk from a sideboard, slung the belt around his neck, dipped a quill in the inkpot, and waited with his hand poised over a sheet of paper. He tried to look official, but there was a tension and a pallor in his face that suggested he had little stomach for what he was about to hear.

"He was right there when I opened the door," Lucrezia said. "Slumped on that divan. Dead." She pointed across the chamber without looking in that direction.

My eyes followed her hand. With a shudder, I noticed that the damask upholstery of the divan that stood against a wall between two windows, a bright pattern of alternating green and yellow stripes, was stained with rust-colored smudges. There were small spots of red on the tiles of the floor beneath it, as well, where some of the blood had dripped and dried.

"Signorina," Stempowski said, again gentle. "Let us start from the beginning. What were you doing here in this chamber so early in the morning?"

I looked at him sharply, a protective instinct rising inside me. What was he insinuating? But then I remembered that it was Lucrezia, who liked to read *Decamerone* and the Greek love letters translated by Kopernikus, and who had flirted with Mantovano during the sleigh ride, even though Stempowski could not know that. I had assumed that flirtation was for sport, but what if it wasn't? Dear God.

I was still absorbing that possibility when Lucrezia sniffled and started her story. "It was still mostly dark when I awoke and felt the need to ... to go"—she hesitated, blushing—"to the privy." I squeezed her shoulder, encouraging her to continue. "I saw the guards, but they were dead to the world on drink. On my way back, I noticed light coming through a crack in the door of Her Majesty's secretary's office." She paused, wiping her eyes with her sleeve like a child.

"It was such an unusual hour," she resumed, "that the first thought that came into my head was that Don Mantovano was in the middle of a tryst, and I crept up to see if I could get a glimpse of the woman." She laughed through her tears, but it was a wistful sort of laugh. "I could already imagine telling the other girls and what merriment we would share at his expense."

She started crying again. I gave her the goblet, and she took a long draught this time. When she was able to speak again, she said that the door had been slightly ajar, as if someone had not wanted to close it all the way for fear of making noise. Putting an eye to the crack and not seeing or hearing anything, Lucrezia pushed the door open a bit, and that was when she saw Mantovano sprawled on the divan. One of his hands was pressed to his abdomen, clutching a handkerchief soaked with blood, the other rested limply at this side. His head was thrown back with a mouth agape as if in a final silent scream.

She ran back to her bedchamber, the sound that Mantovano could no longer utter waking everyone, except for me. I now realized that what I had thought was a dream must have been her screaming.

A heavy silence filled the chamber when she finished, punctured only by the scribe taking down the last of her words with a frantic scratch. His hand, too, was shaking slightly.

"Where is Don—the body now?" I asked.

"It has been taken down to the mortuary crypt."

I had a flash of memory from my previous visit to see another murdered man. I wondered if I would have to go there again. "Did Her Majesty see him?"

The chancellor shook his head. "She was too distraught. She has shut herself in her bedchamber and does not want to see anybody, except for her priest, Don Carmignano, and that doctor."

I felt a surge of concern for the queen. I knew she liked Mantovano, but her attachment must have run deeper than I'd thought if she was unable to look upon his corpse. The extent of her grief must have been great, too, for Baldazzi to have become a needed companion. It was not a good sign.

"What do you think happened here, my lord?" I asked the chancellor.

He raised his shoulders in a sign of uncertainty. "At first glance it seems like the work of a thief."

"Why is that?"

"His ruby ring and his chain of office were missing from his body."

"Oh." As with Zamborski's murder, the explanation of a crime committed for profit did not satisfy me. Yet, under the strain of the moment, I could not think why.

"Thank you, Signorina Alifio." Stempowski's tone turned official again. "Perhaps you should rest now. I am sure Contessa Sanseverino will take good care of you," he added in a way that left no doubt that he was dismissing us.

I would have liked more time to look around. I had a nagging thought that there was something in that chamber that could disprove the burglary theory. But it was not my place to ask for that, or to argue with the chancellor's verdicts.

I helped Lucrezia to her feet, sensing a certain heaviness about her. It was no wonder: she had risen early, suffered a great shock, and the interrogation that followed must have been exhausting. "Let's go to your bedchamber. The girls must be worried about you."

We walked down the gallery in silence. Our steps echoed on the tiled floor, the sound grating on my raw nerves and making my head feel like a busy blacksmith's workshop. We found the other girls huddled by a blazing hearth, talking in low voices. They were fully dressed but wore no jewelry, and their hair was still undone. They made room for Lucrezia closest to the fire, and we all took comfort from the camaraderie born of a shared sense of impending doom.

"Is it true?" Magdalena asked in a trembling voice. "Was Don Mantovano murdered right down the hall from our chamber, and so near Her Majesty's apartments?"

"I'm afraid so."

Fresh tears sprang from their eyes, and they began peppering me with questions to which I had no answers.

"Who is doing this?"

"Why?"

"When will he be captured?"

"Are we going to die next?"

"Of course not," I said impatiently, to cover my own fear. "Stop saying such things."

"There is a killer on the loose, and he is quite vicious, but he seems to be attacking men," I added after a moment, conscious of how meager a consolation that was.

"But who would have wanted to kill Don Mantovano?" Portia asked the question that must have been on everyone's mind. "He seemed so"—she searched for the right word, evidently finding it difficult to describe such a bland figure as the queen's late secretary—"so harmless."

That was apt. Not being very sociable, Mantovano did not appear to have had any close friends or allies at the court. But neither had he been the type to attract enemies. Instead, he had been devoted to the queen, hard-working, and—at least as far as I knew—not mean to anyone. He had also seemed quite pious. I had noticed many times how fervently he prayed during mass, intent on every word of Bishop Konarski's sermons, unlike many of the other courtiers who yawned, fidgeted, or ogled women from their pews. It was a pity, I realized, that he had died so suddenly, without the comfort of the last rites.

I spread my arms in a gesture of helplessness. "As unlikely as it sounds, he must have earned somebody's ill will."

"It certainly wasn't a jealous husband," Magdalena observed sarcastically. I was going to chide her, but it occurred to me that she was right. If Mantovano was known for anything at the court, it was for his ascetic lifestyle. He had a wife who had stayed behind in Naples due to delicate health that made it impossible for her to make the journey north, but to whom, according to the queen, he was deeply devoted. Prior to our sleigh ride, I do not think I had ever seen him talk to a woman unless it was on the queen's business, much less flirt with one. It was difficult to imagine someone less prone to be a carouser. Unless he'd had everybody fooled, he was the last man on earth who would have posed a threat to a husband or fiancé.

"He may not have looked the type, but some men go to great lengths to conceal their secret lives." Helena's words rang out with a strange correspondence to my own thoughts.

I was surprised to hear that from a girl her age, even if I could not dispute its veracity. I studied her, wondering if the lover she had agreed to give up was also a married man. But except for her slightly narrowed eyes, which I noticed were shadowed with dark circles, everything about her was neutral and composed. Unless she chose to share it with me, I would never be able to guess the truth of that affair.

"Chancellor Stempowski seems to think that someone killed Pan Zamborski for his purse and dagger, and that Don Mantovano was killed for his ring and chain—" I broke off as it dawned on me why, just a short while before, something had not seemed right in the secretary's chamber. There was a silver tray on the sideboard, an alabaster vase from the queen's beloved collection, expensive quills, and several golden candlesticks there, none of which the murderer had taken. Instead, he had removed

Mantovano's ring and chain of office, the latter of which was distinctive enough to raise suspicions if he tried to sell it or have it melted down. I took a deep breath. This was not the work of a thief any more than Zamborski's death had been; whoever had done it wanted it to *look like* the work of a thief.

But I did not share any of that with the girls; I did not want to engender more wild speculation. Later, I would seek out Konarski and tell him about it.

"We must let the investigation run its course and hope that the killer will be brought to justice." I tried to convey a confidence I did not feel. "It is not for us to speculate on who did it and why. Try to stay calm, stay together, and keep your wits about you." I rose from my seat and gazed at each of them. "Now do up your hair and put some rouge on your cheeks for when Her Majesty summons you to attend her. She was deeply attached to Don Mantovano, and this will be hard on her. It will be your task to keep her spirits up."

They wiped their eyes and began dispersing to their chests and mirrors to finish their toilette. Lucrezia, who I noticed had grown increasingly heavy-lidded as we talked, went to lie down, and I was glad of it. On a day like this, sleep, if it could be had, was the best—really, the only—remedy.

I motioned Helena to stay. "How are you feeling?" I asked in a low voice. She was pale again. "Is your stomach still bothering you?" I looked pointedly at her bodice.

"I am better, signora."

"So there is no need for Doctor Baldazzi to examine you?" I pressed. "Because you don't look so well."

"I haven't been sleeping much lately," she said. "That first murder must have affected me more than I realized, and now this—" She brought a hand to her throat as if she could not breathe.

I waited until she was calmer, then asked, "Did you hear anything suspicious in the gallery last night?"

She shook her head. "Yesterday I asked Doctor Baldazzi for something to help me sleep, and he gave me poppy milk." She gestured toward the chest by her bed, where, next to a prayer book and a silver comb, there was a small stoppered clay bottle.

"And you took it last night?"

"Yes, a quarter measure in a cup of wine, according to his prescription," she said. "It worked." She gave me a wan smile.

I pursed my lips. To me she looked tired and drawn, but maybe it took a few days.

"You don't have to attend the queen today, unless she specifically asks for you. Take the day to rest." I glanced toward Lucrezia's bed and saw that she was fast asleep already. "These murders are unfortunate, but we must not let them disrupt our lives. Otherwise, we will become victims indirectly."

She dropped her eyes in acknowledgment.

I left her and returned to my chamber. My head was pounding from the wine I'd had the night before and from the morning's developments. I sat on my bed and took a few deep breaths to fight off a rising sense of panic as I recalled the complete silence in the gallery at three o'clock in the morning. I could not remember whether I had seen any lights coming from Mantovano's office. Was it after the murder, or was the killer lurking somewhere in the shadows, waiting for his prey? What if I had looked in the wrong direction and seen his face? Perhaps my body, too, would have been found that morning.

I felt suddenly very tired, and my mind scrambled as various scenarios and images pushed to the fore. I rose to double check the lock on my door, then returned to the bed and lay down, intending to rest for just a moment, but I was engulfed almost immediately by a dreamless black void.

I was awakened some time later by a loud knocking on my door, and when I finally unlocked it, I saw Portia hovering outside. "Her Majesty wishes to see you, signora," she said. "She is very upset, and Doctor Baldazzi is still with her."

Wincing at a dull ache lingering somewhere behind my eyes, I splashed water from the basin on my face, put my head-dress back on, and followed her.

The candles were lit in the queen's bedchamber, even though it was still afternoon, for the day was overcast and gloomy. Bona was resting in her bed, a large and beautiful piece that she had brought from Italy. It was carved out of cedar, gilded, and topped with a white velvet baldachin supported by twist-ing columns in each of its four corners. She was wearing a satin robe over her nightdress, and a linen compress was pressed to her forehead. On a nearby table, a platter with almond-paste sweets dipped in caramelized honey—which I made sure was placed there fresh every night—stood untouched. It was the surest sign that she was distressed, yet her face was dry. Bona Sforza was not the type to cry.

"Your Majesty." I made a deep curtsy. "I am very sorry for your loss. I know how much you valued Don Mantovano's ser-vice and advice. He will be greatly missed."

She gestured for me to rise. "Poor Lorenzo," she sniffed. "Such an honest and pious soul, and so loyal to me. Who would have wanted to harm him?" she asked, though she clearly did not expect me to answer. "Doctor Baldazzi"—she pointed at the physician without looking at him—"tells me that he was stabbed three times in the stomach and must have been alive for some time after the attack, for he was clutching his hand-kerchief to his wounds to stanch the bleeding." She heaved a dry sob.

"Your Majesty must not become too upset—" I started.

She raised her head and sent me a scorching look. She grabbed the cloth from her brow and flung it away, and it hit the floor tiles with a damp thwack. Before I realized what she was doing, she pushed back the damask bedcover and was on her feet. Baldazzi and I started toward her, but she held us back with an outstretched arm.

"This dark, miserable, godforsaken place." She stalked to the window and gazed over the winter landscape of brownish meadows, the steely river, and a stretch of bare-leafed forest on the opposite bank, all dissolving into the approaching dusk. From where she stood, one could also see the top of Baszta Sandomierska. "This land of cold weather, cold people, of men who fear women who speak their minds, and who would keep them confined to the bedchamber and birthing stool all their lives," she seethed.

I exchanged an alarmed glance with Baldazzi.

"May it please Your Majesty to return to bed, for the safety of the heir—" Baldazzi started, almost bending in half, his arms and head seeming to sway as he did so.

"My heir will be fine!" the queen declared. "But I will not let whoever murdered my Mantovano get away with it!"

"His Majesty has already ordered an investigation, and Chancellor Stempowski has interviewed Signorina Alifio. Please, Your Majesty, drink this cup of wine infused with the oil of valerian. It will soothe your nerves." He moved to a sideboard and lifted a Venetian goblet that he extended toward the queen, his hand shaking slightly. For the first time I was impressed with Baldazzi. Usually he was eager to please and full of empty platitudes, but now he did exactly what he was supposed to. Most likely, he was worried that he would be blamed should the queen miscarry.

"Stempowski is an old fool who cannot find his way out of a privy!" Bona exploded as I knew she would the moment Baldazzi mentioned his name. She ignored the proffered medicine. "I will have my own investigation. We will find the culprit and expose him for the coward and traitor he is!"

She started pacing, and I wondered who she was referring to as "we." Was it Baldazzi? If so, he looked too scared to offer any assistance. "But whoever he is, I know why he killed my secretary. Do you want to know why?" She stopped and looked from me to the doctor, her chin raised high as if in a challenge.

All we could do was nod.

"He killed him because they hate me! They have hated me from the day I arrived here to be a queen who understands the affairs of her kingdom and can be her husband's trusted confidante and advisor, not just a broodmare."

I stood frozen and felt Baldazzi go still as well. There was no doubt in my mind that she was talking about Stempowski and his faction.

"In Italy," she resumed, "they value women like me, not just as means of perpetuating dynasties and making political alliances. Matilda of Tuscany ruled over the entire north of the peninsula and won battles against a Holy Roman Emperor; my great-grandmother Bianca Maria donned a suit of armor to join Cremona's troops in their defense against the Venetians; my aunt Caterina Sforza once occupied Castel Sant'Angelo in Rome and defended her fortress at Forlì"—she raised a forefinger high—"also against the Venetians. Italian women have governed, fought, and negotiated with the mighty of this world for centuries! But here?!"

She swept an arm clad in a fashionably flared sleeve, and the ribbons that adorned it trembled. "In this backward country, they cannot abide that I speak my mind, that I dare try to reform their ancient farms that keep their peasants starving and the Crown coffers empty." She paused for a breath. "And that is how they thank me for attempting to save them from bankruptcy, something they have been unable to do themselves!"

"But if that is so, Your Majesty, then who killed Signor Zamborski?" Baldazzi asked in a thin voice.

A corner of Bona's lips lifted in a contemptuous grimace. "I would bet my entire dowry *and* my rights to the Duchy of

Milan that it was done on Stempowski's order too. Everyone knows that he did not want Zamborski for a son-in-law; he had been aiming far higher, for that man's ambition and greed know no bounds. And also"—she threw her head back and gave a bark of laughter—"Zamborski would not have remained faithful to his beloved daughter for a week. Two good reasons to get rid of him."

I had heard that before, but Baldazzi had not, and he looked even more terrified.

As recently as the previous night, I had been questioning the queen's suspicions regarding the chancellor, but with this new murder, the possibility that she might be right stood in my mind again. After all, I had seen the hatred on Stempowski's face. All the same, I silently questioned the wisdom of sharing those suspicions with the doctor, who was a good friend of the Princess of Montefusco. Making such a grave accusation public could not possibly help matters, regardless of the chancellor's guilt.

The first day of January was also King Zygmunt's fifty-third birthday. Traditionally, an evening reception was held in the throne chamber, where courtiers and invited guests greeted the king and conveyed their birthday wishes to him. I worried about whether the queen would be able to attend the ceremony that night, but she summoned me again an hour before it was due to start.

With the help of her parlor maid Dorota, we dressed her in a velvet gown of Prussian blue, a shade so deep it was almost black. Don Mantovano's death had not been officially announced yet, so the queen could not appear in mourning in public without giving rise to speculation, but she wanted to come as close to honoring her late secretary as possible. On her head, she wore a small rounded headdress embroidered in silver thread and decorated with gray pearls. After we had put powder and a little bit of rouge on her cheeks and dabbed her lips with madder-root paste, someone who had just arrived at the court would never have guessed at the heartbreak Queen Bona had just experienced.

In the throne chamber, seated next to her husband under the red baldachin, she was every inch the monarch. She had a smile, nod, or word for everyone who curtsied in front of her before they moved on to wish the king more of God's blessings for a long life and a fruitful reign. I was among the courtiers who queued to greet the king, and I saw that even as she put on a cheerful face, the queen's eyes scanned the room and attendees every now and then. A few times they rested on the chancellor, who stood on the other side of the king, as if she was trying to gauge what went on behind his courtly mask. He looked serious, as usual, but also more watchful of what was going on around the king, which was normally the job of the captain of the guard. The latter stood next to the chancellor, and on both sides of the royal thrones, men-at-arms had been posted in a display of heightened security.

When my turn came to approach the king, I stopped three paces before his throne as he leaned toward his dwarf jester seated on a cushion at his feet. If it were not for the inequality of their station, Stańczyk could have been said to be the king's best friend—someone His Majesty turned to for both entertainment and consolation, even more so than his wife. According to a centuries-old tradition, the jester was the only person who could comment mockingly or critically on the king's actions without risking a severe penalty, which meant that he sometimes expressed truths aloud that nobody else dared to. For that reason, members of the court had come to regard his statements with a certain respect.

I could not hear exactly what the king and Stańczyk were discussing, for they spoke in low voices, but I had an idea as words like "secretary" and "suspicious" reached my ears. I was startled when the jester said, more loudly and in a tone that sounded definitive, "This was no man's fury," followed by a chuckle and what I thought was a wink in my direction. The king, as if taking his cue from Stańczyk, gave me a benevolent smile tinged with sadness, like a dear old uncle, and I hastened to convey my wishes.

But as I moved away from the throne, the jester's words rang uncomfortably in my ears. They reminded me of Maciek's enigmatic last words in the jail cell about a phantom who had stalked his corridor on the night of Zamborski's death. Could the boy have been right, even in his weak mind? For the king's dwarf—a man physically impaired but with a quick mind and a sharp wit—tended to see things that others missed. Was the manner of Mantovano's death, the fact that his killer seemed to have relished the slow agony, a sign of something other-worldly and diabolic?

I took a deep breath, reminding myself not to lose common sense. If I spoke my thoughts aloud, I would sound like a mad-woman. It was far more likely that both victims had died by a human hand, however sinister. But whose hand?

I considered the gathered crowd and, once again, could not help but wonder if the killer was among us. I'd had the same thought the night before at the New Year's Eve celebration. Then, the faces had been smiling and flushed with excitement, and it was hard to imagine. Today, many of the same court-iers bore the signs of those revels in a certain sluggishness of movement and the redness and puffiness of the eyes from too much drink and too little sleep. The mood was less exuberant, but everyone made a good effort for the sake of the occasion. I still could see nobody who would arouse my suspicions in any definite way. Not even the chancellor, I had to admit.

But someone was killing courtiers at Wawel Castle. The murders were not random—of that, at least, I was certain. The subdued mood of the chamber and the tension emanating from the royal dais cast a pall on the court. Now more than ever, it was critical that the culprit be found, for otherwise the entire monarchy might be in crisis.

9

January 2nd, 1520

After the birthday reception, the queen remained seques-
tered in her bedchamber the whole of the following day,
only receiving a visit from the king, who came to inquire after
her health and comfort. She refused to eat the herbed mutton
dish that had been brought for her midday meal, threatening,
not for the first time, to send to Italy for real cooks. She was
tired of the meaty fare favored in Kraków, she said, and she
wanted something light. I took the opportunity to go to the
kitchen to order a bowl of plain broth for her. I had not been
outside since the morning of the *sanna*, and I needed air.

It was warmer once again, with a touch of dampness that
was refreshing, but the clouds hung low and leaden white in
the sky. Even the courtyard's limestone colonnade seemed
darker, making me feel melancholy despite the bustle of servants, courtiers, and knights who came and went in and out
of various buildings. Many of them were still oblivious to the
evil stalking the castle's corridors at night. If only I had been
so blissfully unaware!

Even before I arrived at the door of the kitchen across the
courtyard, I saw men coming out of there carrying barrels of
wine. Inside, preparations for supper had already started, a doz-
en cooks and as many assistants busying themselves around

pots, roasting spits, chopping boards, and bread ovens. In the back of the ground-floor chamber, there were stairs to the upper story, where five women from Italy and France worked every day on the most elaborate confections imaginable. But I preferred the downstairs, with its mouth-watering smells and the warmth of the fires.

The central counter was piled high with chopped cauliflower, celery, and leeks, vegetables rarely eaten by Poles but popular in Italy, from where they were regularly imported. They were favorites of the queen's. That was where I found the chief cook, a woman named Michałowa, who eyed them dubiously. I imagined how hard it must have been for her to get used to the new foods after a lifetime of working with beets and turnips. Of course, the latter continued to be consumed, though one would never guess that from the dark look on Michałowa's face. Still, as with the queen's new fashions, the eating habits of the Polish aristocracy were changing fast, and that must have left many old cooks like Michałowa bewildered. Yet she had no choice but to adapt if she wanted to keep her position. The specter of a contingent of Italian *cuochi* arriving to take over her dominion must have been keeping her awake at night.

"Where are they taking the wine?" I asked, pointing at two more men emerging with barrels from the cellars and heading for the main door.

Michałowa let a huff out of her ample bosom and waddled over to a vat of pottage, her large hips wobbling like jelly under her skirts. She proceeded to stir the soup energetically. "So much wine is bein' sent from Milan that the old cellars under the castle proper had to be reopened." She pointed the wooden ladle in the direction I had come from. "They're movin' the stores there, and a good thing too, if you ask me. It takes forever to carry flagons from 'ere to the banqueting hall, and the servants get an earful from the lords impatient to refill their cups. Tha's what 'appened during the Christmas feast." Michałowa nodded sagely over the steaming vat, her round face red from the heat, then tapped a heavy foot on the floor to indicate the space below. "I always says these cellars are good for storin' nothin' but old sacks. They're too small and used to be crypts." She crossed herself, and I remembered that the kitchen was built on the site of an ancient church. "But tha's where we still keep our beets and parsnips, and ... those things." She snorted, tilting her head toward the leeks and cauliflower.

I opened my mouth to put in the order for the broth but was forestalled.

"I hope the good Lord will let me live long enough to see some other storage built. It gives me the creeps to go down to these cellars. Always expect to trip over some old bones." She crossed herself again. "But even under the castle, there may not be enough room, so much wine is bein' delivered almost every day. And wha's wrong with ale and mead? We've been drinkin' it forever! My father drank it, my grandfather drank it, my great-grandfather drank it. I says as much to the Master Cupbearer the other day, but who's goin' to listen to old Michałowa?"

Well, *I* had to listen for a good while longer before I finally managed to get a word in and state my business. I was on my way out when I felt the urge to have a piece of fruit—a winter diet can do that. Looking around and hoping there would be a bowl of them somewhere, I asked if I could have a few apples for the queen's antechamber.

"They're also in the cellars to keep fresh," Michałowa said. "Marta!" she shouted toward a passing scullery maid, a timid-looking girl of about thirteen. "Go down and bring up some apples and peaches for Pani Caterina." I noted her insistence on the Polish form of address, and I smiled. Any Italian cook to join her staff would have a tough time of it.

Still, my mouth watered at the word "peach." It had been a long time since I tasted one's soft, juicy sweetness, so different from the tartness of Polish apples. I followed the maid eagerly as she headed for the door to the cellar, but Michałowa stopped her. *"Nie tędy!"* Not that way. "They're still bringin' up the wine. Take the other door and take that clean linen sack with you. It's for Her Majesty!"

We went down a passage that led from the main kitchen toward the back of the building, where meat was stored and prepared. Through an arched opening, I could see pig and calf carcasses swinging from hooks in the ceiling, and the long butcher's block covered with pink slabs of meat already cut up. Halfway down the passage, there was a wide door in the side wall, and it stood slightly ajar. Slowing down, I saw that it led outside, but not to the main courtyard; rather it opened onto an area partially enclosed by a section of the castle wall with its own set of doors. The slick flagstones were untidy, dusted with a white powder and littered with vegetable scraps.

I hastened to catch up to Marta, who had already moved down the corridor to another door, smaller and so low that a grown man would have to stoop to enter. She pushed it open and began descending the steep steps to the cellar. I stayed behind, though well out of Michałowa's sight lest she decide to entertain me with another complaint. Looking down, I could see that the cellars were also lit by oil lamps, like the crypt under the cathedral. In fact, they probably looked much the same. The only difference was that the cold air that wafted up to me was not as clean and crisp as that under the cathedral. Instead, it carried the earthy and faintly sweet smell of the fruits and vegetables stored there.

At length, Marta reemerged, the sack in her hands bulging with rounded shapes that made me hungry again. As we walked back, I pointed to the side door and asked where it led.

"It opens to the back of the courtyard," she replied. Then she confirmed what I had already suspected, "This is where we take our deliveries."

The delivery area. This was where goods were first brought in from the town up that cobbled road that led past the jail tower. Somewhere nearby, perhaps behind those other doors set into the castle wall, was the corridor where Zamborski's body had been found eight days earlier. The thought gave me a shiver. Was he killed close to the kitchen, or farther away toward the main part of the castle? Why would he have come to the service wing in the first place? And how was it connected to the murder of Mantovano? I pulled my cloak closer about me and shut my eyes tight for a moment, as if that could stave off the pressure of the ache that had started building inside my head.

When I was again out in the courtyard—the front part of it, where the backdoor delivery activities would never be seen— I spotted a familiar figure coming through the gate from the forecourt, a short cloak swishing in rhythm with his gait. My spirits lifted immediately.

"Donna Caterina." Secretary Konarski stopped when he saw me. "A pleasure."

"Good afternoon." I gave him an apple from the sack, and he accepted it, smiling. Then he lowered his voice, and his face grew more serious. "What a terrible business with Don Mantovano. How is Her Majesty faring?"

"She is hit hard by it. She was very attached to him."

"Of course," he murmured.

"Chancellor Stempowski has his hands full again," I said.

"Yes." He cleared his throat, no doubt remembering our dance conversation from New Year's Eve. "It is not the kind of development he had hoped for."

Is it not? I wanted to ask as we reached the entrance to the castle and stopped under an arch, away from the path of those who came up and down the main staircase. But I did not. Instead we watched as men continued to roll wine barrels across the courtyard.

"What are they doing?" Konarski said more to himself than to me.

"Emptying the cellars under the kitchen and moving all the wine to the castle so it is closer to the banqueting hall," I explained.

"Ah. Just in time for the Feast of Epiphany." A cheerful note stole into his voice. Epiphany was always a big event at the court, with the celebrations rivaling those of Christmas and the New Year.

"Does the chancellor think the same person is responsible for both killings?" I asked, trying to sound casual. I knew I had already tried Konarski's patience, but the case, as terrifying as it was, was also intensely interesting to me. Was it because of the queen's suspicions? The lack of clues? The deepening mystery of it all? Whatever the reason, I could not put it out of my mind. The prevailing explanations, including the one that the queen herself favored, seemed unsatisfactory to me. I still had no idea why, although thinking about it was more likely to give me a headache than to suggest any answers.

"I believe so," Konarski said. Knowing exactly what my next question would be, he added, "He ordered Maciek's release this morning."

"Good." I exhaled. "Does he have any new suspects?" *Any other servant boys that he would make into scapegoats,* I refrained from adding.

"No, but he sent the two guards who were on duty in the queen's wing on New Year's night to Baszta Sandomierska."

Alarm must have been painted all over my face, for he hastened to add, "Only for a week, for drinking on duty. If they hadn't fallen asleep, the murder might not have happened."

It might or might not have, I thought, for if someone really wanted Mantovano dead, he would have found a way to kill him eventually.

"But you will never guess who they had been drinking *with*," Konarski said.

I held my breath.

"Don Mantovano."

"What?!"

He nodded. "The guards testified that Mantovano had come by an hour after midnight with a flagon of wine and a goblet in his hand, though not visibly drunk, and said that he had some work to finish on the queen's agriculture reforms. He offered them a drink, and as they were parched—those are their own words—they accepted it."

"And it didn't seem suspicious to them that he was not drunk on New Year's Eve?"

He spread his hands. "Maybe he had a strong head?"

I shook my head. "No, not Mantovano. He doesn't drink— didn't drink," I corrected myself. "We often made fun of him behind his back for that."

I looked around, bewildered, as if someone could deny what I had just heard. This whole story, at first just sinister, was now becoming bizarre. I remembered that the secretary's desk had been empty of all papers on the morning after his death, and the chair had been pushed in as if he had never sat in it that night. Whatever he had been up to certainly did not involve working on the queen's business. And this despite what he had told us in the sleigh during the *sanna*, and later to the guards. He must have been planning it for some time—but what was it?

"Lucrezia Alifio, the maid of honor who found him, had thought he was having a secret rendezvous with a woman," I said, casting my mind past the lingering headache and back to the interrogation. "Maybe she was right and he had brought wine with him for courage?"

Konarski gave a small chuckle of disbelief.

"I know," I said, unable to suppress a smile myself and feeling bad about it, for we were talking about a dead man. Then I added, more somberly, "Before yesterday morning, I never would have believed he had been drinking, but now—now nothing makes sense anymore."

⁂

Queen Bona, even in the midst of grieving, could not stay idle for long. That evening, she sent a messenger to summon her advisors to her sitting chamber.

After I helped her dress in a black silk gown and put her hair up under a black headdress trimmed with white pearls—the only jewelry she would wear until her secretary was buried—I wanted to leave, but she bade me stay.

"You have friends in His Majesty's household, don't you, Caterina?" she asked, causing me to blush fiercely. By then Don Mantovano's death was no longer a secret, though its cause had not been announced, and fevered speculation had already begun. But even amid that uproar, the news of the time I had spent with Konarski during the New Year's night must have already reached her ears. But what did I expect? At court, gossip spread like the plague, and it was equally hard to contain.

The queen saw my abashment. Taking it as a confirmation, she added, "I want you to stay and hear what my advisors know and what they think I should do." She paused. "I have a feeling they will not want me to become involved in this investigation."

She was probably right about that. Gamrat and Carmignano were fully aware of the tensions between her and Stempowski, and the last thing they needed was to see them inflamed further, which would make their job of advising a headstrong queen even more difficult. I wondered if she had told them about her suspicions. But whether she had or not, I was not sure what all that had to do with me or why she wanted me to stay.

Perhaps the queen could see my perplexity, for she explained, "I want you to keep your eyes and ears open when you go about the castle to see if there is anything else you can add to what they already know."

"I, Your Majesty?"

"Yes." She nodded. "You have more sense than most men at this court. You are also very curious about these murders." There was little that got past Bona Sforza; then again, I was the one who had offered to visit Maciek Koza in the jail.

"They are very puzzling," I admitted, my heart fluttering with excitement. She needed me!

"Indeed." She took a sip from the Venetian goblet I had filled with her favorite Lombard wine. "But what is even more puzzling is how the chancellor has managed to hide his tracks. And you know people who might help you get to that."

So there it was: she wanted me to use Konarski to learn what she or her men might not be able to. I did not relish the idea of taking advantage of his trust in that way, but I could hardly refuse. It was not a request; it was an order.

"Yes, Your Majesty," I said, although I doubted that Konarski would tell me everything that was said within the king's household. He would be selective with me, just as the king's advisors were selective with Carmignano and Gamrat, a subtle but persistent rivalry.

The queen nodded, satisfied, and took some more wine. "If you hear anything, bring it to me immediately, day or night."

"Yes, Your Majesty."

"What is *your* opinion about these murders, Caterina?" she asked suddenly, startling me with that question. "Do you believe those who say that Zamborski was killed out of jealousy and that Mantovano must have had a shameful secret of his own?"

She turned her blue eyes on me, usually steely and assured, and I thought I glimpsed a flash of uncertainty in them. It was so unusual for her to doubt herself once she made up her mind about something that it took me a while to find my voice.

"No," I said at length. "I don't think either of them was killed in a jealous rage." She nodded slowly for me to go on. "I didn't see the body of Don Mantovano, but based on Doctor Baldazzi's description, there was a precision to the attack that suggests it was planned. I believe the same is true of Zamborski's death."

"Ha!" she exclaimed, her regal confidence back. "I knew it!" She set the goblet aside and began thrumming her fingers on the carved armrest of her chair.

I found myself pondering whether this was a good time to tell her about my doubts regarding the Stempowski theory, or whether I should keep them to myself until I had proof. The assignment gave me a chance to earn her gratitude, and it also made me proud. Proud and—yes—excited, for it would help alleviate the daily tedium of safeguarding the girls' virtue. The headache from earlier in the day was gone, and I felt a surge of energy.

I decided to voice what was on my mind, but I had to do it carefully. "There remains the problem of both victims having nothing in common with each other," I began. My pulse quickened as I saw the known facts lining up before me in two neat rows. "That difference—in their nationalities, ages, positions at the court, and, especially, in their lifestyles—is something that the judges will be sure to wonder about when the accused, whoever he is, stands before them." I paused as I heard the logic of it from my own mouth. "The first thing that must be established is a thread that connects the two of them."

Bona swung her head toward me. "What connects them is that beast Stempowski and the fact that they were both inconvenient to him—"

There was a knock on the door, and Magdalena entered to announce that Gamrat and Carmignano had arrived. What the interruption prevented me from saying was that not only were the two men different from one another, but the manner of their deaths was as well: Zamborski had been killed with one stab in the back, while Mantovano had received three thrusts in the stomach. If the chancellor had used an assassin—for he was not even in the castle when the secretary died—would not the mode of the killings be the same?

Those were just a few inconsistencies in an increasingly strange and, it would seem, demonic plot. Stempowski or not, the killer was a madman, quiet and elusive, and we were all at his mercy.

Piotr Gamrat and Antonio Carmignano were so like each other that they could have passed for brothers. Of course, they were only so in their chosen profession and their shared service to the queen, yet because of their short statures, round bellies threatening to snap the seams of their doublets, and small but intelligent eyes, anyone new to the court might have been forgiven for getting them confused.

Their arrival was followed in short order by that of Jan Dantyszek and the poet Adam Latalski. What were *they* doing here? Dantyszek, in particular, with his fashionably sculpted beard framed by a lacy collar above his black leather doublet, upon which was draped a short cape of blue velvet girded off the shoulder, seemed like the last person who would concern himself with so unsavory a matter as murder, even if the victim had been his friend. Latalski—thin-shouldered, pale-faced, and with a mouth perpetually twisted in a wry grimace—looked equally out of place.

I poured wine out of the decanter for the guests, and when everyone was holding a full goblet, the queen ordered

Carmignano to brief us on what he knew about the investigation into Mantovano's murder. The advisor repeated what Konarski had told me about the guards partaking of the wine with the late secretary. I studied the queen's face for a reaction, for it complicated her version of Stempowski's involvement.

"That doesn't sound like Lorenzo at all," the queen admitted after a long pause. "But it was the eve of the New Year, and he must have felt lonely without his wife and children about, so he sought solace in drink, *poverino.*"

The advisors wisely chose to remain silent.

"Panie Dantyszek," she addressed the courtier. "Was Don Mantovano a member of that group of drinkers and eaters of which you are the ringleader? Be honest with me!" she appealed to him, a bit dramatically.

"No, Your Majesty." Dantyszek shook his head with not even a hint of embarrassment. "Upon my word." He put a manicured hand adorned with topaz and emerald rings on his heart. He sounded genuine.

"I thought not." The queen sniffed, looking relieved. "He was as devoted to me as he was to his wife, even though she was so far away. It was a source of great sadness to him."

"Of course." Dantyszek inclined his head, although I doubted that he had any sympathy for that kind of marital longing.

"His Majesty is of the opinion that I should not concern myself with the investigation," she said. I did not know that; they must have discussed it when the king visited her that morning. "He says he has his best people working on it," she added, unable to keep a contemptuous note from her voice on the words "best people." "But I will see that the truth of the matter comes to light. Don Mantovano's loyalty to me over the past six years demands no less."

Given what she had told me in private, this was a cautious and benign-sounding statement. I thought it was wiser that way.

Dantyszek inclined his head in acknowledgment, but he, too, stayed silent.

The queen spoke to her Polish advisor. "Panie Gamrat, do you think that we should stay away from it and let the chancellor investigate?" she asked.

"I do, Majesty." He bowed, and the gemstones adorning his large cap—with which he tried unsuccessfully to mask his balding pate—sparkled. Next to him, his Italian counterpart nodded in agreement. They had clearly already discussed it among themselves. Perhaps Stempowski, too, had encouraged them in this line of advice to the queen. "As they say, too many cooks—" Gamrat started to quote a popular Polish proverb, but she cut him off with a hand gesture.

"Who do you think is responsible for these killings?" she asked directly.

He blinked. "I don't know, Majesty. They are most mysterious."

"Don Carmignano?" She turned to the Italian. He was older than Gamrat, perhaps as old as fifty, but he had a full head of hair, which was all white, as was his beard. He tended to be pompous where Gamrat could sometimes be too cautious, and it was that pomposity I disliked about him.

"It appears that they were religiously motivated."

We all looked at Carmignano with a great deal of surprise, which he visibly relished.

"Would you care to explain?"

He puffed out his round chest with an air of importance, and despite my irritation, I was all ears. This was a theory I had not yet heard.

"There has been increasing strife between those loyal to His Holiness in Rome and supporters of Martin Luther," he said, sending a meaningful glance in Dantyszek's direction. The latter was known to have friends among sympathizers of the reforming German priest—some even suspected him of leaning toward the new religion himself. There must have been some truth to those rumors because I had overheard a conversation Dantyszek had on that very topic with Fugger the banker only a week before at the Christmas banquet.

"We have been getting reports of attacks and killings being committed by both sides, not just in the German lands, but also in the Low Countries, anywhere these blasphemous views"—Carmignano grimaced—"have taken root. We have not seen this type of violence here yet, but we cannot exclude the possibility that this may be the start of"—he hesitated—"similar troubles in this kingdom."

"But is there any proof?" The queen wanted to know.

"Last year, after he returned from a journey to Saxony, Zamborski was involved in a brawl in one of the city's taverns and briefly arrested. It was then that copies of Luther's theses were found in his possession."

"Hmm. I don't remember that."

"His family hushed it up."

"So why hasn't the chancellor announced that to be the motive instead of arresting some half-witted servant?"

"Perhaps so as not to embarrass himself for having nearly allowed his daughter to marry a heretic," Carmignano suggested.

"Of course," the queen scoffed. Then she said, "It would absolutely not surprise me if someone like Zamborski had been mixed up in so godless an activity. But what about my secretary? He was a staunch Catholic!"

"Who can know what darkness resides in a man's heart?" Carmignano said philosophically, shooting Dantyszek another malicious glance. "Not everyone flaunts his heresy openly."

There was a brief interval of silence; then the queen turned to Dantyszek. "What is your view?"

I doubted that the Italian had convinced her, but I could see that she was intrigued, nonetheless. Perhaps, like me, she found these awful developments also strangely fascinating.

Or maybe that was her way of dealing with her grief over Mantovano.

Dantyszek, who had endured Carmignano's subtle attacks with studied indifference, made a show of thinking about it. I guessed that he was preparing a strong rebuttal, and I was not disappointed.

"With all due respect"—he made a small bow toward the Italian advisor that was both deferential and mocking, something only a consummate courtier could achieve with such ease—"I do not think it very likely."

"And why is that?" I could see that the queen was glad to hear it.

"Because such killings look very different," he replied. "Signor Carmignano is right in talking about a rise of religious violence these last few years. It is indeed deplorable. I have traveled extensively throughout the empire, and I have seen such crimes and their aftermath." His eyes swiveled in my direction, concern over my delicate female sensibilities visible in the subtle lift of his eyebrows, but the queen motioned for him to continue. "Almost always those killed for their reformist sympathies are branded in some way, typically with a cross carved into their flesh"—he hesitated, then added in a tone of defiance—"or their foreheads, or even over their hearts."

He glanced at me again, but I remained impassive, even though my insides were gripped by an icy cold. What madness was this that compelled one man to destroy another in the name of preserving the purity of the faith?

"In many cases," he went on, "regardless of whether such mutilations are performed or not, the killers leave rosaries or crucifixes in their victims' hands. It is meant to shame them and send a message to everyone else, to discourage others from becoming swayed," he added grimly.

I was struck by how similar his tone was to that of Carmignano. Watching those two men eye each other warily and with thinly veiled hostility, it occurred to me that such violence was not inconceivable even in this kingdom, where toleration of religious differences ran deeper than elsewhere, deeper certainly that in the empire or in Italy. It was unlikely—for the reasons Dantyszek had just listed—that Zamborski and Mantovano had been killed by a religious zealot. But whether such things might happen in the future, as the break from Rome solidified in the northern lands, was an open question.

"There," Bona said, a note of triumph coloring her voice even as her advisor's face soured. "We can lay that possibility to rest."

She motioned to Dantyszek and Latalski, who had thus far remained silent. "I summoned both of you," she said, "for two reasons." There was palpable tension in the air as the courtiers awaited her next words. They were both ambitious and eager to serve, and she knew it. It occurred to me that she might ask them to work with me in conducting an investigation into the murders on her behalf. It would be odd, not just because of who they were, but also because I'd had the impression that she wanted to keep my mission a secret.

"First, I am now deprived of a secretary, and I will need a new one after poor Lorenzo is laid to rest," she said, and I let out a small sigh.

As if on cue, both courtiers executed their deepest and most elegant bows.

"Panie Latalski, with your excellent Latin and Italian, I will entrust you with that position, if you will accept it."

"It will be an honor, Your Majesty." The poet bowed again, his head nearly touching his bony knee.

"You will be working closely with my advisors." She gestured toward Gamrat and Carmignano. "They will explain your duties and responsibilities and debrief you on the business Don Mantovano was involved in." Her fingers curled tightly around the end of the armrest of her chair until her knuckles went white. "We are not going to let his death slow down the farming reforms; we are going to go ahead just as we planned. It's what he would have wanted."

"Of course," Latalski hastened to agree.

Across the chamber Gamrat and Carmignano exchanged a look, and I knew that they were just as aware as I was of the queen's true—or at least main—motivation. She wanted to send a signal to the chancellor that she would not back down. The gleam in her eye also told me that she could not wait for the official announcement to be made, for she was convinced it would infuriate Stempowski.

As all that was happening, Dantyszek's well-composed courtier's face could barely hide his disappointment. I, too, was surprised that he had been passed over for the post—he had as much Latin as Latalski, and far more diplomatic experience, not to mention charm. But then the queen addressed Dantyszek, and it all became clear. "My second reason is that I will need a trusted messenger to deliver a letter with my condolences to Signora Mantovano in Naples."

"I stand ready to travel wherever and whenever Your Majesty wishes," he replied smoothly, the cloud lifting from his face.

"There are four days until the Feast of Epiphany. I don't wish to cut short your Christmas celebrations," the queen said, and I detected a slight note of sarcasm on the word "celebrations." She did not care much for the *bibones et comedones*, not least because some of the more sanctimonious members of the court grumbled that it was we Italians who had brought loose morals to Kraków with us. This despite the fact that, as Konarski had told me, the society had existed long before the king's marriage. "Come back on the morning of Epiphany, and I will have the letter ready. You will leave as soon as the feast is over."

It was nearly midnight when the queen dismissed the men. As I was undressing her for bed, she told me not to wake any of the girls and sleep in her chamber instead, and I went to fetch my nightdress.

I hurried down the quiet gallery, the chill making me shiver, my own words about not walking alone ringing in my ears. I was almost at my chamber when I saw movement out of the corner of my eye, and a patch of white detached itself from a shadowed alcove and stepped toward me.

A small scream escaped me, and I clamped my mouth with my hand. "You scared me!" I exhaled.

It was Helena, wearing a nightdress, her thick auburn hair falling in loose waves about her shoulders, making her face look small, almost like a child's. Down at the entrance to the gallery, I could see two new guards standing sentinel, very much awake, and I scolded myself for my nervousness. One of them looked in our direction when he heard me, and I raised my hand to signify that everything was fine.

"What are you doing here at this hour?" I asked sharply, wondering if Helena was on her way to or from meeting her lover. The lover she had promised not to see again. But I could not glean anything from her expression—she was calm and inscrutable, as always. "You will catch your death."

"I couldn't sleep," she said.

"What about Doctor Baldazzi's poppy milk?"

"I ran out of it. He gave me only a small bottle. It is a powerful medicine—if you take too much you may never wake." The corners of her lips curled in a slight smile, causing her eyes to narrow, which gave her a feline look.

"Yes, well ... I don't expect that standing in a cold gallery at night will help you with that either. Go back to bed."

"You also cannot sleep, signora?" she asked.

"I was in a meeting with the queen and her advisors." I straightened my spine.

"About the agriculture reform?"

"About Don Mantovano's murder."

Helena hugged her arms about her, her face a mask of apprehension. "Has Her Majesty discovered who did it?"

"No, but we discussed some possibilities," I said with a surge of pride. I felt like I was an advisor too, someone of wisdom and experience whose judgment was sought and respected. "There are some things that don't make sense," I went on, unable to stop myself. "This was no jealousy or robbery—these murders were planned, methodical, and sinister." Helena's eyes widened as I spoke, and I realized that I had said too much. The last thing I needed was to spread more fear or cause more gossip.

"But mainly the meeting was about what happens next," I hastened to add. "Her Majesty needs a new secretary and a messenger to take her letter to Don Mantovano's widow. She entrusted Jan Dantyszek with the mission, and he will be leaving for Naples after Epiphany."

"He will?" She seemed somehow disappointed. A delicate blush bloomed on her cheeks, and I wondered if Dantyszek was the man she was in love with. But what about their hostility during the sleigh ride to Niepołomice? And even if, unbeknownst to the rest of us, it had been a lovers' tiff—perhaps brought about by Dantyszek's blatant flirting with Lucrezia—he was unmarried, so there would be no need for such secrecy. Besides, there was no overt animosity between the girls, as was common in such cases, although I had seen Helena look at Lucrezia with barely veiled disdain more than once when Lucrezia flirted with courtiers—any of them, not just Dantyszek. No, however I thought about it, it did not make sense; the more I tried to understand her, the more she seemed to elude me.

I made to open my door. "Go back to bed," I repeated. "Remember what I said about not walking alone? You know it's dangerous these days, even with guards nearby."

"I have something to ask you, signora." Helena said with a note of urgency. It was as if she had only just remembered it.

"What is it?" I asked impatiently. I was tired and cold, and the queen was waiting for me.

"I had a letter from my father earlier today, and"—she hesitated—"he has been ailing these past few weeks—since the autumn, in fact. I worry about him."

"Oh, Helena." I felt a surge of sympathy for her. My own father had died of the wasting disease shortly before I left for Poland. The memory sent a twinge of pain through my chest. "I hope it's nothing serious."

"His doctors don't know what it is. They keep bleeding him, but he's not improving. He wishes to see me in case he—" Her voice caught in her throat.

I put a comforting hand on her shoulder. "Of course. You have my permission to go. I will pray for his recovery." I blinked, feeling pressure behind my own eyes.

"Thank you," she said. "He sent two of his men with the message. They are lodging in town and are ready to escort me to Lipiny the day after tomorrow."

I was surprised at how quickly this had been arranged, but perhaps the matter was indeed urgent. "Then I hope you will get some sleep before the journey," I said. "It will not be an easy one at this time of year."

"I do too."

"I will inform Her Majesty."

"Thank you," Helena said again. Then she added, before she disappeared into the darkness of the girls' bedchamber, "I hope that whoever did this is caught." She gazed at me levelly. "And that you are safe."

10

January 4ᵗʰ, 1520

I found the note two days later. I had spent a busy morning accompanying the queen and her confessor, Father de la Torre, to a private burial for Don Mantovano. It was held at the Church of St. Agata in Kraków, on a quiet street a short ride from the castle. We were joined by the abbess of the Order of Poor Clares, who held the church in trust, and a group of Italians who had known the secretary well. There were also a few other courtiers in attendance whom I knew from sight but not by name; they must have been the chancellor's men, sent to observe the proceedings and see if they could uncover any clues as to the killer's identity. But if so, they must have been disappointed.

"Into your hands, O Lord, we entrust the soul of your servant Ludovico Niccolo Mantovano," the priest intoned in Latin as we stood before the oak coffin adorned with silver handles and trimmings and draped in rich black velvet. "Look mercifully upon the sins he committed out of human weakness, and grant him the joy of life everlasting in your presence."

He shook the censer, and swirls of pungent incense enveloped us before rising lazily to the vaulted ceiling. There a newly painted image in vivid colors—by one of the city's Italian artists, judging by the style of it—looked down on us.

It was of God sitting in judgment, saints on one side, sinners on the other. Through the smoky haze, I could see the severe aspect of his oversized white-bearded visage, and it sent a shiver down my spine. But I still could not imagine Don Mantovano being guilty of anything serious enough to provoke that divine reaction when he stood before the Heavenly Father's throne.

After the prayer concluded, the priest began chanting the Office of the Dead, and we followed the casket to a side chapel where it was lowered into a crypt below the stone floor. The queen had paid for the crypt space herself, and she was the only one present who seemed genuinely moved; everyone else appeared to be there out of duty or necessity rather than any sense of loss or mourning for Don Mantovano. I found it sad that so few tears were being shed for him, although in truth I felt no great urge to cry either.

Unlike that of Zamborski, whose body had been taken to his family's seat to be buried, the cause of the secretary's death had not been made public. The king feared panic after a second violent death, but rumors were already circulating. The queen was becoming increasingly impatient with the investigation. She had raised the matter again with the king during their private supper the night before the funeral, but it must not have gone as she had hoped because she returned to her apartments in a bad mood, and I dared not ask any questions. I was one of the few people at the court who knew the details of both crimes, and I found myself beset by an unsettling sense of something dark and sinister encircling us and slowly tightening its grip.

Perhaps that was why, when I found the note, I was not entirely surprised.

It happened after we returned from the funeral. The queen went to the nursery, taking Lucrezia and Portia with her, and I returned to my chamber. But as I opened my door and stepped inside, I felt something slippery under my foot. I stooped to pick up a folded rectangle of paper.

My stomach clenched with a bad premonition, even as I clung to a vague hope that the message was left by someone looking for me while I had been out of the castle. But when I unfolded it and read the words written in a deliberately shaky, childlike hand to hide the writer's identity, my hope vanished.

The killer's work is justice.
Stop looking for him or you will be next.

With trembling hands, I refolded the note, which I noticed was written on a paper that bore the crest of the Sforza family, the serpents and eagles, and had therefore come from Don Mantovano's desk. Blood was pounding in my ears as I stood gazing at the windows where the remnants of a thick fog that had descended on Kraków that morning still clung to the glass. When the queen and I had walked to the carriage that was to convey us to the church, one of the servants mentioned reports of a powerful snowstorm that had crippled the countryside to the east, making roads impassable and burying men and beasts as far as the eye could see. Right then, clutching that note in my hands, I would have preferred a blizzard to that silent milky veil that made me feel cornered, trapped, and blind.

I stepped outside, pulling the door closed behind me, and the sound echoed hollowly through the empty gallery. But the guards were in their place at the entrance to the wing, and that made me feel safer. I took a deep breath, walked up to them, and asked if any stranger had come to look for me that morning. They said no. They had not seen anyone knock on my door either.

After a momentary deliberation, I decided that I must inform the queen—she had said to bring her any news immediately, day or night. I reread the note twice on my way to the nursery, which was on the other side of the castle in the southern wing, to see if I could glean any clues or additional meaning from it. But it remained as cryptic and anonymous as the first time I opened it. Nothing gave the author or his motivations away.

I put the note in my pocket before I entered the nursery. It was one of my favorite places at Wawel, full as it was of childish chatter and laughter, and I understood why Bona had gone there after her secretary's funeral. She wanted to be cheered, and I hoped that she was. I hoped I would be too, if only for a brief moment, for the tidings I brought would disturb any peace the queen had managed to find.

The nursery was warm and bright as always, busy with the children's play and the bustle of their nurses. But the queen, sitting on a settle upholstered in blue-and-gold damask and lined with soft cushions, looked melancholy. She still wore the somber gown trimmed with black lace, but her blonde hair was loosely gathered in a golden hairnet, so thin it was almost invisible. With strands escaping about her face, it made her look unexpectedly domestic, but also youthful and vulnerable.

She was gazing into the fire as she held Princess Izabela on her lap. Between the settle and the hearth was a thick Turkish rug on which the king's two other daughters—Jadwiga, who was now six, and four-year-old Anna—were playing. The elder girl was building an elaborate structure with brightly painted wooden blocks. Her sister was combing the hair of a pretty doll in a red silk gown, which I recognized as a Christmas gift from the Queen of Hungary. Nearby was a black rocking horse, and seated on it was five-year-old Beata, brandishing a wooden sword with a good imitation of knights' belligerent cries when they practiced swordsmanship in the courtyard in the summer. She was the king's daughter by his former mistress Katarzyna Telniczanka.

For all her unhappiness—frequently and loudly expressed—about a queen's limited role and expectations that did not go beyond producing heirs, Bona doted on all three princesses. She also took good care of Beata, whose presence at the court she never questioned. She showered the children with expensive frocks and sent them trays of sweets, which even now were scattered on tables and windowsills throughout the nursery. The faces of the girls, including the baby, were smeared with brown streaks of caramelized sugar and white blobs of cream.

I could not help smiling at the sight, and I marveled—not for the first time—at how the queen managed to so successfully combine those two realities. The children clearly adored her. It was evident from the intermittent glances they sent in her direction, full of hope for the attention to which they were obviously accustomed, despite her presently brooding aspect. It was one of the many contradictions in Bona's nature—fiery and unquiet, yet nurturing; elevated by vivid intelligence but also hamstrung by stubbornness and impetuosity.

She turned her gaze on me without a word as I entered the chamber.

"Your Majesty." I curtsied. I hesitated, not knowing how to broach the subject in the presence of the children. "I bring news ... there is something Your Majesty must see. Privately," I added, lowering my voice.

She arched her eyebrows slightly, and I could see that she was bracing herself. But she did not want to act alarmed in front of the others.

"Leave us." She gestured to the nurses, who took the children away, including little Izabela. They removed to the adjoining chamber, which was to be the heir's when he arrived in a few months' time. Then she turned to Lucrezia and Portia. "You too."

With a smile but also a pang, I gazed after the children. Their presence, even if quieter than usual today, was soothing.

If my marriage had turned out differently, I would now have children of my own the age of Princess Jadwiga, or perhaps even older. There were times when that thought filled me with a certain wistfulness. I wondered then if I would have been a good mother. I had once believed so, but the struggles I presently experienced with the maids of honor left me unsure about that. Perhaps nurturing and protecting others was not in my nature.

The doors between the chambers closed, and we were alone. I turned to the queen and saw that she had noticed the way I looked at the children. Our eyes met, and there was a softness in her gaze that I was not accustomed to. Perhaps under different circumstances—if we were both mothers and of a more equal station—we could have forged a bond of friendship over sharing the joys and challenges of raising children. But that was not the case, and there were other matters to attend to. Her face hardened again when she remembered the reason I was there. "What is it that I must see?" she asked, her tone wary.

I took the note from the folds of my gown and handed it to the queen. "I found this under my door after I came back from the church."

I watched her as she unfolded and read the message. She must have gritted her teeth, for a muscle in her cheek twitched.

"The gall of this monster," she hissed, flinging the note aside. She rose with more energy than I would have expected of her in that moment and began to pace the distance between the settle and the window.

"I must report this to the chancellor," I said, readying myself for a rebuke. I had no doubt that she believed the note had come from Stempowski, or at least from someone acting on his orders.

"Yes, you must," she said, and there was an eagerness in her voice that surprised me. "Take it to him and see what he says when he is confronted with it. I would do it myself, but my husband has ordered me not to interfere in a matter best handled by men."

I knew then that it was serious. For one thing, she had used the word "order." Also, when Bona—ever mindful of court protocol and proper hierarchies—referred to the king as "my husband" rather than "His Majesty," it could only mean that she was furious with him.

I spoke into the uncomfortable silence. "I am sure he only wants Your Majesty to be safe, given the condition—"

"I am with child, not dying!" She tossed her head impatiently. "I cannot stay away from this. I *will* not," she added firmly. "Especially if there is a chance that Stempowski will get away with it."

"So, I am to watch for his reaction when I show him the note?" I asked.

"Exactly." For the first time in days, her face broke into a smile as she savored her defiance of the royal command. "Report your impressions to me, and everything that he says."

I curtsied and left the nursery, but I was not sure what it was that she expected to happen. Did she think that the chancellor would break down and confess the truth when I handed him the note, if there was any truth for him to confess? That would be absurd—he was a seasoned diplomat and a high-ranking court official, and I was but a lady-in-waiting.

Yet with the queen's own advisors being against her involvement, and now the king having officially forbidden it, I was all she had.

On the long walk to the State Chambers, my rustling skirts adding to the sense of urgency, I tried to breathe deeply to stave off a tide of anxiety swelling inside me. I wanted to speak to Konarski first, but with the war, the murders, and the mundane business of the realm, the wing was a beehive of activity, and I could not see him. Finally, I knocked on the door to Stempowski's office, and when a clerk opened it, I said I needed to see the chancellor on the queen's order.

Stempowski was not in, but the clerk bid me come in and wait, then went off in search of his master. The office was spacious but sparsely furnished. In the center stood an oak desk, larger but less ornate than Don Mantovano's Italian piece, and also much less tidy. There were piles of papers on it, several quills, bottles of ink, and a block of sealing wax on a silver tray. The only other furnishings were a long sideboard with a flagon of wine and goblets, and two bronze candelabras in the corners opposite the hearth, so tall they had to stand on the floor.

Behind the desk, the entire wall was hung with a tapestry depicting a battle scene, rearing horses and raised weapons so stunningly detailed and lifelike I could almost hear the cries of the men and the clash of blade on blade. Above the field, the coats of arms of the dual monarchy—the white eagle on a red shield of the Kingdom of Poland and the charging knight on horseback of the Grand Duchy of Lithuania—were suspended like twin suns.

"It shows the Battle of Grunwald in the summer of the year 1410, when our king's forebear, the great King Władysław, defeated the Knights of the Teutonic Order." Chancellor Stempowski's voice jolted me out of my admiration. He must have been nearby, or I had been so entranced by the beauty of the tapestry's workmanship that I had lost track of time.

I turned around to find him making a small bow, then moving toward his desk.

"That is very fitting," I said with one more glance at the tapestry.

"They have never regained their former glory, but they continue to be a nuisance as they scheme with Muscovy." He gestured for me to sit in a chair across from his desk, while he took a seat in a heavy high-backed chair of carved oak upholstered in green damask. I noticed that he made no mention of the Order's scheming with the Habsburgs, which was closer and more long-standing than the alliance the knights had only recently forged with the ruler in Moscow. "I hope that Marshal Firlej will deal them a mortal blow this time," he added.

"That is my hope also."

The chancellor's aged but handsome face was difficult to read, which together with his experience, skill, and the king's trust, made him a formidable opponent. How was I to decide what he had done and what he was hiding, if anything? Just now he had spoken like the most fervent supporter of the war, even though a few days earlier, he had tried to slow it down, perhaps even stop it. Maybe he had fallen on the king's side once the matter had been decided, or maybe he was only pretending. Who could tell? Not I, certainly.

"It is a pleasure to see you again, Contessa Sanseverino, even under these deplorable circumstances," Stempowski said. He began to look through a pile of papers, and I studied him again. He was very tall—around six feet, I imagined—and although his chair was larger than mine, his broad-shouldered frame filled it completely. I wondered if he had a military background, for he was built like a soldier, certainly more so than the spare Marshal Firlej.

Finally, he set the papers aside and gave me a considering look. I felt a new surge of nervousness, and it was all I could do not to drop my gaze to where I tried to keep my hands steady in my lap.

"I take it you are here on a matter related to Don Mantovano's death?" His whole demeanor was polite and smooth; someone who did not know any better would never guess at the animosity between him and the queen.

"Indeed."

Before I could say anything more, he leaned back in his chair and smiled, narrowing his eyes, though they remained watchful. "You are young to be acting as Her Majesty's envoy, signora. Why didn't she send one of her advisors?"

The question disconcerted me with its correspondence to my own doubts about myself. Why had the lessons the sisters of Santa Teresa had tried so assiduously to impart in us produced all the wrong results? On the one hand, they caused me to question my fitness for the task with which the queen had entrusted me, but they also made me inadequate for the role of supervising adolescent girls. It seemed I was lacking all around.

I searched for a reply that would justify my current mission. "Her Majesty chose me—I am not so young ..." I stammered, feeling even more ridiculous. "I'm twenty-five."

He laughed one of those laughs that come from deep inside the stomach, as if I had told a good joke. "Same age as my eldest daughter."

A sudden emotion seized my throat as I was reminded of my own father, who had held a middling position at the court in Naples during the turbulent years of the French invasions and the restoration of the House of Trastámara. He had never been as ambitious as Stempowski, nor nearly as wealthy, but it was he, more than my mother, who was responsible for my education. He had always believed that a woman should know more than embroidery and how to conduct pleasant talk at the table. What would he think of me now? Would he be proud, or would he be as dismissive as the chancellor?

"Be that as it may," I said, swallowing the knot and wishing to change the topic, "I found this in my chamber not long ago." I placed the note on the desk between us and withdrew my hand quickly. "Her Majesty believes that you should see it."

The chancellor took the paper and read the message, then flipped it over to see if anything was written on the reverse. He gazed at the writing for a long while, and once again I could find nothing to indicate that he had seen it before, much less authored it. In fact, he seemed just as puzzled as I was.

Or he was pretending admirably.

He rose and went to a small chamber that communicated with his office, and I heard him send the clerk in search of Konarski. The latter appeared a few minutes later, visibly surprised to see me, and the chancellor handed him the note without a word.

He read it, and his face tightened. "Are you and Her Majesty safe?" he asked the question that Stempowski had not.

"Yes, thank you, Master Secretary."

"Secretary Konarski keeps His Majesty informed on the progress of our investigation," the chancellor explained. Then his tone turned official. "So, you found it just now in your chamber, slid under your door?"

"Yes, about an hour ago. It was not there when I left this morning to attend on the queen and accompany her to Don Mantovano's funeral. It must have happened when I was away, but the guards did not see any strangers or anyone suspicious about."

"Hmm." His fingers, gnarled with arthritis, fiddled with his graying beard as he considered this. "And you don't think it's a practical joke, by one of your women maybe?"

I hesitated. "I suppose it's possible, but unlikely. They are serious and well-behaved young ladies," I said, even as I recalled the copies of the illicit books I'd had to confiscate from them. "They would never make light of a situation like that. There was not a dry face among them on the morning Don Mantovano's body was discovered, and they are scared themselves. This is a malicious threat by the killer"—I pointed at the note—"or by someone who doesn't want me to discover who the killer is."

"So, *you* are searching for the killer?" Stempowski raised an eyebrow, even as the rest of his face remained impassive.

I realized my blunder belatedly. "No—" I tried not to look at Konarski. "No, of course not. But I have discussed the various speculations that have been making the rounds."

"Discussed with whom?"

"With Her Majesty, the ladies, Doctor Baldazzi ..."

"And?"

I shifted in my seat. I was not sure why he was questioning me like this.

"I have expressed some reservations—" This time my eyes darted toward Konarski. He looked tense from where he stood behind the chancellor's chair, but he did not signal for me to stop. "For example, regarding the theory that these crimes were committed for gain." I paused, conscious that Maciek's arrest had been justified in exactly that way. But the chancellor nodded for me to go on. "Don Mantovano's ring and chain of office were taken, but there were silver candlesticks, an alabaster vase, and many other valuable objects left behind in his office. To me that suggests that the killer wanted to make it look like a burglary. And Zamborski's murder," I added quickly, before courage deserted me, "while seemingly a robbery too, appears cold and methodical, like ... setting a trap." It was a comparison that occurred to me for the first time in that moment.

Despite his earlier unease, I saw Konarski suppress a smile. Meanwhile, Stempowski sat in silence, still pulling on his beard, which seemed to indicate deep thought. "This case is perplexing, with few clues and many questions for which we have no answers," he said at length. "But I am determined to solve it." He leaned forward, his thick eyebrows lifting to underscore the sincerity of his words. "For this madman killed my daughter's fiancé, and as much as I disliked that loafer—he was good for nothing but drinking parties and dice—my Celina loved him, and her heart is broken." A shadow crossed his face. "The killer has caused her suffering, and I will have his neck for it." He bunched the fingers of his right hand into a fist and twisted it in front of his face as he clenched his teeth.

"Of course," I murmured. *So much for him ordering that murder.* He could still be responsible for Mantovano's killing, however, although that seemed increasingly unlikely too. I would have bet my finest gown and a string of pearls that it was the work of the same man.

I was just about to launch into explaining my other reservations when Stempowski sat back calmly, every inch a courtier again. "Do you know what *I* think, Contessa Sanseverino? I think it was about a woman after all." There was a trace of sarcasm in the way one corner of his mouth lifted. "If memory serves me, it was suggested by that quack of Her Majesty's"— half-turning, he leaned his head toward Konarski—"what's his name again?"

"Doctor Baldazzi, Your Excellency."

"I think that is the most likely explanation," he went on before I had a chance to say anything. "In both cases. And here's why." He raised himself in his chair for a more comfortable and an even more authority-conveying position. "Jan Dantyszek, who was an old friend of Zamborski's, testified that he never showed up for the Christmas banquet. They thought that he was indisposed, and therefore saw no reason to search for him. But what I think happened"—he raised a finger like a priest from a pulpit imparting a tenet of faith—"is that he went to that delivery passage on purpose, to meet someone. But instead of the woman, he came face to face with her husband and paid for it with his life." He let out a bark of contemptuous laughter, and, regardless of what he had said earlier, I could see why the queen would think that he had rid himself of a man he considered beneath his daughter.

Konarski's face wore an inscrutable expression. I was forced to admit, once again, that when it came to Zamborski, that was at least a reasonable theory. But the queen's secretary?

"There is no evidence that Don Mantovano had any liaisons," I said a bit defensively. "Her Majesty swears by his fidelity to his wife and—"

"I know, I know. He was something of a prude." The chancellor waved his hand dismissively. "But do you know that he brought wine to his office on the night he died?"

"Uh …" I could not decide whether I should admit that I did and possibly get Konarski in trouble, but Stempowski was so excited now that he did not notice how flustered I was.

"Not only that," he continued, warming to his theme, "he shared his wine with the guards, who then fell asleep like a pair of newborns at their wet nurse's teats. Do you know what that means?" I was so confused that I could not even shake my head, and Stempowski seemed to relish this. "It means that he laced the wine with something," he finished triumphantly.

"Laced it with what?"

The chancellor shrugged. "I don't know, but Mantovano was Italian, and if the Italians know anything, it is their poisons." He guffawed, momentarily forgetting—or ignoring—the fact that I, too, was Italian. Behind him, Konarski reddened.

A scene flashed through my mind with sudden clarity: a flagon of wine on the table next to Lucrezia's chair on the morning the secretary's body had been found. I had assumed that the chancellor had sent for it to calm her nerves, but had he?

"The wine in Don Mantovano's office—was it there when you arrived to question Signorina Alifio?" I asked, suddenly breathless.

"It was." The chancellor dipped his head in appreciative acknowledgment of my reasoning. "Later that day, after I talked with the guards and they confessed to having accepted a drink from him and then falling fast asleep, I grew suspicious. I had one of my men drink a cup of the wine from the office, and he went on to sleep for fourteen hours." He looked satisfied at how neatly this seemed to explain his thesis. "Signorina Alifio had a few sips from it too, if I remember correctly?"

"Yes. She slept until late that afternoon and was still groggy at supper."

"You see?" He spread his hands. "Now, why would Don Mantovano have put a sleeping draught into the wine he offered to the guards if not to get rid of any witnesses to his meeting with a mistress?"

"Perhaps to get rid of witnesses to his meeting with someone set on extracting information about the queen's business," I said, still rankled by his comment about the Italians.

Stempowski's salt-and-pepper eyebrows met over his nose with a deep frown. "What are you suggesting, signora?" I flinched. This was my second blunder. Thus far I had found no evidence of the chancellor's involvement, but I was rapidly antagonizing him, as was evident from Konarski's alarmed face. "That he was a spy? For whom?"

"I ... I wouldn't know," I stammered. "I just thought ..." I faltered, but he waited, slightly cocking his head. Was he genuinely interested, or did he think that my words reflected the queen's suspicions that he might have a mole among her men? Once again, I felt my own inadequacy to the task, stuck as I was between these two consummate players.

"I have no idea what happened that night," I said, truthfully enough, as I collected myself. It was time for me to stop speculating. "And it does seem that Don Mantovano was ... up to something." It was also time to stop talking before I again said something I should not.

"That much is certain," Stempowski stated sarcastically. He sighed with an air of finality, and I knew that the interview had come to an end. He picked up the note. "I will keep this as we continue our investigation. And thank you for bringing it to my attention."

"Of course." I began to rise from the chair, then something occurred to me. "Perhaps it is worth talking to Doctor Baldazzi? I know he offered poppy milk to another of my ladies when she couldn't sleep. If he gave us—if he gave *you*"—I corrected myself hastily—"a list of who else procured it from him, you could look into whether any of them had a reason to see Don Mantovano dead."

"I already did." The chancellor looked unhappy. "Half the court is taking it, apparently. Besides, there are several different extracts that can put a man to sleep." He frowned as he tried to recall. "Valerian, lemon balm in high concentrations, hypericum ... I forget what else." He shook his head. "Baldi makes them all. It's no use."

I was about to correct him on Baldazzi's name when Konarski interjected. "My Lord Chancellor, may I suggest posting more guards outside Her Majesty's apartments and Contessa Sanseverino's chamber?"

Stempowski hesitated momentarily, then he must have realized how bad a rejection of that suggestion would sound. "I will summon the captain of the guard and give appropriate dispositions," he said without enthusiasm. "And let's keep this"—he waved the note in his hand—"quiet for now."

After we had left the chancellor's office, Konarski insisted on walking me back despite my assurances that nobody would attack me in broad daylight with courtiers, guards, and servants milling about. Servants, in particular, were more numerous than was usual at that hour, and I recognized several of the kitchen staff who would not normally be there until suppertime.

When we turned into the queen's gallery, we passed Lucrezia and Magdalena walking in the opposite direction. There was no smile on Lucrezia's face; it had not returned there once since the New Year's morning. Instead, after acknowledging us with a nod, she continued staring ahead, her expression blank. Magdalena, on the other hand, shifted a curious gaze from Konarski to me and back. Then she tossed her head and jutted out her generous bosom with a lingering look at the king's secretary. Out of the corner of my eye, I saw him return her greeting absent-mindedly.

As we neared my chamber, I wondered who that phantom was who was able to move around the castle with all these people about without arousing any suspicions. For even at night, corridors, hallways, and galleries were rarely empty. Except when there was a banquet.

"Dear God," I gasped, halting in my tracks. I pulled Konarski into a nearby alcove with a narrow window that gave onto the courtyard below. "The Feast of Epiphany is two days from now!"

"Yes." He looked puzzled. "I know."

"Zamborski and Mantovano were both killed when most of the court was attending a banquet—first Christmas, then New Year's. That means that the murderer might strike again the night after next."

Konarski swallowed hard. "You're right." He ran a hand over his face. "Why haven't I thought about this before?"

"What can we do? We don't even know what made him select the first two. They had nothing in common. Anybody can be next." With a clutch at my heart, I realized that it could even be Konarski.

"I will ask the chancellor to order more guards posted, but I am not sure what else can be done unless we have a clue or a firm lead, which we don't."

"Maybe an announcement should be made?" I suggested. "So everyone is on alert?"

He shook his head. "It would only cause fear and confusion, and that's what the king wants to avoid at all costs."

We stood in silence for a while. Outside the window the fog had dissipated, and stray snowflakes fell languidly toward the flagstones that paved the courtyard. For Helena's sake, I hoped that the snowstorm prediction was wrong, for it had only been a few hours since she left for her father's estate.

A sound of footsteps, enhanced by heavy boots, made us both jump. A moment later, three guards appeared, two of whom took up post directly outside the queen's apartments, halberds in hand. Konarski showed the third one the door to my chamber, and the guard planted himself there with an impassive expression.

I turned to Konarski. Before I could say anything, he brought a hand to my cheek, cupping it so gently I could barely feel his fingers on my skin. "You will be fine," he said reassuringly. Up close, his eyes, which I had previously thought dark brown, had a depth to them in which I could see flecks of amber, like that precious resin found on the shores of the Baltic Sea. "I will make sure of that."

I raised my hand to cover his. How I wanted to put my arms around his neck and hold him close, both to give and to receive comfort, for he looked as strained as I felt. But the guards were there, and it would have been unseemly; there was enough gossip going around as it was.

"Thank you, Sebastian," I said in a low voice, using his given name for the first time. "And please ... be careful."

"I will." He smiled, but the smile did not reach his eyes.

He stood watching me as I stepped into my chamber. When I closed the door, I leaned heavily on the dark, iron-studded oak and took a shuddering breath. Outside an early winter night was falling.

I had woken up that morning still believing myself safe, but now it was clear that my life, Konarski's life, and possibly even those of the king and the queen, were in danger.

We were all prey.

11

January 5th, 1520

At noon the next day, a solemn mass was celebrated in the cathedral for the souls of Zamborski and Mantovano.

The interior of Wawel Cathedral was magnificent, with high vaulted ceilings and tall stained-glass windows that, on a sunny day, cast a mosaic of colors onto the walls, the pews, and the floor. It was divided into two parts. The eastern part centered around the main altar, with a triptych altarpiece of gilded wood which depicted scenes of the Last Judgment and the triumph of Good over Evil. It was where the kings and queens of Poland had been crowned for centuries, and the church was so large that the altar seemed dwarfed by the space above. The notes of chants from the white-clad boys' choir drifted toward that space only to come back as faint echoes reflected off the walls. It was so large, in fact, that despite the hundreds of candles blazing around the apse, the ribs of the ceiling were cloaked in shadows into which the swirls of aromatic incense floated and disappeared.

The walls of this section of the cathedral were lined with double rows of stalls intricately carved out of dark walnut. It was there that the members of the royal household—including the advisors, secretaries, maids of honor, and ladies-in-waiting—were seated. The royal couple occupied the central place in front of the altar on damask-upholstered chairs, both dressed in black, the queen's somber-colored gown woven with silver thread under a cloak trimmed with sable fur.

Stempowski and other high officials sat in the closest stalls, and I saw the queen send the chancellor a thunderous look as he bowed upon her arrival. The night before, she was disappointed when I reported on my conversation in his chambers regarding the killer's note, but she was still convinced that sooner or later we would find evidence of the chancellor's guilt.

In the western part of the cathedral, where there was a smaller altar built over the grave of St. Stanisław, the nave and side chapels were filled to bursting with lesser members of the court, while the staff and servants spilled out into the forecourt. It seemed that all of Wawel's residents—from the lowliest to the mightiest—had turned up. Some of it was probably curiosity; by then, everybody knew what had happened in the last eleven days. Yet I wondered how many were aware of the risk awaiting them tomorrow night.

The mass was celebrated by Bishop Konarski. He commenced by leading a slow procession of priests and deacons from the grave of St. Stanisław, his predecessor on the see and a famed martyr, to the main altar to the chant of the choir. In his white robes, his head topped with a miter and a gilded crozier firmly held in his hand, the bishop looked so authoritative and pious, saintly even, that I could not suppress a smile, remembering what his nephew had told me about his weakness for communion wine and pretty maidservants.

The smile must still have lingered on my lips when I looked across to where Sebastian Konarski was sitting in his stall and saw him watching me. He did not look away when our eyes met over the candlelit space; instead, he smiled back, perhaps at the same memory, and it was I who looked away first, my face aflame. He had to have noticed that happening to me quite often by now, and I silently chastised myself for acting like a maid in first bloom. I should be poised and level-headed, as my rank and duties required of me. I straightened my back, vowing not to look in his direction again, and tried to concentrate on the mass.

During the sermon, a melancholy mood assailed me once more as the bishop's eloquent, somber words echoed through the cavernous church. They were wise words about how the body turns to dust but the spirit returns to God, and comforting ones about God's love that made Him send his only Son so that whoever believes in Him shall not die but live eternally. But when he called on anyone—and he paused for a long moment on that word—who might be concealing a dark secret in his heart to confess because God was forgiving and would cleanse those who repented all unrighteousness, I wondered if the man the bishop was addressing was among us. It was very likely that he was. He was someone who had known Zamborski and Mantovano, who had studied their habits and planned their killing, and who was probably getting ready to commit another crime.

Then the cryptic and chilling message from yesterday's note echoed in my mind. *The killer's work is justice.* To him, the murders were not sin; they were not the greatest transgression imaginable. They were, quite possibly, God's work. He was mad, convinced of his righteousness, and therefore the bishop's admonishing words would not stop him, the queen's ladies' scared faces would not deter him, and the Princess of Montefusco's avid eyes sweeping the congregation would not discover him. He was everyone but no one, visible yet hidden, slave to his murderous impulse and free to act on it without anyone getting in his way. But at least in this holy place, surrounded by so many others, we each found a momentary respite, a brief sense of safety.

The mass lasted nearly two hours. When it was over, the king and the queen exited the cathedral. Bona was followed by the maids of honor, but I had arrived late and found myself among the crowd that began pressing at the massive double door as the bell in the great tower above our heads clanged in one final solemn homage to the victims. When I finally stepped into the frosty air, welcoming it after the closeness of the church, I felt a tap on my shoulder. My nerves were so taut that I instinctively dashed forward, away from whoever was behind me, but as the people were slow in dispersing from the forecourt, I did not have much room for maneuver.

I felt a hand on my arm, detaining me gently. "It's all right. It's only me." The sound of Konarski's voice flooded me with relief. "I'm sorry I scared you. You have gone pale," he said as I turned to face him.

At least that was a change from all the blushing I had done so far. "We are all nervous these days." I smiled weakly.

"How have you been faring since yesterday? I hope you had a peaceful night."

"Peaceful enough under the circumstances," I said.

That was not quite true. I had slept fitfully, waking often and imagining I heard footsteps and rustling outside my door. I had two distinct dreams that night. In the first, I followed a cloaked and hooded figure through the castle's dimly lit corridors. The figure seemed to float in the air ahead of me rather than walk, for it had no feet—it was just a cloak, the way Maciek had described it. I woke up briefly and when I went back to sleep, I was outside my chamber standing behind the cloaked figure as it crouched at my threshold pushing the note under my door. I reached out my hand, and the figure turned. The face that emerged from under the hood was that of Konarski. He winked at me and put a finger to his lips, as if instructing me to keep a secret.

When I woke up again, it was still dark, and in that confused state between sleep and consciousness, I was convinced that Konarski was the murderer, and I was terrified. But the light of day had dispelled that fear. What possible motive could he have? He was not in need of money, as far as I could see, and he had no wife of whom to be jealous. But could he be the chancellor's assassin? After all, they did work very closely together. I replayed the meeting in Stempowski's office in my head and decided that while he was a seemingly exemplary assistant, there was something in Konarski's demeanor that betrayed a certain impatience, perhaps even annoyance, with the king's closest advisor, which appeared to go unremarked by the latter. Now as he stood in front of me, his face a picture of gentleness and concern, it seemed like the most ridiculous idea in the world.

"I will send a page every hour to check on you," Konarski said, clearly not convinced by my assurances.

I shook my head. "Thank you, but that's not necessary." I knew that making even more fuss about it would only increase my anxiety. "I just wish for a little sunshine." I glanced up at the gray sky. "I miss the skies over Bari; they can be so clear and blue, even in the middle of winter." I felt a sudden clutch at my throat, and I was worried that I would start crying.

Konarski smiled ruefully. "Give it two or three more months, and you will see blue skies over Kraków again." His hand was still on my arm, and he squeezed it gently in sympathy when he saw tears shimmering in my eyes before I blinked them back.

"My dear Sebastian!" A jolly voice rang out, and Konarski's body jerked forward under the force of a mighty slap on his shoulder. If I had not taken a step back, he would have slammed into me.

He turned, annoyed but also smiling. "Kostek, it is good to see you. It's been a while." He greeted a man who emerged from behind his back dressed in a knight's non-battle uniform: a gambeson and thin chain mail under his cloak, gauntlet gloves on his hands, and a sword buckled at his belt. He was the same height as Konarski and resembled him, but for a lighter shade of hair and eyes that were more hazel than brown. But his nose was equally strong, and he had the same well-defined mouth, although its set was slightly mocking where Konarski's was typically serious.

"My cousin, Konstanty Konarski, from the Baranów branch of the family," my companion introduced him. "Contessa Caterina Sanseverino, the Lady of the Queen's Chamber."

Konstanty—or Kostek, as he must have been known in the family—bowed gallantly, then took my hand and pressed it to his lips in that very Polish gesture of respect for the female sex. "A great pleasure, signora," he said in a low modulated voice, which I immediately suspected he employed with women in general. "A journey to the court at this time of the year is full of hardship, but meetings like this make it all worthwhile."

As he let go of my hand, he gave my figure an appraising glance, which quite mortified me. Next to him, Konarski looked irritated by his cousin's display. "What are you doing here?" he asked sharply. "I thought you were with the army at Koło."

"Ah!" Konstanty turned to him as if only just remembering. "I was, but Marshal Firlej made me his chief messenger and sent me back here to report to His Majesty that the troops have amassed in full and are ready to move north into Pomesania."

"I see."

"We were originally set to start moving on the tenth," he added, "but with the storm approaching, that will likely be delayed."

He looked toward the eastern horizon, and we followed his gaze. There we could see a ridge of darker clouds, which in my southern homeland portended rain, but here and in winter was an unmistakable sign of approaching snow. Across the Wisła, the woods were enveloped in fingers of mist. It seemed that despite the king's prayers, nature was going to throw an obstacle of its own into the war plans.

"I thought I would have time to stop by Baranów on my way back," Konarski's cousin went on, "to see my new nephew. My sister has just delivered her first babe—on January first, of all days. What precision!" He chuckled. "But the weather would delay me too much. I will be heading back to Koło directly."

At this second mention of his family seat, something lit up in my head. "Isn't Baranów close to Lipiny?"

"Indeed, it is. Have you been there, signora? It is a beautiful country, very satisfying hunting grounds," he added with the confident smile of a seasoned hunter—of both game and women, no doubt.

"I have not, and I'm sure it is beautiful. I am asking because one of the queen's maids of honor is from there, Helena Lipińska."

"Of course!" He beamed. "I know the family well. A fine lineage, though much diminished now. They are descended from the Piasts of Małopolska."

I did not know that. Piasts were the dynasty that had ruled Poland before the House of Jagiellon's ascension to the throne in the year 1386. They had several minor branches that held the different historical regions of the kingdom as principalities, including Małopolska, or Lesser Poland, whose capital was Kraków. A distinguished line indeed.

"I was sorry to hear that her father is ailing," I said. "It sounds like quite a serious matter."

"Pan Lipiński, ill?" Konstanty laughed heartily. "Perhaps from indigestion. He likes his venison in the richest sauce his cooks know how to whip up for him."

"Oh." I was confused. "I thought—" I broke off as both men stared at me inquiringly. I did not know what to say, and I did not want to admit that one of my ladies had lied to me.

"I spent Christmas at Baranów before my banner left to join the marshal at Koło, and Lipiński was among the guests at the feast we gave on the twenty-sixth," Konstanty explained.

"He looked fine to me then. Ate and drank everyone under the table, as always. Gambled too." Then he added, more seriously, "Unless it was a sudden apoplexy. God save him. Many men his age succumb to it."

But I distinctly remembered Helena saying that her father had been ill for weeks. "Perhaps I misunderstood," I said, not wishing to prolong the subject.

He gave me another one of his gallant bows. "I regret that I must leave you now, but I have to rush out of Kraków before they close the gates at dusk. I hear they will keep them closed until the storm is over. Cousin—" He turned to Konarski with yet another slap on the shoulder for which Sebastian braced himself this time. "It was nice to see you, however briefly."

"Godspeed."

"And signora"—Konstanty turned to me one last time—"if you are ever in Baranów, be sure to call on us. I would be happy to show you around and take you for a hunt."

I dropped my gaze, too abashed to respond. When I raised my eyes, he was gone.

"Well," Konarski sighed, "that was my cousin Kostek. I apologize."

"No need. He seems nice." I smiled, finding Konarski's own abashment endearing.

Then I remembered Helena, and my smile faded. "Let's go back." I started toward the gate, eager for a refuge from the cold air that was biting at my cheeks.

"You're frowning," he said as we entered the courtyard. "What's bothering you?"

I snorted. "Besides the obvious?" Suddenly my anger at Helena's deception broke through like flood water over a riverbank. I told him, my voice catching at times, about her departure and the false reason she had given for it. I also told him about my suspicions about an affair and a possible pregnancy.

"I'm sorry you have to deal with this also," he said sympathetically. "There is enough trouble to go around without one
of your ladies adding to it with her ill-timed adventures."

"But I cannot help feeling that there is more to it than
that."

He was silent for some moments, thinking. "Do you believe
that she is somehow involved in the murders?"

"What? No!" I protested. "She doesn't have a deceptive nature like some of the other girls"—I thought about the illegal
books again—"which is why this bothers me so much. Helena,
of all people, should have been honest with me. She wouldn't
be the first to get herself into trouble like this. By lying, she
is making this much worse, possibly closing the door to ever
coming back to the court again."

In the entry hall, before we parted in our separate directions, I turned to Konarski, struck by a sudden thought. "But
what if the killer *is* a woman? Have you ever thought about
that?" I started to speak quickly. "What if it wasn't a jealous
husband but a jealous mistress? It wouldn't surprise me at all
if Zamborski had carried on with more than one woman at the
same time and was discovered!"

He laughed. "Don't let your imagination carry you away,
Caterina." When he saw me frowning, he added, apologetically,
"It is an interesting idea, but I just don't see it. Women are not
capable of such violence."

I found it hard to believe, too. Women were supposed to be
weak and timid, soft and nurturing, everything in their nature
priming them to give life, not to take it away. And yet, as the
queen herself showed, they could be quite ambitious, strong,
and forceful in getting what they wanted. Helena, with her
equestrian skills and archery prowess, could hold her own, if
not against a seasoned knight, certainly against many of the
men at the court who were used to comfortable and lazy living.
But murder? No, I could not see that either.

"Besides, you found the note after she left Kraków, didn't you?" Konarski's voice reached me.

I nodded. "So we know it wasn't Helena," I said, trying to sound light. "But we still don't know who it *was*."

And if I was right, we had one more day before he killed again.

∽

When I returned to my chamber, walking past the guard posted outside my door, I was glad of the brisk fire one of the chambermaids had made up in the grate. As I stood in front of it to warm my fingers, the cathedral bell struck three o'clock.

I listened to the distinct metallic notes. One for Zamborski, one for Mantovano, and one for someone who did not yet know his fate.

12

I had the morning of the Feast of Epiphany off. By the fire in my chamber, I breakfasted on wheaten scones spread with butter and sweet comfits. Normally, I found this morning ritual relaxing. My parlor was small but comfortable, cozy with a garden-motif tapestry hung above the hearth. It was a refuge from the bustle of the court and the stresses of my work. But not today.

I had slept poorly again, convinced as I was that something terrible was going to happen that night. I had gone over everything in my mind, beginning with the visit to the crypt under the cathedral, but I could see no clear suspect and no motive beyond the many unconvincing ones that had been put forward over the last twelve days. And with no suspect or motive, there was no way to alert the chancellor, the queen, or the captain of the guard in order to prevent another murder. The day had barely begun, but I was already exhausted.

I went to my jewelry box and took out a small packet Doctor Baldazzi, seeing how tired I was, had offered me the day after Mantovano's murder. It contained wrinkled, burned-looking leaves of some plant which the doctor procured at a great cost from merchants who had returned from the far eastern lands. I followed his instructions and poured boiling water over the leaves. Within moments the brew darkened to a deep brown color with flecks of gold, and it began to give off a delicate aroma. Despite the leaves' unpromising look, the drink had a taste that, although somewhat bitter, was also quite pleasant. According to Baldazzi, it would restore clarity to the mind and energy to the body.

He had also warned me that the Church looked upon this new beverage with a great deal of suspicion, worrying that there might be witchcraft involved. For who knew what incantations were pronounced over the leaves as they were being picked and dried in the heathen lands, where Christian monks or priests were not on hand to ensure that no spirits were being summoned to enhance their potency? So Baldazzi had to be discreet. But he swore that the drink's following at the court—although still admittedly small—was devoted. The physician must have been making a handsome profit off it too, for the packet, only about three spoonfuls, had cost me a silver talon.

It took two cups of the brew to restore me somewhat, and at nine o'clock, I was luxuriating in a steaming bath, letting all thoughts dissolve like the fragrant attar of roses that the maid Marysia had added to the water.

The bath chambers at Wawel Castle were set up in an ingenious fashion. Through a system of lead pipes, water was pumped from the castle well to be heated in vats placed over large hearths. A type of trough connected each stone tub to the wall, and that way the bathwater could be released to flow down a pipe to a special outdoor cesspool. The chief benefit of it lay in the ability to let some of the water out as it cooled, so the maid could add more hot water from the hearth, allowing the bathing to last as long as one wished, which was particularly enjoyable during winter months. It was an uncommon system; the ducal palace at Bari did not possess anything of the sort, and the queen, for all her admiration of France, liked to boast that even King François did not enjoy such conveniences at any of *his* palaces.

I reclined in the tub, the liquid heat caressing my body. My hair was expertly bound up in a linen cloth to keep it from getting wet. Marysia, the maid who worked in our bath chamber, had done that for me, commenting on how straight and thick my hair was, and that it must be an Italian thing, for Polish women tended to have finer and wavier tresses, much harder to tame and to do up into intricate styles.

After she had set fresh water heating on the hearth, Marysia left for a while, and I enjoyed the quietude. The chamber had a single window, and I watched as large snowflakes melted on the windowpanes, not falling thickly yet, but falling at an angle as if whipped by a rising wind. In the corners of the room, candles shimmered in sconces to add more light, and right then it was the most pleasant and peaceful place in the castle, maybe in the whole world.

With timing born of experience, Marysia returned just as steam began to rise from the water in the vat. She filled a jug from it and brought it over, for my bath was already cooling.

As she poured, she said, dropping her voice confidentially, "Her Majesty is angry that Jan Dantyszek hasn't shown up to collect her letter this morning."

"Hmm," I murmured absently, even as I wondered how she would have that information—not about Bona's temper, for that was often easy to hear if one was close enough to her apartments, but about the letter. Then again, the servants' capacity for knowing things their masters considered to be private was prodigious. Marysia probably had it from one of the chambermaids. "I'm sure he will come. It's still early," I said, even though it was not that early at all. Given the hours the queen kept, she must have been waiting for him for at least three hours.

Marysia squatted by the tub, the empty jug lifted high and to the side, and leaned toward me as if to impart a secret. I could see her eyes sparkling with excitement. "What if he's murdered too?" she asked, her dark eyebrows rounding as they traveled up her forehead.

Though said in jest, the words sent a cramp of pain through my stomach. "Hush! Stop saying such things," I said, angry that she had spoiled my moment of relaxation. "It is not a joking matter."

"I am sorry, signora," she replied guiltily, but she was not about to drop the subject. Like all servants, she thrived on gossip, one of the few sources of entertainment to relieve the tedium of their daily lives. In that, I reflected, she was not altogether very different from many of the highborn ladies of the court. "He probably just got drunk last night."

"What?"

"Aldona told me the queen had sent a messenger to his house, and his housekeeper said he hadn't returned home since yesterday." Aldona was one of the chambermaids, so my guess had been correct. Then Marysia added, giggling, "I wouldn't be surprised if he's still asleep, tangled in some tart's bedsheets."

I laughed too, but underneath it I felt a growing sense of unease. Could he indeed be the next victim? Yet there was no evidence that anything bad had happened to him; it was only idle gossip. Besides, the banquet was still hours away. It did not fit the pattern.

"I heard he's not very popular at the court for his reformist sympathies," Marysia resumed, forgetting my earlier admonishment. "Maybe someone took advantage of these two previous murders and offed him, too, for his dangerous talk."

"If you don't stop talking about murder, I will send you away."

"I am sorry, signora," she repeated, contrite.

"Add more rose oil to my water."

"Yes, signora."

She dosed several more drops of the precious essence. As the scent of rose wafted up on the steam again, I sighed and lowered myself in the tub so that the water came up to my neck. I closed my eyes, but my peace was shattered. I would not be able to think about anything else until this matter was cleared up.

I glanced at the maid, who busied herself at the vat again, blessedly quiet for a change. It seemed that everyone was an amateur crime solver these days. And this simple girl was not the worst of them. The queen's advisor Carmignano had already suggested a religious motive with respect to Zamborski and Mantovano. Everyone had dismissed it then, but if any harm had come to Dantyszek, that possibility would have to be considered again.

I ran my hands vigorously over my face and inhaled the flowery scent to dispel my thoughts. Even if Dantyszek was indeed missing, there was no proof it was because he had been killed. I should not let my mind become deranged with conspiracies.

"They say there is a big snow on the way," Marysia said, unable to stay silent for long, as she laid out my chemise and a towel on a stool by the tub. "Biggest we've seen in a hundred years!" she added excitedly. "My sister works in the kitchens and says all the food for the feast was cooked ahead of time and brought to the castle to be warmed here tonight. They shut the kitchens down and won't reopen them until the snow is over and cleared."

"I see." That explained why so many kitchen servants could be seen around the castle in the last two days. There was a special warming room behind the banqueting hall, and a few smaller ones scattered on different floors for that purpose. But they rarely handled the warming of food in such large quantities. It sounded like that snowstorm was going to be a headache.

"I hope Panna Helena makes it home before the snow," Marysia said.

No sooner had those words left her mouth than the cathedral bell rang out. It tolled ten times, and the sound was strangely mournful in my ears. I was reminded of the conversation with Konarski's cousin the day before and wondered again why Helena had lied to me. If she wanted to get away from the court, she could have said so, and she would have been released. The only explanation that made sense to me was that she was indeed with child and wished to leave before her condition was discovered. After sending a letter claiming that she was still tending to her ailing father, she would enter a little convent somewhere, and when she returned in a few months, her father now well on his way to recovery, nobody would be any wiser.

But what about Dantyszek? I remembered the blush rising to Helena's face when I had told her that he would be leaving for Naples soon. Was it a coincidence that the ambitious Dantyszek, always hanging about the court, ready to please and serve, was nowhere to be found so soon after she had left, the letter that could make his career waiting, unclaimed, on the queen's mahogany desk ... ?

I bolted upright, water streaming down my chest and shoulders. It seemed like a preposterous idea that Helena and Dantyszek would have eloped together. They did not even seem to like each other. But they would not be the first to go from enemies to lovers. I had been around courts long enough to know that people were capable of doing the most foolish things while in the grip of passion.

Hopeless anger rose up in me. Helena had made me a promise, broken it, then lied to me *twice*, and was now leaving me to pick up the pieces, to face the queen's rage, and to possibly suffer dismissal. How could she?

I sent Marysia away and stepped out of the bath, wrapping the towel around me. I cleared a section of the steamed-up windowpane with the side of my hand and gazed through it. The large wet snowflakes had turned into smaller ones, falling faster, and there was already a thin layer of white accumulation on the ground. Whether together or separately, how far could the two of them have gone with the weather deteriorating so fast? What would they do if the storm fully broke out while they were still on the road?

I wrapped my dressing gown around me and went to the girls' bedchamber. It was empty as they were all with the queen. I approached Helena's neatly made bed and lifted the lid of her chest, a fine oak piece inlaid with mother-of-pearl. My heart was beating fast, and I had a momentary sick feeling that I would discover something horrible inside—a ruby-studded dagger, evidence of a grievous crime. I took a deep breath and reminded myself of the need to preserve my sanity.

The chest was more than half-full. Most of Helena's gowns were still there, though folded unevenly, as if in some haste. She had probably dug through it to retrieve what she needed for the journey and thrown the rest back in. No bloodied weapon. I sank to my knees in relief, chastising myself for my absurd suspicions. But even if Helena was not a murderess, the contents of her chest provided little by way of illuminating the situation. She was either coming back, pretending that nothing had happened, or she did not care if she left the rest of her belongings behind, although both the chest and the gowns were of considerable value.

I sat heavily on the bed, pressing my fingers to my temples, and went over everything in my mind again, hour by hour. Helena had left two days before in the morning, but Dantyszek had not been seen only since last night. She could have been waiting for him at one of the many travelers' lodgings in town, yet that seemed like a lot of trouble to take. Why not leave on the same day, even at the same hour? With so many people going in and out of the castle—and in and out of Kraków—nobody would ever connect them to each other.

I returned to my chamber and called my maid to help me dress and comb my hair. Then I put my best headdress on and slipped large emerald earrings, my most precious jewelry, into my earlobes. I needed something that would make me feel better as things seemed to be crashing down all around me. I would have to tell the queen the whole truth and accept the consequences, which I knew would involve being sent back home to face an uncertain future. But I would not tell her just yet. I had to make sure that I was right first, although I had no idea how to accomplish that.

In the looking glass, I saw that my face was drawn. My complexion is lighter than the olive-hued skin tones common in the region I come from, and the glow of my bath was receding fast, revealing a pallor underneath and worry lines on my forehead. I pinched my cheeks to bring back some of the color, but I doubted that it would help for long. At one o'clock, the queen would be going to dine privately with the king, and I would accompany her there. Perhaps I would learn more about what was going on. Perhaps, I thought with a faint flicker of hope, Dantyszek would turn up by then.

The queen was furious, I could see that right away. She paced the antechamber as the maids of honor sat still and quiet, not daring to raise their eyes. But she did not begin to talk until we stepped outside. She motioned to the guard who was to escort us to get moving, and she proceeded at a slower pace to put some distance between him and us. Walking slowly was so against the queen's habit that she lost her usual gracefulness of movement and seemed almost awkward as her feet tried to get ahead of her will. But she wanted the time to apprise me of the morning's developments.

When Dantyszek had not arrived by seven o'clock, she sent one of her pages for him. Dantyszek kept a small but fashionable house in St. Anna Street, only a short ride from the castle. His housekeeper informed the boy that her master had not returned home the night before, and she did not know where he was. When she heard that, the queen went personally to the State Chambers to order the chancellor to send men to search his house.

"Of course he tried to assure me that there was no need to raise an alarm yet," she scoffed. "He probably knows that Dantyszek was going to undertake a mission to Naples for me, and he is glad that my plans are being ruined. Perhaps he has ordered him killed too, to prevent him from working for me," she added, but her sarcastic tone told me that she did not mean it. "It was only after I had threatened to appeal to His Majesty that he finally ordered four men-at-arms to his house."

By nine o'clock the guards had returned, reporting the same thing. Dantyszek had not been home since the previous morning, and his housekeeper did not know where he could be found. They had searched the house, and after further interrogation, the housekeeper confirmed that none of his things were missing. His chests had not been packed, his clothes were still in their wardrobes, and his books were on the shelves. It was as if he had just stepped outside for a few hours.

I imagined the poor housekeeper—probably an old woman, scared and confused—watching as the royal guards turned the house upside down only to find no evidence that Dantyszek had planned to go away for any length of time. It was very strange. If he had eloped, surely he would have taken at least a pair of clean shirts with him?

"The traitor!" the queen seethed as we reached the main wing, then she lowered her voice. "Gamrat saw him here in the castle after vespers last night, but he didn't make it home. The profligate! He must have gone with some whore, who knifed and robbed him in a dark alleyway. Serves him right."

"There is no proof he is dead, Your Majesty," I said as much to assure her as myself.

"He seemed so bright and competent. I had such hopes for him," she continued, ignoring me. "I cannot trust anybody here—except for you." Unexpectedly, she reached out and squeezed my hand, her fingers warm and firm.

I was moved by this rare display of affection and felt suddenly guilty for having let her down, compounded by the fact that she did not yet know about it. "Thank you. I am ever Your Majesty's faithful servant." The words, though meant sincerely, seemed somehow deceitful.

"What should we do now?" she asked. She hated being without options, and I could see that.

"While Your Majesty dines, maybe I will make inquiries with His Majesty's household?"

"You mean with Konarski?!" Bona boomed, and it was only God's mercy that there was nobody around to hear that, except the guard who walked ahead of us.

"Yes," I replied, my face on fire. "I would ask him too."

"Do that," she said as we turned the corner and approached the already open door to the king's private dining room. She raised a finger, which she pointed in a general direction behind me before she swept inside. "If Dantyszek is still alive, I will find him and make sure he is punished."

When the door closed behind her, I exhaled with relief, although I knew it would be short-lived. Unless Dantyszek miraculously walked out of any of the chambers along the gallery, apologetic and ready to take on his mission, there would be no good news to give the queen one hour from now.

My anxiety returning, I went down to the State Chambers and knocked on the door to the office that Konarski shared with another junior secretary, a man named Górka who also happened to be Magdalena's half-brother.

"I must talk to you," I said, bypassing the usual greeting, when Konarski opened the door. "Privately."

He beckoned me to enter. "I'm alone. Górka is in bed with the sniffles. Is it about Dantyszek?" he asked as he closed the door.

I nodded.

"Yet another problem we don't need at the moment," he said, and I could hear frustration in his voice. "You probably know that Her Majesty demanded that the chancellor send men to look for him in the city." He gave me a look that meant to convey how that order had gone over with Stempowski.

"I did hear about that," I said. "I think the queen is right to be alarmed. The chancellor may not think this is a serious matter, but I have a bad feeling about it."

Konarski lowered his voice. "What kind of a bad feeling?"

"I believe his absence may be connected to Helena's departure."

He frowned. "How?"

I told him about my suspicions regarding the two of them, and he laughed. "That is highly unlikely. He may be a dandy and a rake, but he is very ambitious," he said, echoing my own thoughts from earlier that day. "His family is up-and-coming, and they entertain great hopes of an illustrious career for him at the court. He would never have done something so irresponsible, not even for love. *Especially* not for love," he added.

"What do you mean by that?" I asked sharply, feeling inexplicably irritated.

His laugh faded, but the smile lingered in his eyes. "Only that Dantyszek is not the type to fall in love for longer than a fortnight."

I sighed, turning to the window, where snow was now peppering the glass, making sharp irregular sounds as the wind rose and died. Konarski's point was well taken. Dantyszek was a ladies' man, and he could have any woman at the court that he wanted—or most of them, anyway. It was hard to imagine that he would have thrown away such a bright future for Helena, or anyone else for that matter.

"I think you are looking for a connection where there isn't any," Konarski said behind me. "Also, you are assuming that she is pregnant, but there is no evidence of that either—"

"I should have had Baldazzi examine her," I muttered angrily.

"What's that?"

"Nothing." I shook my head, exhaling. "Go on."

"And even if she is, if Dantyszek is the father and he loves her, he could marry her in the open. There would be no obstacles as they are of a similar rank. If, on the other hand, he didn't want to marry her, he could have just denied being the father."

I turned and looked at him in dismay.

He spread his hands. "That's how these things go sometimes."

In my irritation I was about to ask him if he knew "these things" from his own experience, when I suddenly remembered the words the queen had spoken a short time earlier. *Gamrat saw him in the castle after vespers last night.*

"They couldn't have eloped!" I exclaimed. "He is still in town! You cannot elope without actually leaving, can you?"

"I suppose not. I have never tried." He smiled, seeing my excitement. "But how do you know he's still in Kraków?"

"Because one of the queen's advisors saw him here yesterday after nightfall, which means *after* the town gates had already been closed for the storm. He might even still be in the castle!" I began pacing the chamber, my mind working fast.

"Do you realize," Konarski said slowly, "that if he is *in* the castle, he's likely dead? Everybody has been looking for him for hours."

That stopped me in my tracks. He was right. I had been so wrapped up in the elopement theory that I had entirely dismissed that other possibility.

"But it's not evening yet," I said, grasping for a less awful explanation. "The others were killed at night and during a banquet. And the killer made no attempt to hide the bodies—he wanted them to be found. If Dantyszek were dead, his body would have been discovered by now, wouldn't it?"

"So perhaps they have eloped after all." Konarski scratched his head; it seemed like we were going in circles. "Perhaps they were stranded in town by the weather and have taken a room at an inn somewhere to wait for the storm to pass so they can make their exit." Then he added, "I know by nightfall even the chancellor will be concerned. He will probably send another party to search for him. If they find him—with or without Helena—I will send word to you immediately."

"Oh, God. Sometimes I hope that this is just a dream and I will wake up and laugh about it."

I pressed my palms to my eyes, feeling close to being overcome. The sound of his footsteps as he came toward me made everything inside me go still. I realized that we were alone together for the first time. He took my hands and pulled them away from my face. The candles were behind his back, making his eyes seem darker, more inscrutable, and completely arresting. I felt my throat go dry.

He let go of my hands and took my chin lightly between his thumb and forefinger. He lifted my head and I watched, transfixed, as his lips parted only inches from mine.

Then the silence around us was torn by the sound of the bell tolling two o'clock.

I took a step back, my hands going instinctively to my headdress, as if it needed adjusting. "The queen will be finishing her meal," I said as the echo of the second metallic clang dissipated over us. "I should go back."

We were still for a few heartbeats, then he moved to the door and opened it for me. He touched my arm lightly as I passed. "I hate to see you worried like this," he said when I finally managed to meet his eyes. "I hope that there is an explanation for Dantyszek's disappearance." A small smile curled his lips. "I will see you at the banquet tonight."

13

January 6ᵗʰ, 1520
The Feast of Epiphany
Evening

A few hours later, the queen—flanked by guards and followed by me and the maids of honor—walked down the gallery and turned onto the main corridor of the second floor of the castle. Konarski had been right: the chancellor had sent another party in search of Dantyszek that afternoon, but there was still no news.

As we walked toward the banqueting hall, I noticed that while there were a few more guards around than usual, it was hardly the kind of heightened security that I had expected. I guessed that the king had decided not to make an overt display of it after all, most likely for fear of stoking panic and interfering with the court's celebrations. It was entirely in line with Zygmunt's nature, but that night I would have felt more assured with a greater number of men-at-arms posted along the galleries.

We walked up the wide central staircase to the third floor. Even before we came to the door of the brightly lit hall, I could hear the buzz of conversations interwoven with the melodies of Kappelmeister Gąsiorek's musicians. The queen had given him special instructions to play a selection of the most popular

Italian, French, and Flemish tunes alongside Polish ones, and I knew I would be in for a treat if I could only manage to keep my nerves at bay.

I was desperately determined to enjoy the evening. I had put on a gown of silver brocade, trimmed at the neckline with frilly lace and slit in the front to reveal the white satin of the skirt underneath. Around my neck I wore a choker of gray pearls, and my waist was encircled with a girdle of the same pearls, falling on the front of my skirt. At the last moment, I had chosen a pair of fitted sleeves because it was a style Konarski had once told me he liked.

As we entered the hall, the conversations ceased and everyone bowed. The queen walked to the dais where she was to be seated with her senior ladies, and although the talk and music resumed, we were still on our feet awaiting the king's arrival. Another pause in music and conversation some minutes later greeted his entrance, then the court was seated at the tables and the feast began.

I could see that my determination to enjoy myself was shared by many others. While the hall was not as full as it had been at Christmas—the foreign guests had long since departed—somehow it was louder. Was it a reaction to the uncertainty and trepidation that many must have felt? An act of defiance against a faceless and a nameless killer, possibly sitting in our midst? Or did they simply feel less formal and constrained, Epiphany not being imbued with the same solemnity as Christmas? After all, it heralded the upcoming carnival season with feasts, pageants, and masquerade balls, the last largely unknown in Poland before the Italians arrived.

Queen Bona was a great lover of masquerade. She had new masks and costumes sent from Venice each year, and the first ball of the season was planned for the middle of February. Like her gowns and manners, masquerades, too, were becoming popular with the local nobility, although by no means everyone. I am quite certain that Chancellor Stempowski had never attended any of them.

Whatever the reason—it may even have been a mixture of those—the men and women of the court were dressed in all their finery, diamonds glittering at their necks and feathers quivering in their hats. They laughed and chattered at an increasing volume, the drink brought up in constant supply from the castle's abundant stores fueling their mood.

I sat at the table closest to the queen's dais together with the maids of honor. I watched the girls' glowing faces and shining eyes, the events of the past few days seemingly forgotten, or at least set aside for a short time. They smiled at the passing gentlemen and exchanged words with those who stopped by their chairs, and even though they cast wary glances at me, I pretended not to notice. I was surprised to find that rather than being worried about them, I felt almost relieved, for it gave me an illusion that things were returning to normal. If a stolen kiss was the worst thing that happened that night, I would count all of us lucky.

The queen, too, managed to put on a display of cheer, even though I knew how anxious she was underneath the smiles she had for her guests. Once in a while her eyes met mine, and from that we drew mutual comfort.

Konarski arrived some time after the king. He was dressed in black leather hose, a black doublet slashed to reveal burgundy lining, and the lacings of his sleeves were embroidered in gold thread. On his head, he wore a feathered cap that sat at a jaunty angle. I smiled when I saw it, for it showed me an aspect of his personality I had glimpsed only once before, during the New Year's banquet. It was a softer and more playful side, which he rarely displayed in the daytime. Except a few hours earlier in his office. I felt a wave of heat rise in my belly at the memory of the kiss that had almost happened, and I regretted having lost my nerve. Who knew when the next opportunity would arise, if it ever did?

Across the table from me, Magdalena noticed my eyes following Konarski to his seat, for she looked away when I turned my gaze on her. I knew that she liked him, and although I had not noticed any interest on his part, it might be only a matter of time if I persisted in my coyness and Magdalena in her simpering.

Konarski proceeded directly to the king's dais, where he took a seat next to Chancellor Stempowski, and thus very close to the king himself. Did that mean that he was about to be promoted to a more senior position? I'd always had the impression that unlike Dantyszek, Latalski, and so many others, he cared little for the privileges that came with attaining a high rank within the royal household. All the same, he seemed to enjoy a high level of trust.

The food, if possible, was even finer than during Christmas, despite the inconvenience of having to shut the kitchens down and use the warming rooms. There was an abundance of game in a variety of sauces, roasted pheasant, sweet hams, smoked eel, and trout encased in clear, delicate jelly, a very Polish dish. Besides that, we could sample an assortment of nuts, fruits, and sweets—candied, caramelized, fashioned of spun sugar into shapes of flower petals, topped with cream, cinnamon dust, or delicate white shreds of coconut, a great rarity brought from the New World.

But I found that I could not eat or drink much. I tasted a dish that looked like some kind of fowl stewed with truffles, but my stomach roiled, much as Helena's had done two weeks earlier. Like her, I kept glancing at the door, although for an entirely different reason. A part of me constantly expected the captain of the guard to appear there, walk hastily up to the king's dais, and inform him that Dantyszek's corpse had been discovered in some dark corner of the castle. Much as the chancellor had done after Zamborski was found.

But the evening wore on, and nothing happened. The party kept growing louder and louder. I cast occasional—and I hoped discreet—glances in Konarski's direction, and at one point I was alarmed when I saw that he and the chancellor were gone. But they returned soon thereafter, and I was flooded with relief. It appeared that despite the festive occasion, those two were still working, most likely on the upcoming war with the Teutonic Order.

Shortly after that, I became aware of a conversation that made my hand, in which I held a spoon with a piece of frangipane, stop halfway between my plate and my mouth.

"Dantyszek still hasn't shown his face," a man at a table behind me, whose face I could not see, said to his neighbor loud enough for me to hear. It was the kind of volume a man's voice assumes when he has had so much to drink that he believes anything he has to say is of utmost importance to everyone around him. "He was supposed to travel to Gdańsk on His Majesty's business."

Despite myself, I chuckled at the inaccuracy of the information—that was how gossip started. I was about to take a bite of my frangipane when the other responded, his speech just as loud but more slurred than that of his companion. "He'll be in trouble when they find him. Serves him right, too, for his reformist ideas." Then he had a flash of inspiration. "Maybe he's drinking somewhere with his German friends?"

Clearly not everyone expected the worst to have happened to Dantyszek, but then they did not know as much about the killings as I did. I imagined that few besides myself, Konarski, the chancellor, and the captain of the castle guard were aware of the pattern of these murders occurring on feast nights. I had not even told the queen about it.

"The chancellor sent men earlier today to make inquiries around the town, then he ordered the castle searched from top to bottom, including the servants' floor and the attic. And nothing!" the first man said.

I was not aware that such a thorough search of the castle had been performed. Nobody had come to search our wing all day. I leaned back in my chair to hear better.

"Did he search the cellars?" the slurry voice asked. He guffawed. "Maybe he's been holed up down there sampling Her Majesty's Italian wines all day. I wouldn't blame him; they are *eccellente.*" He attempted to mimic the Italian pronunciation and burped.

The spoon fell from my hand and clattered against the plate, the frangipane tumbling onto the cloth. The man had meant the castle cellars, but there was another set of cellars—empty of wine now, in a separate building that had been vacated for the last few days because of the storm. As this realization flashed through my mind, my chest tightened, and I was suddenly unable to draw a breath.

I pushed my chair back. Everybody was so preoccupied with their conversations that they did not notice my reaction, which was just as well. I looked toward the dais, but Konarski, the chancellor, and the king were in deep talk, and I was unable to catch Konarski's attention. Nor could I walk up and interrupt his conference with the king to tell him of my terrible suspicion. If Dantyszek had been seen in the castle after the town gates had closed last night, if the chancellor's men had not found him in Kraków, and if the search of the castle that afternoon had revealed nothing, there was only one place he could be.

A minute, then another, stretched into eternity, and Konarski was still talking with the king. Impatience tugged at me, and a sense of premonition coiled around my stomach like a snake. I had to go and see for myself if I was right, even though there was a chance that I might find a dead body or a dying man. Given the amount of time that had passed since Dantyszek's disappearance, a dead body was the most likely result. This killer did not keep his victims alive; he dispatched them swiftly. But then, this had already been enough of a change of pattern that it was just possible that Dantyszek might still be alive.

I sprang to my feet. To my right, Beatrice Roselli turned to me. "Is everything all right, signora?"

"Yes." My voice was taut and sounded unconvincing even to me, but Beatrice was flushed with wine and did not appear to notice. "I have to ... can you tell Signor Konarski that I—" I broke off. There was no way to say this without causing hysteria.

"Signor Konarski?" She grinned, then cocked her head to one side, arching her eyebrows coquettishly. "*Il segretario carino?*"

Across the table Magdalena gave me a look of amusement with a hint of challenge. It suggested that she was beginning to suspect something, but also that she did not consider me a serious rival. She was probably correct in that, but right then I had no time to ruminate over any of it.

"*Non importa,*" I said. *Never mind.* "I'll be right back."

I hurried toward the door and was about to step out into the gallery when I saw Doctor Baldazzi and the Princess of Montefusco. A full head taller than the doctor, the princess was fanning herself dramatically, while her left wrist rested in Baldazzi's hand, presumably so he could check her pulse. With eyes half closed, she looked like she was about to faint, although her color was high—whether from wine, rouge, or her obvious good health, I could not tell.

I took a step to pass them when another memory emerged from the recesses of my mind. My heart slowed with dread as the implication of it dawned on me.

"I must speak with you," I turned to Baldazzi, trying—and failing—to keep the urgency from my voice.

The medic looked uncertainly from me to the princess, his eyes red and bleary. I noticed that when he'd had wine, his movements lost their usual jerkiness and became smooth and fluid, almost graceful. Under any other circumstances it would be amusing, but not now.

"It will only take a moment," I spoke apologetically to the princess, who seemed to have recovered from her weakness and was now eyeing me suspiciously.

"If you need a love potion to ensnare that pretty secretary of His Majesty's, you had better ask a wise woman in the town," she smirked. "Doctor Baldazzi is a *real* physician." She gave him a smile in which she managed to combine both fawning and condescension, and he grinned like a child praised for finishing an exercise properly.

"It's not about that," I replied, too defensively. Was everyone in the castle aware of my infatuation with Konarski? "Please, Your Highness, it's important."

"Have you already had luck with him, then, and need a different kind of remedy?" She cackled. "In that case, it can wait until the morning—believe me." But she let go of her grip on Baldazzi's arm.

I pulled him out into the gallery, where it was a little quieter. When we were out of the princess's earshot, I dropped my voice. "How many bottles of your sleeping draft did you give to Helena?"

"Who?" Baldazzi looked confused.

"Helena," I repeated, trying not to lose my patience, even as I wondered how reliable any recollection might be that came from his mouth right now. "The queen's maid of honor who had trouble sleeping lately? How many bottles of the poppy extract did you give her?"

He thought for a moment, his eyes slowly coming into focus. "I cannot remember." His head swung from shoulder to shoulder in an inebriated emphasis.

I inhaled. "Please. Think."

"I don't know—two?"

"Two? Or one?"

"Two," he said with greater conviction this time, then he smiled the blissful smile of a drunk. "The pretty girl with red hair and catlike eyes. She came on New Year's Eve, and I gave her a small bottle along with her monthly dose of belladonna. Then she came for more poppy just the other day." He swallowed a hiccup.

I paused, confusion now adding to my dread. My chest was so tight I could only draw shallow breaths. "Belladonna? For what?"

"For her womanly courses. She came to me a few months ago saying they had become painful."

"But it is a poison, isn't it?" I almost shouted, my panic mounting. I was trying to remember what I knew about belladonna. It was an herb whose extract was commonly used by women to bring about an enlargement of the pupils for beauty reasons, but it could also induce hallucinations and even death in higher doses. "It can kill a person, can't it?"

"Not the amount I gave her." He raised a hand in a gesture that was both calming and defensive. "I only measured out a spoonful into a tiny vial and told her to take no more than two drops a day. That's just enough to relieve pain and relax tension, although"—he lowered his voice to a conspiratorial whisper—"I suspect the real reason she wants it is to make her eyes shinier. She must be in love—that would also explain the trouble sleeping. Youth, eh?" He shrugged indulgently.

I let go of his arm, and he frowned. "What is it, signora? You look like you've seen a ghost." He blinked at me intently.

But I could not utter a word. It was as if an iron fist were pressing on my throat, even as my mind, with an awful clarity, saw it all.

I knew what had happened.

The only thing left for me to find out was why.

I raced down the stairs, the frantic clicking of my heels on the stone steps echoing hollowly around me. I slowed momentarily on the landing as I saw the tempest of snow raging on the other side of the mullioned window, then continued down two more levels to the entrance hall. At the foot of each flight of stairs, there was a pair of guards, each man standing straight, staring ahead, and gripping a steel halberd in his hands. Their presence calmed me a little. I briefly considered asking one of them to come with me, but I had no power to order them to leave their post, and no time to go in search of such permission.

When I arrived at the main door, the guard there gave me a quizzical look without moving or changing the impassive expression of the rest of his face.

"I need to go outside," I said. "To check on something."

"There is a snowstorm, my lady," he said matter-of-factly.

"I know, but it is urgent. Please let me out. I am acting on Her Majesty's orders." The moment those words left my mouth, I realized that I should have told the queen where I was going. She would be worried when she noticed me gone. But it was too late to go back now. Dantyszek might still be alive.

The guard hesitated briefly, then grabbed the long iron handle. Men-at-arms were not trained to argue but to follow orders, and I was thankful for that. "Be careful, my lady." He pulled the massive oak door ajar.

I had expected the storm to be bad, but I was not prepared for the howling wind and the vortices of snow that welcomed me as I slid through the narrow opening. It was as if those swirls wanted to take me in their arms and carry me away on some wild dance. I steadied myself and took a few cautious steps, holding as tight as I could to the iced-over railing, but when I arrived at the bottom of the stairs, my satin boots immediately sank into snow that reached to the middle of my calves. I shuddered as the icy wetness seeped over their tops, soaking my stockings and clinging to my legs.

The courtyard was dim—no torch would remain burning for two heartbeats in that weather—but there was enough illumination from the castle's windows for me to orient myself. Then I heard a rumbling, followed by a loud crash directly above my head. For a second or two, the courtyard lit up brightly. It took me a moment to realize that it was that rare phenomenon I had heard about but had never seen—I had, to be honest, thought it was a myth. But there it was—thundersnow. It seemed that nature was determined to unleash all of her fury with that storm. If I had guessed correctly about what I would find in the kitchen, it was the worst night for it.

I was now out of the relative protection of the arcade, out in the open with the wind blowing squalls of snow every which way. My skirt whipped about my legs, and my feet were buried in snow so that I could only take slow, dragging, painstaking steps. I had not taken five of them before a mighty gust tore off my headdress, and it tumbled away from me. I stopped, my hand instinctively reaching out to grab it, but it disappeared in the whirling white cloud, and I abandoned any attempt to go after it.

I squared my shoulders against the wind and the cold, belatedly realizing that I should have gone to get my cloak first. But I could not return for it now. Something was pushing me forward like an invisible hand at my back, urging me to continue on my way.

On a normal day, the walk of about a hundred steps took less than two minutes, but it felt like hours before the red brick of the kitchen building loomed out of the storm. There was a faint orange glow in the windows, and I guessed it was from one of the ovens left burning to prevent the water in the vats from freezing and to allow for a quicker restarting of the kitchen fires when the storm was over. What that meant was that kitchen help had to have come here every few hours to feed the fire, and they would have noticed and reported it if something was amiss. But that had not happened, and I was beginning to doubt my reasoning. Maybe I was going crazy and would only catch a nasty cold out of this if I was lucky, or freeze to death if I was not.

I came to the front door and turned the handle, but the door was locked. I groaned in frustration. *All that effort for nothing,* I thought as I stood there buffeted by the wind, rattling the handle as if the meager effort of my freezing hands could ever dislodge the iron lock. But even if it could, I am not sure I could have opened the door because of the blown snow that covered the bottom part of it with a thick layer. Then I remembered the side door that was used for deliveries. It was worth a try.

Groping along the wall, bent forward against the wind, my eyelashes so heavy with snow I could barely keep my eyes open, I moved to the corner of the building and then around and up toward the side door. It was a bit quieter here, it being a nook between the kitchen and the south wall of the castle where the wind did not whip as much as in the open courtyard. But my face was getting numb from the cold, and my breathing was becoming difficult; it was necessary for me to get indoors quickly.

I grabbed the handle of the side door, which was larger and heavier than the front door, but to my surprise and no small relief, it budged. Somewhere in the back of my mind, I registered the fact that it was unlocked and should not have been, but I was too desperate to get out of the cold to give it any more thought. I took hold of the handle with both hands and pulled with all the strength I could muster. There was less blown snow here, and slowly I managed to open the door wide enough for me to slip inside. As I did so, the bell began striking the hour, but between the howling wind and my own preoccupation, I could not keep track of the number of strikes. I thought it was ten, but it may just as well have been midnight. All I knew was that it was late, so very late.

But hopefully not too late.

My first sensation on entering the kitchen was that of blessed warmth compared to the freezing air outside, although the low fire in the oven could not have provided much heat at all. The snow on my face and hands began to melt, and my hair, uncovered and ripped loose from the hold of the pins, hung long and sodden on both sides of my face. I ran my hands through it to wring out the excess water and looked around. It was nearly dark, the only light coming from the oven, but it was just enough to see around. I noticed a lantern on one of the tables, and I lit the wick of its candle from the sluggish flames in the oven.

I knew there were two doors to the cellars—one from the main kitchen leading to the former wine storage area, and the other off the delivery passage to where fruits and vegetables were kept. I guessed that if someone had brought Dantyszek here, it would have been to the empty wine cellar. Both doors were closed, however, and it was completely quiet. It was as if the kitchen was deserted for this tempestuous night.

Again I wondered whether my imagination was getting the better of me, as Konarski had once suggested, and whether I should not just turn away and make my way back to the castle. Maybe Dantyszek had been found one way or another in the time I had been away. How long had it been? I could not tell. I had lost track of time, and the storm made it impossible to gauge it from any external signs. It could have been ten minutes, or it could have been an hour or more.

But that indefinable urge kept pushing me. Was it fate, or was it my training as an overseer of unruly girls, having to pay attention to every detail, leaving nothing to chance? To this day I do not know, but I walked across the kitchen, swallowing a lump that had formed in my throat, and turned the knob on the wine cellar door before my courage deserted me altogether.

The cold air that flowed from the passage below chilled me in my wet clothes, but I was greeted by silence. I took a deep breath, then began descending the stone steps slowly, stepping on the balls of my feet so the heels of my boots would not make a noise. I held my lantern aloft, although oil lamps flickered at intervals along the walls. One could never have enough light when searching for a missing man in a cellar that used to be a church crypt.

I stopped at the bottom of the stairs to orient myself. To my relief, I was not facing a maze of passages like the ones under the cathedral, but rather a corridor with cells on both sides of it. Those cells, I realized with another shiver, had once served as burial chambers for Wawel court officials during the Piast dynasty. I put the thought out of my mind as I took stock of the layout of the space. There were four cells on both sides of the corridor in front of me. Behind me, an arched opening connected to the other part of the cellar, with a separate set of stairs leading upstairs. Judging by the ripe and earthy smell wafting on a current of air, that was where cheeses and vegetables were stored.

The first three cells on each side had had their doors removed for easier access, and I stepped into the closest of them. It was empty but for two leftover barrels in a corner. I could see that the actual burial spaces were under the stone floor—much like Don Mantovano's recent grave—and still had names and dates engraved on them. Fortunately, there were no bones scattered about, as Michałowa had feared. The cell was perhaps seven paces long and five paces wide, large for a non-royal crypt, but I could see right away that even all eight of them combined would be insufficient for the amount of wine that was consumed at Wawel.

I returned to the corridor, raised my lantern high again, and held my breath as I strained my eyes and ears. The last set of cells had oak doors that were closed. All was quiet—except for the squeaky noises of mice coming from the food storage area—and dim in spite of the lights flickering on the walls. I moved toward the stairs, my heels echoing on the flags of the floor as I stopped walking with caution. I had put my foot on the first step when I thought I heard something, an indefinable sound, a sort of grunt. My first thought was mice. I ran the lantern in a circle around me but saw no vermin anywhere; besides, they did not make grunting noises.

I listened, and after some moments I heard the sound again, a little louder, and accompanied by what I thought was a clink or a scrape of metal. This time I had no doubt that someone was here, someone human, and I felt the little hairs on my arms stand on end.

Returning to the balls of my feet, I walked slowly down the corridor, my heart hammering in my chest, and shone my lamp into each of the open cells. They were all empty but for a few more barrels and scattered rags on the floor. Then I reached the cells with the doors. They were solid fitted oak doors, hard to penetrate with either light or sound, but as I approached the last cell on the right, I heard a muffled protest that sounded like someone trying to speak with a hand clamped over his mouth. I crouched and gazed at the bottom of the doors. There, through the narrowest of cracks above the threshold, I saw faint light seeping through. I took a step back as I fought to swallow a cry.

This is the moment to run back and call the guards, one voice told me. There could be no doubt anymore. Then another voice asked, *but what if he is injured and needs help?* I never considered what kind of help I might be able to provide because the hand that had been at my back since I left the banqueting hall was again pushing me on. Even if I wanted to turn away, I would not have been able to do it. It was as if I were in a trance as I stepped toward the door.

I put my hand gingerly on the handle, and the moment I did that, a strange calm descended on me, my heart and my breath slowing. I pressed down and pulled it toward me, but the door did not move. Was it locked? Another muffled sound from the other side, more desperate now, and something like a shuffling of feet. I pressed the handle again and pushed it this time, and the door yielded. It opened to the inside. The rusty hinges groaned in protest.

The cell was smaller than the ones without doors, and it was lit by a single candle standing on an overturned crate. Immediately, I was assaulted by the stale smell of an unventilated space, and of a mix of sweat, urine, and mice droppings. I instinctively put my hand up to cover my mouth and nose. Then I saw a man sitting in the far corner on a makeshift bed made of old sacks, much as Maciek Koza had in Baszta Sandomierska. His hands were bound behind him, and his mouth was stuffed with a rag.

I knew right away it was Dantyszek, his fine hair now matted and in disarray. But I was relieved to see that he did not seem to be injured or dying. He tried to spit the rag out, but it was secured with a strip of cloth tied across his face and knotted at the back. He moved his head around, shaking it, jutting out his chin, making those urgent noises, his blue eyes bulging out of his head, but I could not understand what he was saying. I moved toward him, holding out my hand to pull down the gag, but I had not made it halfway through the cell when I heard the door behind me slam shut with a crash that seemed to echo through the cellar.

I whipped around, and the lantern in my hand clattered to the floor, the little flame extinguishing itself in a small puddle of hot wax.

I was trapped in an empty building, underground, with a killer who was pointing a silver dagger at me, a dagger with a ruby-studded hilt.

14

At first, in the small circle of light cast by the remaining candle, all I could see was that dagger. And a hand.

Something was wrong with that hand.

Or would have been, if I had not already guessed the truth. It was a woman's hand.

In the next moment the person in front of me took a step forward, and a face emerged from the shadow.

"Helena!" I stepped back toward the corner where Dantyszek was sitting, the meaning of his wordless sounds suddenly all too clear. He had been trying to warn me to go back, not to step inside the cell. Now his tone had changed from desperate and pleading to angry.

She stood before me in the same brown traveling dress I had last seen her in two mornings earlier, but the starched white lace of her neckline and her wrists was gray and stained. She was no longer wearing a headdress but kept on the linen coif, strands of hair falling out from under it and hanging limply around her face. That face seemed thinner now, its angles sharp in the low light, and her eyes were rimmed with dark circles. They shone with the same unnatural light I had seen in them when she returned to the table after her absence during the Christmas banquet.

My thoughts were scattered in a thousand directions. Why was she holding Dantyszek captive? What was she going to do with him? And—like a buzzing fly, absurd in its obviousness but maddeningly insistent—where did she get Zamborski's dagger?

I kept moving away from her, and she flicked her wrist, pointing the dagger next to Dantyszek. "Sit."

I did as she told me, but I kept my eyes locked on hers the whole time. When I was on the floor, my back against the wall, she took a seat on a stool across from us, the dagger still pointing. It was a solid double-edged weapon, at least six inches long. In the hands of someone who knew how to use it—and somehow I knew that she did—it was a fearsome and deadly instrument.

We stared at each other for a long time, but her face was inscrutable. Her eyes, too, became distant and detached so that I was no longer sure if she even knew who I was. It occurred to me that she might have gone insane, and I decided not to upset her or make her angry. I would wait until she spoke first. Maybe that way I would have a chance of getting Dantyszek out of there alive.

The silence continued for what seemed like a very long time, and even Dantyszek went quiet. Then Helena spoke, her voice calm and even slightly amused, "I suppose you would like to know how I found myself here in this cellar with him?"

I nodded. I had already guessed that she had drugged him with the poppy milk, the same method Mantovano had used with the guards on the night of his death. In both cases, she was the one who had procured the bottles from Baldazzi. But how had she managed to get Dantyszek down *here*? For although she was young and strong, she could not possibly have dragged an unconscious man all the way to the kitchen and down the steps to the cellar without being seen by anybody.

"Well, it's a long story." She laughed with relish, and I realized that she was proud of what she was about to say. Once again, I wondered if her sanity had left her. "I lured him here with the promise of the one thing a man like him would never refuse—an amorous encounter."

I heard Dantyszek take a ragged breath and try to spit out his gag again, to no avail. I kept staring at Helena.

"When you told me about his upcoming mission to Naples"—she waved the dagger in Dantyszek's direction without looking at him—"I knew I had to act quickly. The storm and the emptying of the kitchen came just in time, and with the help of a few coins, I procured a spare key to the side door from one of the kitchen maids."

For a moment, I wondered if it had been the girl Marta, the same who had given me the sack of fruit a few days earlier. But it could have been any one of the two dozen servants who worked there. Besides, that was the least of my worries right then.

"I had sent a message to him to meet me upstairs in the kitchen at midnight last night, and when he arrived—punctually, of course"—she laughed again—"I gave him a cup of wine to welcome him. I had mixed it with Doctor Baldazzi's poppy milk, and after he drained it, I told him there were empty cells downstairs that we could go to in case someone returned to the kitchen to feed the fire in the oven. By the time we made it here, he was barely awake, and before he could put his hands on me, he fell like a log to the floor. After that, tying him up was easy."

Dantyszek moved sharply, and I heard the clink of metal again. I realized that one of his legs was chained by the ankle, the short chain fastened to the wall. What kind of a church crypt had this place been?

As if guessing my thoughts, Helena said, "During the previous century, the good fathers used this crypt as a prison for witches. I learned as much as I could about it before I implemented my plan, mainly from Michałowa. She knows all kinds of stories and is only too happy to share them."

That I could believe. Normally, I would not have put much faith in the veracity of Michałowa's tales, but the chain and the hinges sticking out of the wall three feet above the floor that had likely supported some sort of a bench or cot suggested that it might indeed have been a prison cell once. If so, the women held here must have gone through terrible suffering.

I shuddered as I looked up at Helena. She was not insane. She had planned this out from the beginning to the end, leaving nothing to chance. Her mind was sharp and clear, but it was also in the grip of some powerful and sinister force. I recalled my early sense that nothing was what it seemed in this story. Appearances could be deceiving: that was what I had thought about Latalski and his possible association with the *bibones et comedones*; that was what Konarski had said about Maciek; that was also what I had felt when I found out that Mantovano had been drinking wine on the night of his death. Yet the true deception was right before my eyes this whole time—in an innocent-looking young woman whose calm demeanor belied an unspeakable darkness in her soul.

The deviousness of it took my breath away.

"But why, Helena? Why are you doing this?" I asked.

For the first time a shadow of pain crossed her face. She rose from her stool and began pacing the cell to the door and back. I could hear her breath quicken. "To make you understand," she said at length, her voice catching, "I would first have to tell you about Zamborski and what a monster *he* was."

Something lodged in my throat like a stone that I could neither swallow nor spit out. I suddenly realized that up until then—and despite all evidence to the contrary—I had still held a tiny glimmer of hope that the kidnapping of Dantyszek was not related to the murders. That Helena would say something to make that clear, to cut herself off from those other crimes. She might have found the ruby dagger abandoned somewhere and was now using it for this prank—in poor taste, to be sure, but with a perfectly good explanation. Like jealousy. Maybe they had been lovers after all, Dantyszek had left her, and she wanted to take her revenge by frightening him?

But now I saw this last illusion evaporate like a fog that lifts only to leave one staring at the stark, horrible, inescapable reality of a devastation beyond repair.

"It is all his fault. It all started with him." She stopped in the middle of the cell, her hands by her sides. She gazed into the flame of the candle, her sea-green eyes wide and still, her face frozen. Only her lips moved as she spoke, which made her look like a sleepwalker, talking from somewhere deep within herself, slowly and dispassionately. "It happened on Midsummer Eve. We all went down to the riverbank to float flower wreaths and light bonfires. It was always my favorite holiday, when nature is at its most lush and green. It is so warm, the air so clear, and the scents so heady that it makes you think that summer will never end, that we will never grow old, never die, and you are simply happy, so happy to be alive."

I could see her eyes glaze over, but it was a moment before I realized that they were brimming with tears.

"We were having a delightful time, the other maids of honor and I. You were there too." Her eyes swiveled in my direction, and two tears ran down her cheeks. "For once you were enjoying yourself, not watching over us like a hawk." There was a slight mockery in her voice, but I ignored it as my mind reeled back to that June celebration. She was right—it was a joyous occasion, a tradition in these northern lands that went back hundreds and hundreds of years, all the way to pagan times. The Church frowns upon it, of course, which is why it is so popular with young people, who come to eat, sing, and dance outside all night. Yet something terrible had happened last year, and I was frantically trying to remember if I had seen or heard anything out of the ordinary. But I could not.

Helena must have seen the struggle in my face. "You didn't see it. Nobody saw it. Zamborski came up to me and took my hand to lead me in a dance. I was in a cheery mood and I'd had more wine than I am used to, so I didn't notice when we moved outside the circle of the other dancers, away from the light of the bonfire and toward the shadow of a copse of trees some distance away. There we stopped, and I thought he wanted to kiss me, so I laughed and turned away, but he grabbed me by the arm. I told him to let me go, that I wanted to go back to the others, but he said that what I wanted was something different, something I didn't know yet but would enjoy when I tried it.

"He pulled me into the copse, and I cried out but nobody could hear me through the music and laughter and the roar of the bonfires up and down the river. It is that sound that haunts me at night even more than his breathing in my ear as he pushed me to the ground and forced himself on me."

"Oh, Helena." My hand went to my mouth. "I had no idea. I didn't notice anything—if I had seen—" I could not go on, knowing how inadequate my excuse was, how belated the assurance.

"When he was done, he said I had got what I deserved for besting him at the archery contest earlier that day, that even though I had won, I was still a weak woman who needed to be shown her place." She wiped her tears, flowing freely now, with the back of her hands. It was a childlike gesture and it broke my heart, for it reminded me how young she still was. "And then he said that if I ever told anyone about it, he would say that I had seduced him, and that I had been drunk. And then everybody would think that I was a whore, fit for a tavern rather than a royal court. Oh, how I wish I had been drunk that night," she said bitterly. "Maybe I would have no memory of any of it now."

I made to rise. I wanted to put my arms around her, to comfort her, but as soon as I moved, her body jerked as if jolted from sleep, and she swung the hand that held the dagger in my direction.

"Stay where you are," she said through gritted teeth, her eyes flashing like the blade in the candlelight.

I raised my hands in a gesture that I hoped would calm her and sat back against the wall. "I am sorry for suspecting that you were having a liaison and that you were with child," I said, guilt coloring my voice as I realized how unfair my words had been, how ironic and painful to her.

She laughed scornfully. "You were worried about it two weeks ago because all you care about is your position with the queen, but I almost went insane with fear last summer, thinking of the possibility of having to bring a bastard child of a rapist into the world. I spent three terrifying, sleepless weeks until my courses arrived, but even so my mind has not known a moment of peace since then."

She went back to the stool and wrapped her arms around her chest in a protective gesture, like she had done the night I found her in her nightgown in the gallery after the council meeting with the queen. She began rocking forward and backward, the dagger still clutched in her hand. "Every time I saw him in the castle—and it was almost every day—his air of self-satisfaction, his smirk, his nod whenever he caught me looking at him, his brazen flirting with women as if to show me that he could do whatever he wanted with whomever he wanted, and that nobody could stop him . . . it tore something inside me over and over again. And I knew that it would never close and heal as long as he was alive."

"So you sent word to him to meet you in the delivery passage during the Christmas banquet, and you killed him."

This time, her laughter was full of satisfaction; there was even a hint of relief in it. "Well guessed, signora. I did kill him, with my own hands and his own dagger." She hefted the weapon in her palm, gazing at it fondly.

I was about to ask how she managed to do that without drugging him too, when it all became clear to me. "You left our table in the hall—which I assumed was because you felt unwell—then you went up to the servants' floor because you thought it would be empty at that hour, and through their corridor, you made it to the other side of the castle, where you used the servants' staircase to reach the delivery passage. Zamborski was already waiting for you, or you had to wait for him, and when you finally met, you embraced him. He was kissing you when you pulled his dagger out of its sheath, reached your hand around, and plunged it into his back as you stood in front of him. That explains why his wound was in the middle of his back, not higher up between his shoulders."

That had been the nagging thought I had in the cathedral crypt that night after Christmas when the queen demanded to see Zamborski's body. That was why I had not believed that a romantic rival had killed Zamborski in a fit of anger, or that he had been accosted and dispatched by a thief after his property. The strike had been quick and stealthy, but most importantly it had been inflicted by someone who was much shorter than Zamborski—in other words, a woman.

"It also explains why there was no blood on your gown and you were able to return to the table without arousing suspicion," I added, running my hand over my forehead where I could feel the wetness of perspiration despite the chill that pervaded the place.

Helena gazed at me intently for some moments as if seeing me for the first time. She wagged her finger at me playfully. "You are clever, Donna Caterina. Cleverer than I thought, given your obsession with guarding our virtue from *ourselves* and your timid pining for Secretary Konarski." I opened my mouth to protest, although I was not sure about what, for she was right on both counts. But she went on, ignoring me and growing more somber again. "Yes, that is exactly how I killed him. It made me sick to kiss him, but I kept thinking that that kiss would be his death, and that was what helped me endure it. It was a means to an end."

All the remaining pieces fell into place. It was Helena that Maciek Koza had seen in the servants' corridor as she was returning to the hall from killing Zamborski. What he had thought was the hem of a man's cloak was a sliver of her dress—dark blue that night, but easily appearing black in the dimly lit passage—as she turned the corner away from him. With a bitter sense of irony, I remembered my fleeting thought as he had said it that it might have been Helena—or Lucrezia—returning from a secret rendezvous. How close I had been to the truth in that moment, and yet how far, for even that brief idea had not extended to me suspecting one of them of murder.

Suddenly, the forgotten words Stańczyk the jester had spoken on the evening of the king's birthday reception rang in my ears as clearly as if he were standing next to me in the cell. *This was no man's fury.* How naïve was I, and how clever the dwarf! It was no phantom or ghost who had sown terror in the castle those last few weeks, but a living, breathing—and much wronged—woman.

I looked away, my gaze falling on Dantyszek. He was staring at Helena steadily, without anger but without much sympathy either. He was almost defiant.

"What about him?" I asked. "Did he hurt you too?"

"No. He's not the kind of beast Zamborski was, at least not to my knowledge. Though you never know," she added with an indifferent shrug.

"Then why hold him?" I grasped at it. "Why not let him go?"

"*Because,*" she said with an impatient intake of breath as if she were speaking to a child or a simpleton, "he makes the behavior of men like Zamborski possible. As the leader of the *bibones et comedones,* he glorifies and encourages the pursuit of women, and the likes of Zamborski look up to him."

Dantyszek pulled on his chain again, and I could sense his exasperation returning. His hands tensed as he tried to break the tie binding his wrists, but the rope was fastened securely and tight, one of the many practical skills Helena must have learned from her father. Dantyszek let out a muffled groan of frustration, but he was weakening, and his chest worked laboriously with each breath. He had not eaten for more than twenty-four hours, and I doubted that Helena had given him anything to drink either.

"He needs water." I pointed with my chin to a pewter jug in the corner by the crate where the candle was standing. "Can I remove his gag for just a moment so he can have a few sips?"

She shook her head. "The water is for me. He doesn't need it anymore. He doesn't have long to live."

Dantyszek slumped next to me, and for the first time, I began to fear for my own life. If she meant to kill him, she would not let me out of there alive to let the world know what she had done. A cold dread spread through my core and to my limbs, rendering them heavy as lead as I realized that the most likely outcome would be both of us dying at her hand. When she was done with us, and before the kitchen staff returned, she would make her way out of the castle and out of Kraków, perhaps dressed in my clothes for a better disguise, and nobody would ever know she had been there that night. Meanwhile, our bodies would remain in the dank cellar to rot or be eaten by vermin, undiscovered for months or years to come. Eventually, all that would be left would be bare gray bones, indistinguishable from the others buried in this crypt centuries ago. This image stood so vividly in my mind that I began to shake.

"You are cold in your wet clothes, signora," Helena observed, then her tone turned ominous. "You shouldn't have come here. It was a bad idea—"

"I was looking for him because the queen was impatient to dispatch her letter to Naples," I hastened to explain to prevent her from saying what I knew she was going to say next: that I would share Dantyszek's fate. It was a pathetic explanation, but I wanted to distract her and keep her talking about anything but what she was going to do to us. Until help arrived ... but what help? Nobody knew we were there, and it must have been the middle of the night by then. The banquet was over, and everybody had gone to bed, relieved that another body had not been found.

"He is not going to Naples, not only because a dead man cannot travel, but also because the letter of condolence to Signora Mantovano is full of falsehoods," Helena said matter-of-factly.

"What do you mean?" I asked as my ears hopelessly strained for any sound of footsteps outside. Had I left the door to the cellar open? I tried to remember desperately, but I could not.

"What I mean is that the letter likely states that Mantovano was not only a dependable and competent secretary but also a faithful and loving husband. In reality he was a cad and a lecher, no better than Zamborski, Dantyszek, and the rest of that wretched society. Actually"—she put a finger to her chin and looked up in a mock gesture of wondering—"he may have been even worse because they at least never pretended to be virtuous and pious. When was the last time you saw *him*"—a quick swing of the dagger tip toward Dantyszek—"sing praises of the Holy Virgin in a front stall of the cathedral, Mantovano's favorite pastime? No, he prefers to wink at the flesh-and-blood virgins in the stalls across from him. The pleasures of the bed are the only gods *he* worships."

She roared with laughter and slapped her thigh the way a man would. When her mirth abated, she affected a look of inquiry as she leaned forward, asking Dantyszek directly, "Or should I have said 'preferred' and 'worshipped,' given you aren't going to do either anymore?" Her lips curled into a smirk at the look of terror in his eyes.

"Don Mantovano wasn't a member of the society, so why kill him?" I asked, again to distract her.

She turned to me. "He was not, but not because he didn't share their inclination toward vice. He was simply too much of a hypocrite to be open about it." She paused and savored my stupefaction. What was she saying—that he had raped her too? I found it hard to imagine, for Mantovano had been a slip of a man, and much older, and he would have been easier to fight off than Zamborski.

"He did not violate me, but he did something just as vicious," Helena resumed. "After Zamborski had left me in that copse, I straightened my skirts as best I could and came out staggering, for my legs were barely able to carry me. And who was the first person I encountered? None other than Don Mantovano, looking like an evil sorcerer in a black hat and cloak, even on a hot summer night. And that perpetually sour face! Not for him the dances and merriment; he preferred to scurry in the shadows like a rat." She spoke more calmly now. "He must have seen Zamborski coming out of there before me, for he wagged a finger at me without a word. But I was too distraught to say anything. I just ran back to our chamber, shed my clothes, and curled up in my bed even as the celebrations were still going on down by the river. But I could not sleep— each time I closed my eyes, I saw the flames dancing under my eyelids and heard Zamborski's groans in my ears.

"A few days later, Mantovano found a way to speak to me as the other maids of honor were entertaining the queen. I was on duty refilling the decanters of wine and setting out sweetmeats on the trays around the antechamber. He came up to me on the pretense of trying one of the sugared almonds and told me that he would keep my tryst with Zamborski secret from the queen if I agreed to be his mistress." She shook her head as if she found it hard to believe it, and I felt the same. The idea of Mantovano as both a blackmailer *and* a lover strained anybody's imagination. "I stared at him, not knowing what to say. I was mindful of Zamborski's warning, and the lewd smile on Mantovano's bloodless lips and the gleam in his fish eyes made it clear to me that even if I told him the truth, he would not believe me or care. For him, it was just an excuse to get what he wanted. He had found my weak spot, and it didn't matter how I had come by it."

She fell into a pensive silence, and I reeled from this additional revelation. I felt great pity for Helena, alone and unable to seek help from anyone, assaulted in different ways by men whose position at the court allowed them to act with impunity.

"So you became his mistress and killed him when you couldn't stand it anymore?"

"No." She shook her head again. "I never did what he wanted of me. I would have killed myself first. No, I held him off for as long as I could. First, I told him I had to think about it, and when he pressed me again a few days later, I said that I suspected I was with child. It was after I already knew I was not, but it was a convenient excuse. Then, in the autumn, he cornered me again during the banquet for the French ambassador and said that as I was not quickening, there was nothing to stand in our way. Fortunately, the next day he fell ill with some stomach ailment that kept him away from me for a fortnight. By the time he was well enough to return to his duties, Advent had begun, and I told him to wait until Christmas was over. Pious hypocrite that he was, he agreed to that. By then, Zamborski was dead, and if Mantovano had had the wit to figure it out, or if he had decided to rediscover his fidelity to his wife and stay away from me, he would still be alive now. But he did not. In fact, he sent me a note urging me to make my decision the day after I had killed Zamborski. I replied, saying that I would meet with him after midnight on New Year's Eve, when everyone was either in the hall celebrating or drunk and asleep."

"The wine he gave to the guards was laced with Baldazzi's poppy milk," I stated what I already knew was true.

"A whole bottle had to go into that flagon," she said proudly. "They were big men."

So that was another lie: on the morning of Mantovano's murder, she had pointed to the clay bottle by her bed and told me that it was for her, and that she had only used a quarter measure. If I had bothered to check that bottle, I would have found that it was empty rather than three quarters full. Would it have led me—or the chancellor—to solve the murders sooner? Would it have prevented this last desperate act that was unfolding and might yet cost more lives?

"Whose idea was it?"

"Mine, of course. Mantovano had few ideas of his own. Most of his life he had done the bidding of his betters, and on the last night of his life he did mine." She smiled triumphantly. "It didn't even occur to him to make sure that the guards were not aware of our encounter." She cocked her head. "Or maybe it excited him to think that they would know and wonder what was going on behind closed doors." She waved her hand dismissively. "It doesn't matter."

I thought about how increasingly angry and desperate she must have been during those months following Midsummer Eve. Both of those men—one by his mere presence, the other by his pestering—made it impossible for her to forget the violence that had been done to her. As time went on, it must have been her life or theirs as the only way of regaining her shattered peace, and she had chosen the latter. But depending on the outcome of this night, she might still see her life forfeit in the end.

"That handkerchief, by the way"—she arched an eyebrow with a rakish smile—"the one that the queen thought Mantovano had pulled out of his pocket to stanch the bleeding? It was mine. I brought it with me to wipe the dagger and clean my hands afterwards. But I was careful to select one of my new ones that had not yet been embroidered with my initials. After I stabbed him, I wiped my hands, then stuck the handkerchief in his. He did try to press it to his wounds, but he was too shocked and his blood was flowing too fast."

"Were you not afraid that he would scream and awaken everyone? The queen's apartment is just two doors down." No sooner had I spoken those words than I knew. "Was *that* what the belladonna was for?"

Helena looked impressed. "You really *are* clever," she said. "Chancellor Stempowski should have entrusted you with this case. Instead, he is using men who are incompetent, and he doesn't care because he is secretly happy that Zamborski is out of the way. Luckily, though, it allowed Mantovano to pay for what he did to me. But to answer your question," she added, "yes, I have been saving the small amounts Doctor Baldazzi gave me of what you Italians call belladonna. Here we call it *wilcza jagoda*, wolf's berry, which I like a lot more. Our name is stripped of the unnecessary sentimentality; instead, it conveys the plant's stealthy and ruthless nature. It looks innocent, but it is deadly." She chuckled softly as she smoothed her dress. "The amount I slipped into the wine I brought with me to his office was just enough to take away his power of speech but leave him conscious until the end."

I felt nauseous and, despite everything, could not help but pity Mantovano. It must have been a terrible way to die.

"So he did drink wine after all," I said, more to myself than anybody else.

"He didn't enjoy it, but he was nervous. It was probably the first time in his boring life that he was going to cheat on his wife. And it turned out to be the last," she added with feigned sadness.

I did not respond, and she grew pensive again, but it was a wistful kind of pensiveness, as if the memory were precious. "I waited for him to die—it took almost ten minutes, the most exciting ten minutes of my life! You cannot possibly imagine that feeling, the pure, most sublime exultation of it. I was the judge and jury and God, all in one." Her eyes lit up with such intensity that it bordered on ecstasy, and I thought that maybe she had finally gone insane.

"Sometimes I wish I had taken my time with Zamborski, too, but he died quickly," she resumed regretfully. "As Doctor Baldazzi said, I punctured his lung—though, of course, such precision was purely accidental—and he suffocated fast." She fell silent, but the glow lingered on her face. She was reliving it. "After Mantovano had gone still, I poured the wine with the belladonna out of the window, took the goblet, and went back to bed. But I could not fall asleep again. I was too excited. Some hours later I heard Lucrezia stir and get out of bed, and a few minutes later she started screaming."

We gazed at the guttering flame of the candle. It was burning low now, and soon we would be in complete darkness. The moment of reckoning was coming. "So much death already, Helena. Was it really worth it, beyond the momentary satisfaction?"

Her eyes appeared to glaze over as she stared past me at nothing. "Oh yes," she said quietly but firmly. "Those two did not deserve to live, and I would do it all over again."

"What about your immortal soul?"

"I don't care about it. I don't believe in it anymore."

A wave of exhaustion swept over me, the result of nearly a fortnight of this nightmare, and this day that had begun so long ago that it seemed like another year, another lifetime altogether. I wanted to lie down, put my head even on the dirty sacks that made up Dantyszek's pallet, and close my eyes, block out this awful place. But I knew I could not do that, for then I would lose the last vestige of control, such as it was, over what happened to me. If I slept, I might not wake ever again.

"Maybe *I am* evil." Helena's words, pronounced with quiet wonderment, reached me.

"You are not," I said, surprising myself with the vehemence in my voice despite my tiredness and fear. "You were wronged, and you took revenge on your tormentors. I understand that even if I don't condone it. But you were not born to be a murderess; otherwise he would be dead already." I tilted my head toward Dantyszek, who seemed to have drifted off into slumber, his breath shallow. His eye sockets and cheeks were sunken, and his skin had assumed a gray tinge that I could see even in the poor light. If we did not get out of there soon, Helena would not have to worry about dispatching him. "You know it would be wrong to kill him ... or me."

She turned her eyes on me, and once again I saw them shimmer with tears. "I don't want to kill you, Caterina, but you leave me with no choice. I left you a note to warn you to stay away from this. If only you had listened." She sighed, then added in an almost apologetic tone, "If I let you go, you will tell Konarski, and they will come after me. I cannot let you ruin my plans when they are so close to completion."

The mention of Konarski brought a dull ache to my chest. I would have given everything I had to be able to see him one more time, to kiss him the way I had failed to do earlier that day. He was the only man who had ever managed to stir something in me that other people seemed to feel so often and so readily. Whether it was love or lust, I did not know, but I wanted to feel it again, and now it was too late. I would die in this stinking, dark, airless cell. But the worst part of it was that he would never know what happened to me, and he would eventually forget that I had ever existed.

Hot tears pushed at the back of my eyes, and I pressed my hands to them to keep them in check. I would not let her see my grief. For the first time since I had ended up in that cellar, I began to feel angry.

"A lot of people suffer in this world." I took my hands away from my face and looked at her defiantly. "For most people, especially us women"—I pointed a finger from myself to her and back—"life is not fair. I was married to a man I neither knew nor loved, and some of the nights I spent with him were not that different from the way Zamborski treated you, or the way Mantovano would have if it had come to that. Most women go through it; your fellow maids of honor will meet that fate one day, and the blessing of a priest will do little to make it easier. Only a few lucky ones escape it, and that is mainly if they choose a convent over married life. Maybe that's where you should have gone in the first place instead of coming to court—"

"Be quiet," she said through gritted teeth. "Be quiet."

I knew I was being cruel, but I was too mad to stop. "You are trying to turn yourself into a martyr, but being a martyr means that *you* die"—I hardly knew what I was saying anymore—"rather than go around murdering people, especially innocent ones—"

She jumped to her feet. "Shut up!" she shouted.

Dantyszek woke with a jolt and gazed fearfully from one of us to the other, his eyes so wide I could see the bloodshot threads in them. "He is *not* innocent!" She made a jabbing gesture in his direction, and he recoiled. "Sooner or later he's going to do to someone what Zamborski did to me, if he hasn't already. I am doing the world a favor."

"What about Maciek Koza? That poor boy they threw into jail for your crime. You were ready to let him die for it."

She scoffed. "I knew he would be let out the moment Mantovano's body was found."

"But if you kill us and flee, someone else will be made to pay for it. Someone as powerless and defenseless as he is."

She laughed mockingly, the sound harsh in my ears. "*If they ever find you—*" She broke off as a crashing noise rang out above our heads.

We all froze.

For a moment I had trouble recognizing what was happening. It sounded like someone—or rather several people, judging by the number of voices and footsteps—was overturning tables and stools upstairs in the kitchen. My heart lifted again with hope as the cell fell deathly quiet, and we each held our breaths while gazing at the door. But soon the desperate thought came back to me: had I left the cellar door open? If not, they might not guess that we were down below in the space that was supposed to be empty and unused.

Suddenly I heard a scream. "Help me! Help! We are here! Help!—" Then I realized it was coming from me. I scrambled to my feet and lunged for the door, but Helena was swift. I felt her hand grabbing at the back of my neck, but she only managed to get hold of my necklace, and her fingers twisted to tighten it like a garrote. Yet before I even had time to react, the pressure on my throat eased as the silk thread snapped, sending the pearls scattering on the stone floor with a soft tinkling sound like a fairy's laughter. It was enough to slow me down and allow Helena to reach the door first.

Behind us, Dantyszek took up yelling. The sound was hopelessly inadequate through the rags in his mouth, but it was enough to cause Helena to lose her head. I saw the indecision in her face—should she defend the door or kill Dantyszek before the prize of the evening eluded her? I took advantage of her hesitation and pushed her aside with as much force as I could summon. She staggered away, clearing the path for me, but as I reached for the handle, I could see out of the corner of my eye that she had not fallen. She regained her footing quickly, her hesitancy over, and charged at me just as I was pulling the door open.

I started screaming again, my throat quickly becoming raw and painful. I was aware that she still had the dagger, that she had not dropped it, and my back felt terribly exposed. I let go of the door and turned around to protect myself from the blade. I still remember the roar of fury with which she raised the weapon over her head and aimed. All I could do was to raise my arms to protect my face, and that was how she slashed across the soft bottom part of my left arm.

I was wearing a fitted sleeve for the evening, nothing but its brocade fabric and the chemise underneath to protect me, and the blade went into it as easily as if it had sliced into butter. For a moment I was stunned that it did not hurt, that nothing really happened, until a liquid warmth began pouring out of me, spreading and swallowing my silver-white sleeve, the stain deep red like spilled wine.

The scream died in my throat, and I fell against the door. It closed with a thud, and a terrible silence ensued, broken only by faint moans as Dantyszek struggled against his restraints. *They can't hear him, they can't hear him!* The desperate words kept circling through my head because I was no longer able to produce any sound. Helena stood panting in front of me, the dagger raised high again, and she would no doubt have plunged it into my chest if I had made any move. But my ears began to ring, and I could no longer hear the footsteps and voices upstairs; I was overcome by a light-headedness and knew that I would not remain on my feet for much longer. In my last conscious act, I fell sideways so as not the block the door. I slid against the wall, crumpling in a heap like a rag doll.

The last thing I remember is Helena taking a step toward me but looking at the door, her head cocked. By then I could no longer hear anything, not even Dantyszek's moans or her

rapid breathing, and my vision darkened. Then my consciousness slipped away.

✍

When I came to, the scene was much the same, except that
the person who was leaning over me was squeezing my arm. I
let out a groan of fear and protest, but I was too weak to fight.
The figure kneeled down by me, and with relief I realized that
it was not Helena.

"You'll be all right." The voice came faintly through the
ringing in my ears as the pressure on my arm increased. The
words were familiar as was the voice, but I could not place it. "I
will bind up your arm—"

The person looked around in search of something, and
in the light of the candle still burning by Dantyszek's pallet,
I saw Konarski's face. Whatever it was that he was looking
for was not there, and he called to another man who I now
saw was leaning over Dantyszek, untying his wrists. The man
was dressed in the uniform of the castle guards, though he did
not have his halberd on him.

"Hold her arm here—like this." Konarski showed him, and
I saw that he was scared. "She's bleeding out . . ."

I glanced at my arm, now overspread with a creeping dark
stain, wet and heavy. "My sleeve," I said plaintively. "It's ruined."
I heard tears in my voice and was stunned that after all I had
been through, that was the thing that was going to make me
break down.

"Never mind the sleeve," he said. "Hold still."

The guard took a firm hold of my arm, pressing just below
my armpit the way Konarski had showed him.

But my tears were falling in an unstoppable flow. "Where
is Helena?" I sobbed. "She tried to kill us."

"I know." Konarski quickly took off his doublet and pulled
his shirt up over his head. He began to tear it into long strips.

"Where is she?!" I heard a note of hysteria in my voice as I wiped my eyes with my uninjured hand. I was gripped by a terror that she was going to come back and finish me and Konarski, and the guard too.

Konarski began tying one of the strips above where the guard's hand was pressing. "She was taken back to the castle. She's not going to hurt anyone," he said through gritted teeth. "Not anymore."

"What about Jan?"

He pointed with his chin toward the pallet as he tied a knot on my tourniquet. "He's fine, too, just a bit sore, and his wrists are bruised." Then he paused, still crouching beside me, and looked me in the eyes with an intensity I had never seen there before. I thought he was going to kiss me, but he put his hand on my cheek. "It's over, Caterina."

He put his doublet back on, then stooped to lift me, for I was unable to stand on my feet. "I will take you to the infirmary. The queen sent for Doctor Baldazzi, and I will have him come to see you immediately."

"The queen ..."

"She is safe. Don't worry."

"But ..." I wanted to say that I needed to explain to the queen that Dantyszek had not betrayed her trust, that it was I who had failed in my duties, and that Helena's crimes were also my fault. But my tongue would not form the words. My thoughts were slowing down as sleepiness overcame me.

Making a supreme effort with my remaining strength, I clung to him like a child as he carried me upstairs to the kitchen, which looked like a horde of Tatars had just been through it.

As another guard opened the front door for us, Konarski told him to run to the queen's apartments and tell Doctor Baldazzi to come to the infirmary. When we were out in the courtyard, I gulped the cold clear air like someone who had emerged from under water at the very last moment of her endurance. But as much as I inhaled, I could not rid myself of the foul smell that lingered in my nostrils. It seemed to have soaked into my clothes, my skin, my very core.

The snow had all but ceased, but the wind was still blowing, sending white dust swirling off the piles on the ground. Konarski walked slowly, knee-deep in the snow. Eventually we reached the infirmary, which was on the ground floor of the northern wing, right next to the entrance to the castle cellars where we had watched the servants carry barrels of wine not a week earlier. The infirmary was normally staffed by three nuns from a nearby Benedictine abbey, but only one was on duty during the night.

She led us to an empty bed in the far corner on which Konarski placed me gently. The moment I felt the softness of the hay mattress under me and the blankets he wrapped around me, a softness I had thought I would never feel again, the tension and fear finally released their hold on me. Exhaustion swept over me like a giant wave. The infirmarian and Konarski exchanged some words, but I could not make anything out. For the second time that evening, everything went black around me.

15

February 1520

For the next two weeks, I battled a fever from the cold I had caught that night, my body alternately shivering to its very core and swimming in waves of heat. It was made worse by the gash on my arm, through which I had lost a significant amount of blood. Fortunately, Doctor Baldazzi stitched it up well after having cleaned it with wine and vinegar. He also brought me salves and unguents of his own making, for which he procured dried herbs from apothecaries all over Kraków. He claimed that his recipes were the best for protecting wounds and speeding up their healing. Whether they did or whether it would have taken just as long without them, I do not know, but they certainly took some of the sting and tightness off my raw flesh.

Still, it took a month before I no longer needed bandages and was able to wear a gown again rather than a loose infirmary smock with a shawl draped around my shoulders when I had visitors.

And I had many of them. The parade of officials, well-wishers, and plain gossip-seekers would have been endless once my fever had abated had I not asked the infirmarian sisters to keep them out. After the maids of honor had visited me, I wished only to see Chancellor Stempowski, who was interviewing witnesses in preparation for Helena's trial, and Sebastian Konarski.

The latter came to visit me every day, even when I was too ill to talk to him and when my head was too clouded with fever to know who he was. On the first day that I was well enough to sit up in bed, the shawl wrapped around me like a cocoon for propriety's sake by one of the sisters, he told me how he had managed to find us in the kitchen cellar on the night of the Epiphany.

At the royal table in the banqueting hall, the chancellor and the king had been discussing the delay of the army's march north out of Koło due to the snowstorm. Not only would it have to wait until the weather cleared and roads became passable again, but the king, after having finally agreed to send artillery, had changed his mind again for fear that the valuable equipment would suffer damage. It was a decision that would necessitate many dispatches to be drafted and dispositions sent out the next morning, and Konarski could not excuse himself, even when he noticed that I was gone. He grew increasingly worried when I did not return, but he could only go to look for me when the war business was settled and the king rose to retire to his apartments.

As soon as that happened, Konarski went to inquire with the queen, who had already sent Magdalena to look for me in my chamber. Moments later, the girl returned, saying that I was not there. The queen was about to raise the alarm and order the captain of the guard to search the castle when the Princess of Montefusco, reliably attracted by any sort of commotion, turned up. After learning of my disappearance, she announced that she might be able to help, for she had seen me talking with Doctor Baldazzi in the gallery not two hours earlier. After that speech—which had looked animated but whose content she had regrettably not caught—I ran down the main staircase as if I had all the hounds of hell at my heels.

"All the while she was saying that," Konarski recalled, "she was looking at me in a way—it's hard to describe"—he frowned as he cast his mind back—"as if she thought I knew where you were but was pretending not to. And at the end she winked at me." He looked puzzled. "She is a strange woman."

In the old days—and I could not believe that that meant only weeks earlier—I would have blushed crimson to the roots of my hair. But now I only closed my eyes, my cheeks remaining blessedly cool. Something had changed in me. I felt that—on the inside at least—I had aged many years. I had so much guilt and pain and grief to overcome that I could no longer afford to become upset by things that were of little consequence.

That was my new maturity.

Konarski paused in his story and asked me if I was feeling unwell, but I shook my head and told him to go on. Upon hearing the princess's revelations, he resumed, the queen sent for Baldazzi, who had already gone to bed, but whom she ordered to be woken and brought before her in his nightshirt and cap if need be. But Konarski did not wait for that. He ran down the stairs, just as I had done earlier, shouting questions at the guards on each floor, finally learning from the sentry at the main door that I had gone out.

By then, the snow was winding down, and he could discern nothing in the pristine whiteness of the courtyard at first. Then he noticed something dark sticking out of a pile of snow. Grabbing a torch, he went to investigate. It was a headdress, and he guessed that it belonged to me. Nearby he could still see the faint outlines of the tracks I had left, almost completely covered by snow, but they were enough to guide him to the kitchen.

He took four men-at-arms with him. They tried the main door, but they found it locked. They would have turned back—my tracks around the building having been completely obscured by snow that had blown against the wall—had one of the guards not had a sweetheart among the cooks and known about the side entrance. Once inside, they found one of the two doors to the cellars slightly ajar, but they did not think much about it, and after searching the ground level, they were about to go to the upper floor. That was when they heard me scream just before Helena slashed me with the dagger. I must have screamed louder than I thought, or the underground passage carried the sound well. Maybe it was both. Either way, I am glad I did it, for otherwise I would have died that night.

When they got down to the cellars, they heard the door of the last cell being locked from the inside. Fortunately, the lock was old and rusty, and it only took a few kicks from one of the guards to send the door crashing open. That must have happened when I was unconscious, for I have no memory of any of it. The next thing I remember is Konarski kneeling over me and trying to stanch my blood flow.

When he finished telling me the events of that night, I reached out and put my hand on his as it rested on the edge of my bed. "Thank you, Sebastian," I said, emotion distorting my voice. "I owe you my life."

He smiled but shook his head. "We should all thank *you*."

I gave him a puzzled look. "One of my ladies killed two men and I had no idea, no inkling that would have helped me to prevent it," I said bitterly. "I failed to protect Helena, and I failed in my duties to the queen. How do *I* deserve anyone's gratitude?"

He squeezed my hand gently but removed it when one of the sisters sent us a disapproving glance. "If it hadn't been for your questioning and your refusal to accept the convenient explanations"—he dropped his voice—"explanations that the chancellor, the queen, and even I really wanted to believe, Helena would have killed Dantyszek. It took a lot of courage to go against all that and to keep searching for answers. You saved his life, and you put an end to this nightmare."

In a low, halting voice—emotion was still choking it, and I had to wipe my eyes with the shawl intermittently—I told him what had transpired in that cellar, everything Helena had told me about the harm that had been done to her. Earlier, Konarski had told me that while she had confessed to the two murders, she had refused to give any explanation for her actions. Now he listened, his face falling as I recounted the awful details of how Zamborski had dragged Helena into the copse by the river while everyone else was laughing and dancing around the bonfires. And how Mantovano had taken advantage of her misfortune to blackmail her afterwards.

"Those bastards deserved everything that happened to them." He ran a hand over his face when I came to the end. "It's a pity that she must follow them to the grave."

We were quiet for a long time, watching the watery sunlight of a February day filter through the small square windows of the infirmary, marking pale patches on the opposite wall. Normally, a winter sun, even one so weak, would put me in a cheerful mood, but right then I did not care. The windows had iron bars in them like those in Baszta Sandomierska, where Helena was being held awaiting her trial. Everything around me—and inside, too, for my injured arm still felt tender—reminded me of those terrible events. Would I ever be able to find joy again after all that had happened?

One of the infirmarians brought me a tray with cheese, bread, and watered wine. I nibbled at the food, but I had no appetite.

"You should eat more, Caterina," Konarski's concerned eyes swept my face. "You look thin."

I knew I did. I had caught a glimpse of myself in Magdalena's small hand mirror when she came to visit me, and saw my sunken cheeks and the dark circles around my eyes. A few weeks earlier, Konarski had wanted to kiss me, but I doubted that was the case anymore. The thought threatened to bring fresh tears to my eyes. I tore a bigger piece of the bread and took a sip of the wine with it to moisten it because it felt hard and dry in my mouth, even though it was still warm from the oven.

"So the chancellor wants Helena to be tried for murder?" I asked when I had finally managed to swallow the food.

"I'm afraid so."

"Can it not be argued that she was pushed to the extreme and committed those crimes in a state of distress, desperation, and justified anger?"

A smile crossed his lips. "If you were a man, you would make a fine lawyer." Then he grew somber again, but there was a sympathy in his eyes that had not been there before I told him Helena's story. "You can make that case to the chancellor if you wish, but I doubt it will change anything. We found too much evidence of planning for it to be argued that they were spur-of-the-moment crimes." He paused, and I knew what he was thinking: it was I who had once argued—to none other than Stempowski himself—that the murders had been methodical rather than spontaneous. "And with multiple victims, it will be even harder to persuade the judges of it," he added.

He then told me that a search of Helena's chest had yielded a nightdress with a sleeve and front spattered with blood, and empty medicine bottles with stains of what Doctor Baldazzi identified as poppy milk and belladonna. They were hidden at the bottom under her gowns. Again, I cursed myself for not having been more thorough in my own search. But I had only looked into that chest and saw its disturbed contents on the morning of Dantyszek's disappearance, too late to have prevented it, and certainly too late to have stopped the murders.

"The chancellor had her things searched on the morning *after* she was arrested," Konarski said. "But on the afternoon of the Epiphany, when we were looking for Dantyszek, the ladies' chambers were excluded."

I recalled his own words when I had suggested, after the mass in the cathedral, that the killer might not have been a man at all, a timid guess I had promptly dismissed but the court jester had made instantly and with such confidence. "Because nobody thought a woman could have committed such violent acts," I finished for him.

He nodded, and I saw something approaching admiration in his face. "Helena has a mind equal to that of any man. She planned it all so meticulously. Her traveling trunk was found at the Red Cockerel inn, where she'd had it sent the day before she was supposed to leave for home. By the way, Mantovano's ring and chain of office and Zamborski's purse were in it," he added. "The chancellor believes that she never left the castle on the morning of January fourth but went to the kitchen directly, and that she spent the night there, sleeping on that makeshift bed that she later had Dantyszek sit on. Until now," he said, "we didn't know how she got inside because she is refusing to speak, but you are saying that she had a key from a kitchen maid obtained in exchange for a bribe?"

"That's what she told me."

"But how did she manage to make her way there without being noticed?" He scratched the short dark beard he now wore, which suited him just as much as the lack of it had before. "The kitchen was empty by then, but someone should still have seen her walk over there. The courtyard is always busy. I suppose she was very lucky in that, if you can call it luck."

I grabbed his hand at a sudden realization but dropped it when a sister paused in her work and looked toward us again. "I know how she did it!" I dropped my voice. "It was very foggy—I remember because that was the morning of Don Mantovano's funeral, and the carriage in which I rode with the queen to the Church of St. Agata had to proceed very slowly due to poor visibility. We couldn't see the gate until it was right in front of us, and in the forecourt, the cathedral was completely invisible. Oh,

God." I put my hand to my mouth. "She may have been walking right by us as we rode out, and we wouldn't have seen her."

"That was also the day you found the threatening note," Konarski said. "How did she leave *that* in your chamber?"

"She must have slid it under the door on her way out. It would have taken her only a few seconds, and the guards pay more attention to who enters the queen's wing than whoever is already there."

I leaned my head against the wooden headboard and closed my eyes, feeling very tired. Things looked bad for Helena. Even if the judges were to believe that Zamborski had assaulted her and that Mantovano then blackmailed her, they would not be likely to accept that she had killed them on impulse, for, in truth, she had not. She had worked on her plan for weeks, perhaps even months.

"I will let you rest." Konarski's voice came as if from afar.

I opened my eyes and nodded.

He looked toward the infirmarian who was feeding broth to a patient on a bed on the other side of the chamber, glancing at us every now and then. He looked back at me, and we exchanged a small smile of understanding.

"Will you come again tomorrow?" I asked quietly.

"Of course." He rose and was about to turn to leave.

"Sebastian—"

"Yes?"

"I would ask you a favor—would you go to the tower and ensure that she is fed and properly clothed?" The image of Maciek on a December night, shivering in his shirt next to an empty plate, stood before my eyes. "You will have to bribe the guards, but I will pay you back."

He shook his head. "No need."

"And if you see any evidence at all that she has been … mistreated … by any of the guards—" My voice caught as I tried to stave off another image.

He leaned over me and touched my cheek, heedless of the nurses. "She won't be. I will make sure of that."

Two days later, Chancellor Stempowski came to officially interview me. With him, he brought a scribe who wrote down everything Helena had told me about her crimes. The chancellor wanted to know if I had any idea who the servant was who had given Helena the key in exchange for ducats, and I said I did not. I had wondered about that too—was it the little scullery maid Marta or the sweetheart of the guard who had led Konarski to the side door of the kitchen? Perhaps it was Michałowa herself? In truth, it could have been any one of the dozens of people who worked there. What was clear was that Helena had not and would not reveal that person's name. Whether it was her conscience or one final act of defiance on her part, I would never know, but it would keep her accomplice from being branded a traitor and banished from the court for life, or worse.

The morning after the interview, I was called to a private chamber reserved for high court officials during illnesses that required constant care. Inside, Queen Bona was awaiting me. She was alone.

I dropped into a low curtsy, my weakened body protesting dizzily. I would have fallen if the queen had not stepped forward, taken me by my healthy arm, and lifted me up. Her grip was strong and firm, unsurprisingly. She sat me on the bed and took a chair opposite, too large and too ornate to have been a permanent part of the sick chamber's furniture.

I had not met her eyes yet, too embarrassed and a little scared. She and I had always gotten along well, but the queen had a quick temper, and I had heard the verbal lashings she gave others often enough. I waited for her to speak—or shout—first.

"How are you feeling, Caterina?" Her voice was mild, but her face was stern when I finally looked up. For once, she was difficult to read.

"Better, Your Majesty. Thank you."

"I'm glad." She reached for a tray of nougat that she must have brought with her and offered me the sweet squares. She knew it was my favorite confection.

I took one, but I could not taste it as bile rose to my throat. "Doctor Baldazzi did a fine job sewing up my arm," I said instead. "The wound hasn't corrupted and is mending well."

The queen grunted. "I am glad to hear that, too, especially as he has never helped *me* in any way."

I dropped my gaze. *That is because you have never been truly ill.*

"You are missed."

My head snapped up. I was so surprised, I could not find the right words. "Has Your Majesty been—" I started. "Has Chancellor Stempowski informed Your Majesty of—" I faltered.

"Yes," she said grimly.

I could not resist the impression that her tone had as much to do with what she had learned about Helena's motivations as with the fact that her hopes for Stempowski's downfall had been dashed. At least for now.

"I am so sorry." I wrung my hands. If I had the strength, I would have fallen to my knees to beg her forgiveness for letting it all happen, but at that moment, I was not sure if I would be able to rise again.

Bona was silent for a while as I fought to keep my emotions in check. "I want you to know that I do not blame you for this," she said at length. I looked up at her, my eyes widening in disbelief. She went on, "I know how hard it is to keep an eye on those girls. They flirt and they tempt, then they raise a great lament if they find themselves trifled with and cast aside. Men cannot be expected to resist charms that are offered so freely."

I felt a heat of indignation rising to my cheeks. "Helena was not like that!" I protested vehemently. Then I changed my tone. "She didn't provoke Zamborski or Mantovano. She was their victim," I added quietly, but I held her gaze.

She raised a skeptical eyebrow. "We will never know that for certain. After all, the dead cannot speak for themselves."

I looked away, trying to hide my dismay. Of all people, I had not expected the queen to defend Helena's tormentors. But I was hardly in a position to tell her that. "I believe her," I said. "I saw her pain when she told me about it. She did not lie."

There was something in the silence that hung between us that told me the queen was not convinced. Or perhaps she did not want to be.

"Be that as it may," she said, her tone definitive, "Helena's fate is sealed. A murder is a murder."

I could not find a response to that. Instead I said, surprising myself, "If Your Majesty wishes me to leave my position and return to Bari, I will."

"I do not. You may stay if that is what you want."

Not long before, I would have been relieved to hear that. But now I was not sure anymore. "I don't know if I am the right person for this role," I confessed, articulating a doubt that had been building inside me for months. "Perhaps I don't have the—" I broke off, not knowing how to explain it. The right mindset? Set of convictions? Lack of empathy? I was too close in age to those girls and still remembered what it had been like to be full of romantic notions, eager to experience the thrills of first love, dream that my future would not be determined by what my family considered to be convenient, prestigious, or financially desirable. These young women knew what awaited them, they knew there would likely be no love—or even attraction—in the match eventually made for them, and that was their way of rebelling just a little before they submitted to their fate. I did not want to stand in their way.

But of course I could not say any of that to the queen. "Perhaps this requires someone with a different approach," I said. "Someone older and more experienced."

Bona waved her hand. "I think you are just fine." She was never one to pick up on subtle cues. "The girls respect you, and I am confident that when we put this deplorable episode behind us, you will guide them with a firm hand and keep them from getting themselves in trouble. We will have them dress more modestly and behave with more decorum, and this sort of problem will never happen again."

I folded my hands in my lap and pressed them together so hard my knuckles turned white. She still thought it was their fault. She was not going to do anything to protect them. She would order a few small and meaningless changes, and then all would be forgotten and things would return to the way they used to be.

"And if you are worried about how this will reflect on you," the queen went on, "well, there are so many rumors by now that only a few people will ever know the truth. Many seem to think that Helena killed Zamborski and tried to kill Dantyszek because of their reformist sympathies—her father is a staunch Catholic known for his speeches against reformists in Baranów, where that movement has been on the rise. They also say that poor Don Mantovano had to have been secretly a Luther supporter and that she found him out. It is preposterous, of course, but better that than if they believed Helena's story about his supposed infidelity to his wife. It would have been most unseemly," she concluded.

I kept staring at my hands. There was no hope of persuading her. Not only because of her stubborn nature, the difficulty she had in letting go of her beliefs once she had formed them, but also because it was clear that she did not care for the truth if it was inconvenient, and she certainly did not care about Helena.

I took a deep breath. "I will think on it, Your Majesty. I still have a long way to go before I am fully recovered, and I must prepare to testify at Helena's trial." The thought caused a painful constriction in the pit of my stomach.

"We will discuss it again after ... it is all over," she said more softly.

She rose and I followed her out of the chamber, wiping the tears that finally spilled when her back was to me.

When I returned to my bed, I curled up on my good side and covered myself with the blanket up to my forehead. I had told the infirmarian that I did not wish to see anybody else that day. A black melancholy descended on me, and if I had felt stronger, I would have gone to my chamber, packed a few belongings, gone out the gate, and never looked back. I would make my way to Bari, throw myself at my mother's mercy and her matchmaking schemes, and live out my life as a lady on some minor rural estate, supervising winemaking or olive harvests.

But I could not do that. I was still too ill.

And there was Konarski.

16

March 15ᵗʰ, 1520

I went to see Helena in her jail cell in the early morning. It was still dark outside; only the first red streaks of dawn could be seen on the eastern horizon on the other side of the river.

It was our first private meeting since the events of the night of the Epiphany. Helena was calm, almost serene, and although she was thinner than before, she did not look unwell or emaciated. Konarski had paid the guards to take care of her, and they must have. The rushes on the floor were much cleaner than the ones I had seen in Maciek's cell, and there was even a small coal brazier in a corner that made the air tolerably warm.

A week earlier, I had testified at her trial. She had been just as calm throughout those proceedings, refusing to speak a word or answer any questions beyond the short confession she had made to Chancellor Stempowski after her arrest. Dressed in a plain linen gown without a headdress, her auburn hair pulled tightly back from her face and covered by a simple white coif, she sat quietly between two guards. She did not look at anybody—not the judges, not me, nor any of the witnesses that had been called forward, including Jan Dantyszek. Neither did she acknowledge her father, who had come down from Lipiny. He was a pitiful sight, white-haired and gaunt, a broken man who was a shadow of the jovial baron of voracious appetites Konarski's cousin had once described to us.

The trial started at nine o'clock before a packed chamber of the royal court, which was located on the ground floor of a somber two-story building next door to Baszta Sandomierska. But after the chief magistrate had read out the indictment, based mainly on what I had told the chancellor while still recovering in the infirmary, as well as the contents of Helena's chest, the crowd began to thin out. The spectators realized that this would not be a case of a religiously motivated crime in which they could take sides; nor would it offer a sordid tale of an affair ended in murder committed in a jealous rage that could be water for the gossip mill. It seemed the fact that Helena had not wanted the men's advances took the excitement out of it.

By the time we returned from the midday break, only a few stalwarts remained, including the Princess of Montefusco. Thus the queen had been right in her own way—the truth did not matter. I imagined how, for years to come, people would talk about those events in the way that suited them best and that created the most dramatic effect. A legend would grow around Helena that would have little to do with what really happened. In that, I would be proven correct.

From the whispered conversations around me, I could sense that the predominant feeling toward Helena was one of hostility. Her refusal to speak in her own defense and her indifferent demeanor were taken to mean a lack of remorse, which in turn fueled talk of her evil nature, a rot that had penetrated her to her core. She had committed the murders out of a lust for blood, she had enjoyed them, she must be a witch ... I had to dig my fingernails into my palms to stop myself from screaming as I sat on a bench awaiting my turn to testify.

I knew that what I would tell the judges might send Helena to the executioner's block, and the thought of it had tormented me for weeks, preventing me from sleeping and taking away my appetite. When I finally stood before the six men in their black robes and chains of office, I was still so weak that I had to lean on the railing, and the chief magistrate had to send for a chair for me despite the rules to the contrary.

After I finished recounting the events of that fateful night, it was the turn of the lawyer assigned to Helena's defense to present his case. He was a short thickset man with neatly combed graying hair poking from under his cap, and his large black robe made him look like a fat crow. I cannot remember his name, but I still remember his tired-looking face dominated by heavy bags under his eyes. To his look of tiredness was added that of boredom so that it was hard to imagine anyone less suited for the job than he was in that moment. He was not sitting near his client, nor did he consult with her during the proceedings, although, to be fair, she did not appear interested in his services either. I knew from Konarski that she had refused to meet with him.

He stood up from his table, on which he had been shuffling papers all throughout my testimony.

"The accused Helena Lipińska's weak and feminine nature is what predisposed her to react irrationally to a difficult situation," he stated by way of an opening.

The judges nodded sympathetically as I tried to guess where he was going with it. A "difficult situation" was an understatement for what had happened to Helena. That said, I was sure that the judges would see it as a mitigating circumstance if the lawyer made a convincing case. I barely dared to breathe as I waited for him to explain why it warranted leniency.

"On the night of the twenty-fifth of December, the Feast of the Birth of Our Savior, she finally became guilt-ridden due to the carnal act committed outside of the lawful bonds of matrimony and attacked Kasper Zamborski with his own dagger in a manner that resulted in his death."

"But—" I began to protest before a strong pull of Konarski's grasp on my wrist made me sit back down on the bench. The chief magistrate frowned at me, then motioned to the lawyer to continue.

"It was a crime committed in a moment of hysteria, and thus I ask the court to show mercy to the accused."

I turned to Konarski, appalled. "How can he say such a thing? He has completely ignored what I have just told the judges," I hissed, making a supreme effort to keep my voice low.

He shook his head and pointed with his chin at the door. I understood his meaning immediately: if I disturbed the proceedings, I would be escorted out. I could not let that happen, not until I was able to speak again.

The lawyer went on in that vein for a good deal longer, occasionally wiping sweat from his forehead with a kerchief, his torturous argument, if indeed it was an argument at all, leading nowhere.

When he rested his case, I rose, and this time Konarski did not try to stop me. By now I had brought my emotions under control and spoke calmly. "Your Honor, I wish to say one more thing if you will graciously permit me to speak."

I was aware that there was a good chance the magistrate would refuse me. But whether on the strength of the role I had played in discovering Helena's crimes or because I was close to the queen, he reluctantly allowed me to speak. "Go ahead, Contessa Sanseverino, but pray be brief. We haven't got all day," he added sourly.

"Thank you." The few remaining spectators turned to me with curiosity, a sentiment that was notably absent from the judges' faces. I took a deep breath. "I feel obliged to repeat what I already made clear in my testimony, namely that the 'carnal act' that was just referred to was not one that Helena Lipińska had invited, encouraged, or to which she had willingly acquiesced." I looked pointedly at the lawyer, who scowled back at me then resumed shuffling the papers, an action that did not seem to lead to any specific outcome. Underneath his robe his shoulders moved with a barely perceptible shrug.

"In the months that followed, she endured anger and shame that eventually pushed her to seek justice in the absence of any other recourse. Should you condone or license a murder committed under such duress? No. But you can show understanding and compassion, for hers was a crime born of another crime, and of fear and desperation, not of a wicked and wanton nature.

"I appeal to Your Excellencies to imagine what it would be like for you to learn that your wife"—I locked eyes with one of the judges—"or your daughter"—I turned my gaze to another—"or your sister"—I nodded toward the chief magistrate—"had fallen victim to a similarly foul deed?" I pointed at Helena with a final and desperate appeal. "Do not let this young woman who was so cruelly mistreated be counted among the traitors, footpads, and other villains who have passed through the king's prison on their way to the block or the scaffold!"

As I uttered those words, Helena's father, finally overcome, let out a loud cry and fell forward from his bench. He was caught by two younger men seated on both sides of him—probably relatives, for Helena had no brothers—who guided him out of the chamber as he groaned and his legs kept buckling under him.

That was the only time Helena betrayed any emotion. She squeezed her eyes shut, and the muscles of her throat worked to try to stifle a sob until her father was gone.

The magistrate cleared his throat and turned his red-rimmed watery eyes on me. "Are you finished, signora?"

"I am."

"We shall now close these proceedings," he announced. He did not look at Helena. In fact, few of them had paid much attention to her throughout the trial. "We shall retreat to our chamber to deliberate on the sentence for the accused."

I remained in the nearly empty courtroom with Konarski, Lucrezia, Carmignano, and the princess until the judges came back an hour later and the verdict was pronounced.

Helena was found guilty of the murders of Kasper Zamborski and Ludovico Mantovano, and the kidnapping of Jan Dantyszek with the intent of killing him. As a member of the *szlachta*, a noblewoman, she was to be beheaded rather than hanged.

Lucrezia squeezed my hand, and I saw blood drain from her face. From the chill that assailed me despite the warmth of the chamber, I knew that the same thing had happened to me. The princess rose without a word to any of us and swiftly walked out, no doubt to be the first to deliver the news to the queen.

On my other side, I heard Konarski's voice. "You did all you could to save her. You spoke very bravely in front of the judges."

"I did nothing." I shook my head, staring as the guards led Helena out through a side door and back to the tower. "I did nothing."

Helena's father was not there when the magistrate read out the sentence in his flat, indifferent tone, and that was a small blessing at least.

◈

On the morning of March 15th, the scheduled day for the execution, I went to see her in the jail.

We stood in silence for a long while, Helena gazing at me steadily without any hint of anger, fear, or guilt. It was as if she were incapable of feeling anything, or perhaps she was simply reconciled to her fate. And just as in that moment when I found her in the cellar with Dantyszek, too many questions crowded in my head.

"I should have asked to see that letter from your father summoning you home," I said finally. In the past few weeks, as I had blamed myself—and despite what Konarski had said in the court chamber—I had come to believe that at least some of this calamity could have been avoided if I had been more diligent in my duties.

That March morning I felt the guilt sharply, and although time would blunt its edges, it is a sentiment that I have carried with me to this day.

The corners of Helena's lips lifted in a small smile, but her eyes remained lightless. "You should have. Maybe then Dantyszek would not have missed two days having his beard trimmed and perfumed, and the two deaths would have gone unsolved due to the ineptitude of the chancellor's men."

I could not help but admire her wit, and on a day like that. A purr of laughter curled in her throat, white and exposed in the square neckline of her gown. "Your suspicions about me sneaking out to see a lover would seem to have been confirmed," she went on in a slightly mocking tone, "and you would have chastised me about it again, but then you would have forgotten about it because, like our king, deep down you don't like confrontation."

She was correct in that too, but still I was disheartened to find myself so transparent. Yet this was not about me. "Why did you not tell anyone back in June that Zamborski had violated you?"

"Because—as he himself said—nobody would have believed me." She was still speaking in that cool, detached tone, so different from the passion and vehemence of two months before. She had lost her gambit, but she had taken her revenge and regained her peace of mind. Nothing else seemed to matter.

I wanted to deny her words, but I found myself unable to do so. Not after my meeting with the queen in the infirmary, and not after I had seen the judges conduct her trial. And how would *I* have reacted without the trail of death left in the wake of Helena's rage? Would I have offered a sympathetic ear or dismissed it as a misunderstanding, or, even worse, her own fault? I could not answer that in good conscience.

"You see?" She smiled again, seeing the uncertainty in my face. Was I truly not able to hide anything from the eyes of the world? "But even if they had believed me, they would not have cared. They would have said that I had flirted with him and enticed him because they see the maids of honor like Lucrezia or Magdalena, the sweet eyes they make at the courtiers, and what is a man to do?"

I was struck by the similarity between her words, even if spoken mockingly, and what the queen had said, and again I could not deny it. But there was something else I wanted to know. "Even if that happened and you were dealt with unjustly and sent home with your reputation ruined, surely that would have been better than what is awaiting you today?"

She tilted her head, the gesture almost teasing. "Would it?" she asked, narrowing her eyes. Then she straightened up again. "No, it would not." Her voice hardened. "And I regret *nothing.*"

I opened my mouth to say something about her soul, but I thought better of it. It was a matter between her and her confessor if she chose to avail herself of one.

"But I am glad that it ended with just Zamborski and Mantovano," she added unexpectedly. "You were right, Dantyszek *was* innocent. And who knows"—she paused, and something sinister in those three words made my skin prickle—"if I hadn't ended up in this cell, if I had returned to the court in a few months—which is what I planned to do after killing Dantyszek and leaving the city secretly—I might not have resisted killing again."

I felt the blood in my veins turn to ice. "What do you mean?" I asked, my throat so dry the sound was barely audible.

"I *mean* that I am not sure I could have stomached Lucrezia or Magdalena's thoughtless, reckless behavior," she replied with a hardness in her voice that told me she was not jesting.

"But as it is, your curiosity has sealed my fate," she added with a hint of amusement. "And saved *them*."

I could find no words to respond to that. There was nothing left to say between us, and the sooner this sad story was behind us the better. Then I could start trying to put my life back together from the pieces into which it had shattered, and she ... well, I did not know what awaited her afterward. Perhaps nothing at all.

I turned to leave, but her words reached me again. "Thank you, Caterina."

I paused with my hand on the door's rusty iron handle. Her voice was quiet and sad, the kind of sadness that envelops you like a heavy, wet cloak, making it hard to breathe. I was not able to look at her.

"For speaking up for me, even though my case was hopeless, and even though I would have killed you had things gone differently. There aren't many people out there—especially at the court—who would do that." Her voice caught at the end.

Still staring at the rushes on the floor, I said, "I hope you find peace, Helena. I will pray for it."

And I have, every day since then.

I left the cell. But before I descended the narrow staircase, I leaned against the cold stones of the wall and let my tears flow for the last time.

Executions were carried out across the road from the tower, on a low hill that sloped gently toward the meadows on the riverbank. It was the same riverbank where, on a summer night nine months earlier, the first act of this tragedy had taken place against the background of dancing flames, laughter, and singing. The day was cool, and patchy clouds scuttled across the sky, now flooding the world with sunshine, now plunging it into a somber shade. But there was an unmistakable scent of spring in the air, sweet and moist, a spring Helena would never see again.

A block had been set up where the scaffold normally stood—noble executions were rare and tended not to draw as many spectators from the town and surrounding villages unless the condemned was well known. Neither Helena nor her victims were, and the crowd was small and quiet. It consisted mainly of a gaggle of older women, some just curious, but a few looking grim as they stood shaking their heads and whispering to one another in low voices. I had feared the hostility that I had seen in the court, but those people stayed away or found another distraction to keep them occupied, or perhaps they were there but had discovered some sympathy in their hearts. Whatever the reason, I was thankful.

I came with Lucrezia, the only maid of honor who had expressed the wish to attend. I had advised her against it, but she insisted. In the past few weeks, she had taken to dressing more plainly and abandoned most of her jewelry, especially the strings of pearls she had once loved. I doubted that the queen's newfound strictness accounted for it, for although Her Majesty had given the girls a speech, none of the others had taken such drastic steps, and gradually things were returning to the way they used to be. No, Lucrezia's was a more profound transformation, whose nature I had not yet fully grasped.

A little apart from us stood Piotr Gamrat, the queen's Polish advisor, dressed somberly in black but wearing, as usual, one of his elaborate caps to hide his growing baldness. Next to him was Chancellor Stempowski, his arthritic fingers clasped over his stomach and his lips set in a grim line. I wanted to be angry at him, but I could not. Perhaps I had no emotions left in me, or perhaps it was because he had ultimately just done his job, efficiently and dispassionately, as had the judges, in the only way they all knew how.

Two other members of the court were in attendance: the Princess of Montefusco and Doctor Baldazzi. Rather than wearing a typical garish gown and dripping with diamonds, the princess looked very different in black lace that enveloped her from head to toe. There was no rouge on her face, and she kept dabbing her eyes with a silk handkerchief, although from where I stood, they looked dry enough to me. I had a strong suspicion that she was there mainly to have something to talk about for the next six months, but perhaps I am too harsh. After all, it was her inexhaustible curiosity and the desire to be at the center of events that may well have saved my life.

Doctor Baldazzi, on the other hand, looked genuinely stricken. I had run into him at the entrance to the tower earlier that morning, after I came down from my last meeting with Helena. He was on his way up to see her and offer her a vial of valerian oil to dissolve in wine, which would calm her and dull her senses. I waited downstairs, and he returned not ten minutes later saying that she had refused any help. She would not go to her death dumb like a beast to slaughter, she had said, but she would be her own mistress and face it on her own terms. Now he looked pale, there were beads of sweat on his forehead, and he could not hide the shaking of his hands.

I looked around for Helena's father, but he was not there, and who could blame him? Dantyszek was absent, too—after the trial he went home to continue his recovery, but I suspected that he would be back in Kraków once the dust settled. He was not one to stay away from the glamour of the royal court for long. In that, too, I would be proven right.

The cathedral clock struck midday, and all eyes turned to the tower, looming cold and rusty red at the southern foot of the castle hill. How many had suffered and died in there, and would Helena's ghost join them today? Unlike the unfortunate town councilors of the previous century, she was not innocent. But was she truly guilty if she was forced so violently onto the path that had brought her to this place? Again, I hoped that there was nothing for her afterward—if no joy, then also no more pain. I knew that was what she wanted too.

Shortly after the bell fell silent, the side gate opened, and the first person to emerge was the executioner. He was a bull of a man and was dressed in a black leather jerkin whose seams appeared on the verge of snapping over his thick arms. His thighs were like the trunks of an old oak, the powerful muscles knotted underneath the tight hose, and his brown leather boots had dark stains on them that could only have come from one source. His head was covered with a fitted cap with holes cut out for the eyes and mouth, and he carried an axe that looked almost like a toy in his meaty hands, although it was sharp and deadly.

I shivered when I saw him, and Lucrezia clung to my side with a low whimper. I think in that moment, both of us regretted coming. Then Helena stepped out, flanked by two guards with halberds, and I was glad I was there, even though my heart hammered against my ribs as if it would crack them. If Lucrezia and I had not been there, Helena would have died with only those impassive servants of the state and a coterie of curious crones around her. I hoped that seeing our familiar faces, faces of those who bore her no ill will and were not indifferent, would make it easier for her, less frightening.

I could see that she was frightened. Her lips were white, they moved as if in a silent prayer or some other exhortation, and she could not tear her wide eyes away from the wood block, stained dark like the executioner's boots. But she continued walking, never stopping or even slowing her pace, her legs never buckling under her, and I was glad of that too. I would have hated to see her manhandled by those guards or by the executioner in her last moments.

She stood in front of the block. Her hair had already been gathered up into a tight bun, and her neck stood exposed. She wore the same plain black dress with a low neckline in which I had seen her that morning, and no cloak. A gust of wind swept from the east, carrying the fresh scent of pine from across the river where the forest was awakening to a new life after the winter's slumber. Helena's dress fluttered, clinging to her hips and legs. With her pallor and her slim figure, she looked dignified and soulful, like a martyr from an old painting or a stained-glass window I had seen in a church somewhere. But unlike a painted martyr, she was a woman of flesh and blood, and just then it seemed like such a waste of a young life and a good mind, and for what? Already she was known as the unnatural female killer, that transgression far graver than the cause of her crimes.

Looking at her in those last moments, I doubted that she thought of herself as a martyr—a martyr died to prove the world's injustice or to affect a change with her sacrifice. But there had been no talk of a new code of conduct for the courtiers, no attempt to help women find redress if they were wronged. The only time I had mentioned it to the queen, she said that given the number of short-lived affairs that occurred at the court, it would be difficult to tell real cases from those motivated by jealousy or revenge. Then she repeated that if we kept a close eye on the girls and ensured that they behaved properly, such a thing would never happen again. If Helena's death had a deeper meaning, I could not see it.

The executioner motioned for her to kneel. She locked eyes with me then, and I would remember their look—both resigned and defiant—for the rest of my life. I admired her in that moment. I do not think I would have the strength to remain so poised, not to scream, or struggle, or faint. I knew that she saw that admiration in my face, for her lips were touched by a ghost of a smile. Then, after a small hesitation, which, no doubt from long habit, the executioner patiently observed with the axe crossed at his chest, she laid her head on the block so that her chin rested in the little indentation, just above a wicker basket that had been placed below. It, too, had rusty smudges all over it. That whole cursed ground, the very earth beneath our feet, was soaked in blood. My chest felt as if it were encased in tight armor. I could not draw a breath.

It was then that I heard footsteps behind me, rustling on the remnants of last year's grass. They were familiar footsteps; I could already pick them out from among hundreds of others. That alone allowed me to take a breath again, albeit a shallow and painful one. The executioner planted himself on Helena's side, his heavy legs wide apart, and raised the axe over his head. I could not have moved if I wanted to. I felt a hand on my arm, the same way he had held it that night we walked back from visiting Maciek in the tower. But this time his grip was stronger. He knew before I did.

The executioner froze for a brief moment with the axe in position. I closed my eyes, shutting them tight as if that could somehow also block my ears against the sound. But it could not. The blade cut the air with a swish that ended in a dull thud, and I gasped, staggering to one side. If Konarski had not been there, pulling me against him, I would have gone down. He held me so that my back was to the block, but he could do nothing about the awful sounds of the men moving about, lifting things, moving them, and then the squeaky noise of the cart being pulled away down toward the tower. Next to us, Lucrezia sobbed loudly, and I could hear wailing from where the women were gathered.

I did not cry, but for a while I could not control my breathing, which came fast and shallow as if I had run a great distance. My fingers dug into the leather of Konarski's doublet so hard I was afraid I would tear it. We remained like that for a long time, until the women's cries subsided and their footsteps retreated and died in the distance, until the princess and Baldazzi, Stempowski and Gamrat, and even Lucrezia left to return to the castle.

Then we, too, made our way back slowly as the bell struck the half hour, a mournful and solitary sound. Clouds came and blotted out the sun, and an increasingly angry wind tugged at our cloaks. I was glad of the wind; there was something purifying about it. A few weeks before, in the infirmary, I had wondered if I would ever be able to find peace again. Now I knew I would, one day. There was time to grieve and time to be comforted. Tragedies passed, lives ended, but nature—whether in a storm, sunshine, cloud, or a gust of wind—was eternal, impervious to the evil perpetrated by us who are but brief guests here.

Behind us, the low hill stood empty, absorbing the fresh blood and quietly waiting for more, patient but never satisfied.

EPILOGUE

Bari, Kingdom of Naples
March 1560

I stayed in the queen's service until Prince Zygmunt—now King Zygmunt August—was born the following summer; then I took my leave and returned home. By then the queen understood how miserable I was in my position, and I think she also knew the reason for it. But we never spoke of it, for, in truth, it would have made no difference. When it came to women and their role within families, Bona—that most rebellious and independent of Polish queens—was very traditional. It was her upbringing, and her role as a monarch intent on preserving the power and securing the future of a kingdom that had always functioned in certain ways, that made her that way. Perhaps that is understandable. But I had no such obligations; despite my own precarious situation, I could choose whether to be a part of it or to retreat from the court and make another life. I chose the latter and she released me, and on the first day of September of the year 1520, I left for Bari.

The Teutonic War was never the kind of success that Poland had achieved a hundred years earlier. The early offensive stalled due to bouts of bad weather, but artillery was eventually sent from Kraków in the spring, and it assisted Marshal Firlej's troops in capturing several northern strongholds. But instead of insisting on the Order's immediate surrender, the king accepted a ceasefire, which Grand Master Albrecht von Hohenzollern promptly broke once Danish and German mercenaries arrived to help him. And so the fighting continued until a truce was signed in April 1521, even though Poland was in a position to demand a full peace treaty. It was none other than Chancellor Stempowski who managed to persuade the king not to push for it, and the truce was widely criticized. Who knows how many more times that ages-long conflict would have flared up had it not been for the Reformation? It was that, more than the military efforts of Poland and Lithuania, that finally weakened the Order sufficiently to lead to its secularization and disbandment in the year 1525.

Helena's father died within a month of his daughter's execution, and so ended that ancient and proud line that traced its origins to the previous ruling dynasty. The estate at Lipiny passed to some minor relative, and then was sold off at auction with part of it acquired by Konarski's other uncle—Konstanty's father—who lived in Baranów.

Lucrezia Alifio, as I have already said, changed in a way that made her hardly recognizable. The queen soon forgot about her new strict rules of behavior, paying no more attention to them than she had before. But it was as if Lucrezia had donned a garment of perpetual mourning. She sold off her colorful silk and brocade gowns and all of her jewelry, and with the proceeds, she paid for an antependium depicting the scene of Christ's Resurrection for an altar in one of the cathedral's chapels. She never spoke about her transformation, at least not to me, but she was the only one of the queen's maids of honor to never marry. She remained in Bona's service until she died in 1547.

Doctor Baldazzi returned to Italy the same year I did. I never understood the queen's dislike of Baldazzi, for despite his oiliness and his many quirks, he was a competent physician, at least for those who were genuinely ill. And it is doubtful that she made a good bargain by replacing him with Giovanni Andrea Valentino, a medic from Modena who later turned out to be a spy for the Dukes of Mantua and Ferrara.

Giovanna d'Aragona, Princess of Montefusco, went on to marry twice more (she had already been widowed by the time she joined the court in Kraków). She outlived those husbands, too, the last one having succumbed on their honeymoon. The last I heard of her, she had moved to Paris, but that was many years ago, and I have no knowledge of what happened to her after that.

Adam Latalski served briefly as the queen's secretary, but whether because of the dullness of the state bureaucracy, the intrigues of the court, or Don Mantovano's unquiet spirit that some claimed haunted the chamber where he had died, the poet left the position within a year to return to his literary pursuits and to teach rhetoric at the University of Kraków. To my knowledge, he never did translate *Il Cortegiano*.

What of Dantyszek, you will ask? Like a phoenix, he rose from the ashes—or as near to ashes as he had come on that fateful night—to become one of the queen's most trusted envoys, advisors, and indeed friends. He penned a poem titled *Epithalamium Reginae Bonae*, in which he praised the attributes of his patroness's mind and spirit. He also served on many diplomatic missions for her, including one that involved (unsuccessfully) securing her Milanese inheritance after her mother died. For seven years, Dantyszek was the Polish ambassador to the imperial court, where he staunchly advocated Bona's anti-Teutonic policies. He traveled far and wide, from Spain to England to Arabia, and wrote extensively about those lands before embarking on a no less distinguished ecclesiastical career.

Yes, Jan Dantyszek became a priest in later life. Thus he laid to rest any suspicions that he may have abandoned his Roman allegiance. He reached the rank of Bishop of Warmia, and in that capacity was even nominated as a papal legate to His Holiness Clement VII. From the news that has reached me over the years, I gather that he, too, underwent a deep transformation. With great dedication, he took to eradicating loose morals among his flock, and he was ever vigilant when it came to the celibacy of the clerics under his jurisdiction. The latter, I suspect, was a more challenging task.

Had the brush with death changed him? Was he remorseful? Or was it a natural consequence of aging, a time when many of us become more reflective and critical of the excesses of our youth? Who knows, but he turned out to be one of the few protagonists of this sad story to go on to rebuild his life and make it better than before, and that must be a good thing. He died in October 1548.

Time proved Queen Bona to be a capable administrator of her crown possessions, which she expanded vastly over the subsequent years. Through a wise and fruitful management of those lands, she increased the Jagiellonian fortune and filled crown coffers with gold while helping to overhaul the outdated farming practices throughout the commonwealth and enabling the construction of new roads and bridges. But as her successes grew, so did the hostility of the aristocracy. Chief among them, Stempowski remained a thorn in her side until he died, some time in 1532. He and many other wealthy, greedy, and complacent landowners considered the queen's economic activities unnatural for a woman, and her gains illegitimate for a foreigner. But she pressed on, never wavering, and she became richer than the lot of them. Nonetheless, for those achievements, she paid with an unjustly blackened reputation—and more.

When I returned to Bari in the autumn of 1520, I did not go alone. I was accompanied by Sebastian Konarski, whom I married in a small ceremony in the cathedral's St. Mary's Chapel that August. Except for his uncle the Bishop of Kraków, who presided over our vows, there were only two other people in attendance, both as witnesses—the queen and Konstanty Konarski, my husband's incorrigible cousin and a veteran of the last Teutonic War. Before he died in 1542, he had visited us several times in Bari, leaving, Sebastian often said, a trail of offspring in his wake. We laughed at that, but it is quite possibly true.

By remarrying, I lost my widow's income from the Sanseverino estate. In recompense, the queen sent me off with a chest full of linen, shirts, and nightgowns of Flemish cotton embroidered with silk and gold thread; a Persian rug; a silver ewer and a matching bowl; a pair of silver candlesticks; and several rolls of cordovan leather wallpaper printed with artichoke and ostrich egg motifs, the latter from her own dowry that she had no use for at Wawel. With this trousseau of sorts, and a small pension Konarski received after King Zygmunt elevated him to the rank of *eques auratus*, Knight of the Golden Spur, we settled on my family's much diminished land and became almond farmers.

I was glad to be back in the house in which I had spent my earliest years, before the convent and my first marriage, with expansive views of groves, vineyards, and white cliffs rising from the blue-green sea. But there is one thing I have not done since the day I returned: I have not gone down to the cellar. I tried a few times early on, but it was as if my body hit a wall, invisible but hard, at the threshold. No amount of willpower would quell the blind panic that rose inside me at the prospect of descending into that dark and chill space below ground. And so I never have.

That small inconvenience notwithstanding, I was luckier than the other ladies in the queen's service, indeed most women I know, in that I was able to choose the man I married. Widows have somewhat more freedom in that regard, and I had no father to stand in my way, though I doubt he would have.

My mother grumbled at first and looked upon my new foreign husband with a good deal of suspicion, but even she eventually took to him. He has a way of making people love him.

We had three children. Our eldest is a daughter, Aurora—a name I chose to pay a subtle tribute to Helena, who had died nearly two years to the day before she was born. She is named in the memory of that dawn when we had our last conversation. I choose to remember Helena not as she was at the execution block, pale and wide-eyed. In my mind, she is forever serene and unbroken, the way she was on that morning I last visited her. I told Aurora the story only a few years ago. She is a widow herself now—her husband having been set upon and knifed by brigands on his way from doing business in Rome— and we cried together. Then I told her that I was proud she had shown the same dignity through her own ordeals as Helena had done all those years before.

Sebastian and I also had two boys. The first we lost in infancy; then, when I was almost forty and thought I would have no more children, Giulio arrived. Although he was christened with the Italian name, at home we call him Julian, the way his name would be said in Polish, for he was named after his paternal grandfather.

He was a healthy boy for the first few years of his life, then he began to suffer bouts of fevers that are common in our southern lands and to which some people appear to be more prone than others. He would recover from each bout, but within months he would inevitably become ill again. We brought many doctors to see him, but none of them knew how to prevent these recurrences, and the weakness was beginning to affect his growth. I was starting to despair at the prospect of losing another child when a letter arrived from Lucrezia, with whom I had carried an intermittent correspondence over the years and to whom I had mentioned my son's health troubles. She suggested that we bring him to Kraków, where the royal physicians might be more helpful, for King Zygmunt was old and ill by then and had surrounded himself with some of the best medical minds of Europe.

It was a big decision, and we worried about how we would be able to support ourselves in Poland, but we were desperate to save our son. We even considered writing to the king to ask if Sebastian could reenter the royal service. Then news reached us that my husband's last surviving brother had died without an heir and left his estate outside of Kraków to him. Within days, we packed up our household, left the farm in the caretaker's hands, and made our way back north.

Thus my path was to cross that of Queen Bona once again, something I did not expect to happen when I left her court twenty-five years earlier. Not only that, it would send me on yet another journey with profound consequences for the queen, and—as it turned out—for the monarchy as well. Perhaps one of these nights I will write the story of that reunion, the mission with which she entrusted me, and the strange and dark events that occurred in Lithuania in the year 1545.

I am now back in Bari again, having returned permanently four years ago. For the past few weeks, sleep has often eluded me, and when I do sleep, I am tormented by nightmares. This anniversary of Helena's death, like no other before it, has brought back the terrible memories from forty years ago in all their vivid, horrible detail.

Why are they haunting me again now? Maybe because I am old. For I am past my sixty-fifth year, and although I still feel well enough and my eyesight is surprisingly strong, I am slower than I used to be, and I tire more quickly. When I lie down and try to sleep, the images I had banished to the farthest corners of my mind assault me and keep me awake. Perhaps writing this will help me reclaim some of my lost peace.

I once saved a life, and there is a great deal of satisfaction in that. My only regret is that I was not able to help Helena, and this will not cease until I am no more. But what I will leave behind is this testimony, that it may serve as a warning. Those who heed it will be all the better for it; those who do not should expect that sooner or later their deeds will catch up to them.

Perhaps one day a world will dawn in which similar accounts will no longer need to be written.

Historical Note

During the Christmas season of 1519, King Zygmunt Stary (the Old) was away from Kraków. He had decamped to Toruń (in Royal Prussia) to be closer to the theater of the expected military activities against the Teutonic Order. Queen Bona, pregnant for the second time, remained behind at Wawel. I took liberty with this historical fact by placing the king with his wife in the capital during the two-week period in which this story is set.

The group known in Latin as *bibones et comedones* really existed at King Zygmunt's court. I was a bit surprised when I stumbled upon it in my research, but it makes sense. The Renaissance was a period of repudiation of the medieval philosophy that glorified earthly suffering as preparatory to eternal happiness after death. As the arts and the sciences of the humanist era focused more on this world, its beauty and its inner workings, many people also began to consider the pleasures of the flesh as important. As a result, sexual behaviors and attitudes that had been condemned or marginalized in earlier periods became more widely accepted. In addition to drinking and lovemaking, the society's members occupied themselves with producing poems and pamphlets that satirized life at the court.

Chancellor Aleksander Stempowski, although a fictional character, is based on the real-life Crown Grand Chancellor Krzysztof Szydłowiecki. The latter was King Zygmunt's childhood friend and trusted advisor who was also a Habsburg partisan, and a political (and possibly personal) enemy of Queen Bona's.

The queen's agricultural reforms did not begin until somewhat later in her tenure, but the nobility's resistance and hostility (including that of the chancellor) to her deep involvement in a range of state and foreign affairs are a fact. The conflict came to a head in the mid-1530s and gave rise to a negative and largely undeserved reputation of the queen as a meddler, gold-digger, and even poisoner.

Most of the main characters in this story are fictional, with the following caveats and exceptions:

Kasper Zamborski is a composite character based on several historical figures known to have been members of the *bibones et comedones* society.

Jan Dantyszek was a real person, a distinguished courtier, diplomat, and later a high-ranking church official who in his youth was a drinker, womanizer, and one of the most enthusiastic members of the *bibones et comedones*. The storyline involving his kidnapping is fictional, but everything else about him as presented in this novel is true.

In 1519, Antonio Carmignano was the treasurer of Bona's court in Kraków. Piotr Gamrat did not join the queen's circle until 1524, and, like Dantyszek, he later embarked on a church career. He became the Archbishop of Gniezno and Primate of Poland, but was criticized by his contemporaries for leading a dissolute lifestyle. Bona, however, valued his loyalty (he was the only advisor who never betrayed her trust, she is said to have once claimed) and promoted his ecclesiastical career.

Of course, Queen Bona (1494-1557) and King Zygmunt (1467-1548) are historical figures, although the storylines involving them are fictionalized. That said, I tried to imbue the Bona of this story with as many traits of the real queen as possible. She is portrayed as highly intelligent, loyal to her friends and servants, a lover of music and art, but also a woman who was haughty, argumentative, and irascible. The latter traits often pitted her against the Polish nobility, which was more conservative in its attitudes toward women and their role within a family (even if it was a royal family) than was customary in Italy at the time.

Chancellor Szydłowiecki, as already suggested, was a major Habsburg supporter within the king's circle of advisors. It was a misguided position given the almost invariably antagonistic attitude of the German Habsburgs toward Poland, not just during Szydłowiecki's lifetime but for centuries afterwards. He seems to have been quite vain and greedy, and some historians believe he may have been a spy for Emperor Maximilian and perhaps even for the Teutonic Order's Grand Master (and King Zygmunt's own nephew) Albrecht von Hohenzollern.

Young Beata, who was raised alongside the king's legitimate children, was indeed a daughter of his former mistress Katarzyna Telniczanka. The child's "official" father, however, was Telniczanka's husband, whom she married in 1510, after the end of her affair with the king. Nonetheless, contemporary rumors claimed that Beata was the king's child. It is a testament to Bona's generosity of spirit that she allowed the girl to be part of the royal household and later took care of her and her young daughter after Beata became a widow after just a few months of marriage to Prince Illia Ostrogski in 1539.

Thank you for reading *Silent Water*. I hope you enjoyed it. Would you kindly take a few minutes to support independent publishing by leaving a review on Amazon and/or Goodreads? I will greatly appreciate it!

If you want to learn more about my Jagiellon mystery series and stay up to date as I work on the sequel to *Silent Water*, feel free to get in touch via my website's Contact Me form at www.pkadams-author.com or my Facebook Author Page at www.facebook.com/PKAdamsAuthor.

You can also follow me on Twitter @pk_adams

Acknowledgments

I would like to thank Jena Henry, C. P. Lesley, Quenby Solberg, and Jake Conner, who read the full manuscript of *Silent Water*—as well as Elaine Buckley and Ann Marie Carmody, who read extensive excerpts—for their very insightful comments. This novel would not be what it is without your honest and generous feedback, and you have my deepest gratitude.

I am also grateful to Jenny Quinlan for designing another excellent cover, and to Deborah Blume for making the map of Poland-Lithuania under the Jagiellon dynasty. I am in awe of your artistic skills!

About the Author

P.K. Adams is the pen name of Patrycja Podrazik. She has a bachelor's degree from Columbia University and a master's degree in European Studies from Yale University. She is a blogger and historical fiction reviewer at www.pkadams-author. com. Her debut novel, *The Greenest Branch, a Novel of Germany's First Female Physician*, was a semifinalist for the 2018 Chaucer Book Awards for Pre-1750 Historical Fiction. She is a member of the Historical Novel Society and lives in New England.

Excerpt

MIDNIGHT FIRE
A JAGIELLON MYSTERY 2

On the Road to Kraków
Early June 1545

We set out from Bari on a journey that we hoped would save our son's life toward the end of May in the year 1545.

It was altogether different from the grand progress I had made twenty-seven years earlier as a lady-in-waiting to the young Bona Sforza, heiress to the Duchies of Bari and Milan. She was on her way to Kraków to meet her new husband, Zygmunt, King of Poland and Grand Duke of Lithuania. We stopped in Venice to watch carnival festivities, stayed in Graz long enough for a hunt, and sojourned at the court in Vienna, where Emperor Maximilian treated us to a feast in a manner that befitted a future queen. At our final destination we were greeted by cannons booming from the city walls, cheering crowds, and the entire Polish court awaiting us outside of Wawel Cathedral.

This time, we rode in a simple carriage as part of a train of merchants, stopping overnight at travelers' inns, eating the watery stews they all seemed to offer or our own provisions or whatever unspoilt food we managed to buy in villages along the way. But I was glad of the swift pace, for each day brought us closer to the renowned physicians in Kraków who might be able to help our ailing boy.

Glancing at Giulio as we rattled over yet another rutted road, I shuddered to see how frail he appeared. The recurring fevers that afflicted him, starting when he turned four, had stunted his growth and weakened his limbs. He did not look like a boy of nine. How could he? He spent more time in bed than playing outdoors with other children. As a result, his skin had a pale, almost translucent quality, an effect only enhanced by his dark brown eyes with flecks of amber. Those eyes, so like his father's, glowed unnaturally large and bright in his thin face. My old friend Lucrezia Alifio, who still served as a lady-in-waiting to Queen Bona, insisted that the royal physicians in Poland could lessen his suffering, perhaps even cure him. Watching Giulio now, I hoped that this journey would prove her right, for none of the Italian doctors we consulted had succeeded in helping him. I also hoped that Lucrezia told the truth when she wrote that Her Majesty would be glad to see me and happy to help my family in our predicament.

"Do you know what I'd love to see when we get to Konary, Caterina?" Sebastian Konarski, my husband of twenty-five years, said from his seat across the rocking carriage. "I'd love to see the woods still as thick as they were when I was growing up. We'll need a lot of timber for the repairs," he added, appraising the large pines, ashes, and beeches rolling past our carriage windows.

It is not a thing one would normally admit, but the inheritance of Sebastian's family estate after the death of his elder brother Feliks was a godsend to us under current circumstances. Just five miles outside of Kraków, it gave us a place to live and an income to enable us to stay in Poland for as long as necessary to see Giulio restored to health. Sebastian's hopes for abundant wood had a high chance of coming true. Northern Europe was, after all, the land of endless forests. The woods we were traveling through had started in the Austrian territories and continued through Bohemia, which, according to the calculations of the leader of our caravan, should be coming to an end soon. Any moment now, we would cross the borders of the Kingdom of Poland, with less than a hundred miles separating us from Kraków.

The day was hot, but the broad canopy of leaves kept our path in a pleasant shade. After a while, the buzzing of insects and the twittering of birds soothed Giulio and his nurse Cecilia into asleep. Giulio curled up on the same seat Sebastian occupied, and Cecilia's head lolled on her ample chest next to me. After ten days on the road, with fitful nights tossing and turning on uncomfortable pallets and long hours of riding in a carriage with little to relieve the tedium of the journey, I rejoiced to see them able to sleep at last.

"It surprised me to hear that Feliks let the estate decline so much," I said, referring to the letter we had received from Konary's caretaker two weeks before our departure from Bari. We wasted no time in making our decision, putting our affairs in order, and setting out for the north. "But after the death of his son and then his wife," I added on reflection, "perhaps it's no wonder he lost interest in managing his affairs." I winced, realizing that, wrapped up in my own family's troubles, I had not stopped to consider the blows life had delivered to my late brother-in-law. His only son, Adam, thirsting after a soldierly adventure, had joined the army of Jan Tarnowski and headed east to the Grand Duchy to fight alongside the Lithuanians against Moscow. During the battle of Homel in 1535, the boy, only eighteen years old, was struck by an arrow and killed.

"Feliks never recovered from Adam's death." Sebastian's eyes strayed to Giulio with a concern I often saw in them but which he almost never expressed aloud, for fear of adding to my own worries. I had once appreciated his restraint, but these days it seemed like a way to avoid talking as we had in the early years of our marriage—about everything, happy and sad, honestly and openly. I missed those days.

The carriage rocked and shuddered as the wheels hit a rut, and the jolt awoke Cecilia with a start. She opened her eyes, blinked, saw that her charge was still asleep, and promptly nodded off again. I turned to the window, where the forest appeared to be thinning. More sunlight streamed through the tops of the trees, most of which looked like pines. I could not mistake those tall, narrow silhouettes. A sudden breeze hit my nostrils with the pungent odor of sap, which trickled in long rivulets down the ancient trunks.

As the air filled with that sharp, invigorating scent, I recalled with astonishing clarity the March morning when one of Queen Bona's maids of honor, who had been in my charge, was executed outside the royal jail for murdering two men of the court. In the moments before the executioner raised the axe, just such a breeze swooped across the river. Cooler than today's, it too smelled of pine and spring and life. In all the years I lived in the south of Italy, I had seldom encountered that aroma. I did not realize, until now, how its absence had helped me bury the past for so long. But inhaling that fragrance brought back the memories of the injustice Helena Lipińska had suffered and the revenge she took, for which she paid with her life. I knew even before leaving Bari that my return to Poland would force me to revisit that dreadful winter of 1519, but I had not expected it to be so soon or so sudden. The weight that settled on my chest told me that I had overcome my guilt and grief, but not completely. They lurked deep inside me and would last the rest of my life.

We sat for a long time in silence as I contemplated my son's sleeping face and the sheen of sweat on his forehead. I hoped he was simply exhausted, but I feared another bout of fever.

After so many days on the road, we were all ready to stretch our limbs and sleep in a comfortable bed, without having to rise at dawn to spend hours jolted about in a carriage.

At length we entered a sizable village, with solid, lime-washed cottages, busy animal pens, and sounds of clanging metal coming from a smithy somewhere out of sight. After the tiny hamlets of Bohemia, where ramshackle huts were shared with skinny pigs and scrawny chickens, and where people barely eked out a living farming small plots of land, this was the surest sign that we were now in Poland.

"One thing is certain," I said, feeling a new surge of hope. "The countryside has never been so prosperous as it is now due to the queen's reforms." When we left a quarter of a century earlier, Bona had just set out to overhaul the outdated farming practices, to build roads and bridges, all of which would in due course bring a significant increase in revenue for the Crown and make the Jagiellons' fortune one of the largest in Europe. In Bari, which she continued to rule through her representatives, we had only ever *heard* of her successes. Now we could see them with our own eyes. Perhaps we might even benefit from them.

"It will be good for us, too, once we're settled in Konary." Sebastian's words echoed my own thoughts.

But I could not help sounding a cautionary note. "After we complete the repairs."

Sebastian leaned forward and took my hand in his, squeezing it briefly. "Don't worry about that. Whatever the state of the buildings, I'll do everything in my power to restore the estate to what it once was." The fine lines around his eyes softened as he rubbed Giulio's foot. It was a measure of the boy's fatigue that he did not even stir.

With a sting of longing for happier days, I wondered when Giulio had become the main recipient of my husband's affection and caresses. I did not blame Sebastian. Our son's poor health had long been our main preoccupation, leaving little time for ourselves and for each other. And in all fairness, whatever tenderness I missed from Sebastian, he probably missed it from me in equal measure. I sighed, setting the concerns about the state of our marriage aside for later, because whatever he said, I did worry about the renovations, especially their cost.

To save money, Sebastian would supervise the repairs and even spoke of doing some of the work himself. But he was a gentleman by birth who had spent his youth as a royal secretary at the court in Kraków. True, in Italy we had farmed almonds, but Sebastian only managed the estate and kept its books, so the prospect of him doing manual labor made me uneasy. Still, I drew comfort from the calm assurance with which he seemed to approach this new challenge. Having no other choice, I decided to trust in Providence.

We found Konary's buildings in better shape than I feared. On examining its books, however, it became clear that for years the farm had generated barely enough income to cover basic upkeep. We would have to spend much of the money we had brought with us to fix leaky roofs and broken shutters, replace rusty hinges on the doors of the grain storehouse, and clean out the barn occupied by a handful of animals, although large enough to accommodate a hundred head of cattle.

A few days after our arrival, we took the estate's only carriage—its chipped paint and worn wheels suggesting that it, too, would require replacement soon—and drove to Kraków. We wanted to visit Sebastian's sister Emilia, who lived with her prosperous merchant husband on a street not far from Wawel Hill.

As we emerged from the wooded tract, I gasped at the familiar panorama of the city with its slanted red roofs. Kraków had spread out in every direction since the last time I saw it. But the proud bulk of the castle above the silver ribbon of the Wisła still dominated the capital, timeless as the river itself. Its shape had changed somewhat due to the demolition of the east wing in the 1520s and subsequent new construction; yet it was still the Wawel I remembered, encircled by a stone wall that looked gray in the rain and almost white in the sun, with the copper-domed bell towers of the cathedral watching over the royal residence.

The castle held a special and conflicted place in my heart. Within its walls, terrible crimes had been committed on my watch, lives and futures destroyed. But I had also met Sebastian there and begun a new, unhoped-for, and happy chapter in my life. I looked at him, and only then did I realize tears were rolling down my cheeks. He smiled, but I saw a shadow of emotion pass over his face. For him, too, this journey brought a mixture of joy and grief.

As we approached, the bells of the city's churches rang out, but within the gates the subdued atmosphere in the streets struck me. As a crossroads of major trading routes and the kingdom's capital, Kraków was normally loud and bustling, but on that beautiful early summer day a strange hush hung over it. People seemed to move slowly and talk in soft voices. When they turned their faces in our direction, I saw worry lines or tears swiftly dabbed away.

Sebastian and I exchanged a puzzled look. The bells rang more loudly now, as they once had for Bona's arrival. But this time I heard something somber in their sound; their rhythm lacked the energy and joy I remembered. The slow and mournful cadence sent a shiver through me. Could it be for the king? Zygmunt—now nicknamed Stary, the Old, to distinguish him from his namesake and heir—was approaching his eightieth year and fast declining, according to Lucrezia.

"I hope it's not for His Majesty's soul," I said to Sebastian, who had served in Zygmunt's household during those dark events of 1519 and 1520.

"Me too," he replied, but I could see that he was worried. He liked and respected the old king, and I knew that Zygmunt's demise would cause him a great deal of sadness.

"Lucrezia wrote that his body is stronger than his mind," I added by way of reassuring him and myself. "There didn't seem to be any signs of impending death."

Before Sebastian looked away, I read in his eyes the same concern I had: the king's death might indefinitely delay our petition.

We continued the rest of the way in silence until we at last pulled up in front of Emilia's sizable stone-and-timber house, red-roofed like most of its neighbors. On this elegant street and in front of its polished exterior, our carriage looked even shabbier than it had in Konary. A maid in an immaculately starched white apron promptly appeared in answer to our knock. Her eyes, too, were red-rimmed and blurry from crying.

My stomach flipped. "What has happened?" I asked, steeling myself to hear my fears confirmed.

"A great tragedy, mistress." The maid struck a lamenting tone as she wiped her eyes with the cuff of her dress. "Our gracious queen has died."

Printed in Great Britain
by Amazon